Praise for *Southern Exposures*

"Ann Jeffries definitely has a skill for storytelling. There is vitality and high drama in Southern Exposures. The author did an excellent job with honing in and focusing on the three main, important characters of which the drama surrounds. I fell in love with the Alexanders. Job well done!"
—Jessica Tilles, Author/Editor

"Loved the way [Ann Jeffries] described the activities...I felt as though I was there witnessing everything [that she was] describing. [She] immediately got my attention with the colorful... attention to details. The book is very warm. The characters have to face challenges and each does it in a different way. Loved the focus on loving family— members of the family loving each other and believing in each other."
—Brenda Irons LeCesne, Esq.

"There are a lot of promising plots within the story. I thoroughly enjoyed... this [novel]. I think [Ann Jeffries'] ability [to] create emotion is a true talent. [She] did a great job creating suspense. The [characters'] stories seemed most authentic and enter- taining. Language and dialogue [o]verall... is a strong area for [Ann]."
—Karen R. Thomas, President, Creative Minds Book Group

Praise for *An Unguarded Moment*

"Ann Jeffries does an excellent job of weaving her characters' stories together and keeping the reader captivated."
—Nancy Engle, Author of *Murder at Mount Joy*

"An engrossing and sensuous love story that immediately grabs your attention and keeps you involved till the last page."
—Abraham Leib, Esq.

ANN JEFFRIES

Touch Me In The Morning

Family Reunion—In the Wisdom of the Ancestors Series

Published and Distributed By
New View Literature
820 67th Avenue N, #7603
Myrtle Beach, South Carolina 29572
www.newviewliterature.com

Cover and Interior design: TWA Solutions
www.twasolutions.com

ISBN: 978-0-9915003-7-6

Library of Congress Control Number: 2014907678

First printing May 2014

Acknowledgments

$\mathcal{L}$ ife does not give us an opportunity to be anything other than a combination of ancestors from back through the ages to the beginning. I lucked up and got the right combination. For that, I will forever be proud of and grateful to my parents, grandparents, great-grand parents, ad infinitum. The Ancestors and The Creator also smiled on me by giving me a son and daughter who I can both love and respect. For these gifts, I am eternally thankful.

Ted and Tracy, you are the sunshine of many generations and of my life. May the quiet joys that we shared over many seasons of our lives continue to fill your hearts.

The journey continues and the struggle for perfection will never end.

"Most of us can recall the special warmth which characterized our families and, most of us, if honest, also see that our success and survival depended on the family from which we came."

—Dr. Wade Nobles, 1978
Director, Center for Applied Cultural
Studies and Educational Achievement

1

"What are we going to do, Satarah?" Jennie Jones, a young, petite nurse asked shrilly in her Butterfly McQueen sound-alike voice juxtaposed with her silky, platinum blond hair, milky complexion, and big, pretty, brown eyes. Those eyes were currently wide with fear and apprehension. "If we don't get a doctor to come soon, he's going to die."

Satarah Whitfield did not spare the young nurse a glance as she continued to chatter like a magpie. Actually, Jennie was wearing on Satarah's already frayed nerves by standing there wringing her hands and bouncing from one New Balance shod foot to the other. She could not hear the boy's lungs properly with Jennie whining and yapping at her. Satarah was well aware of the consequences to the young boy on the Emergency Room table, if she did not take immediate action. As the head Emergency Room nurse and a Nurse Practitioner, Satarah had to make a life or death decision, and soon. She made the boy as comfortable as she could, but he was likely in shock and his injuries were severe. A nurse for eleven years she knew the procedures necessary to save the child's life, but if she attempted to act, she, as well as the other two nurses in the small examination room, could lose their licenses. Or even worse, be prosecuted if the boy died at her hand.

"Pressures dropping, 80 over 50," Mary Ella Baker reported as she monitored the child's vital signs on the sophisticated medical equipment hooked up to his body.

Both of the boy's legs had sustained fractures as well as one arm. Satarah checked his cold fingers and toes again. They were not pinking up which meant that his blood flow was not getting to his extremities, he had a blood clot or any number of things could be happening. Without X-rays, a CATscan or a MRI, she could not determine whether there was head trauma or internal bleeding. Effectively, she was functioning in the dark, but there was no doctor available to make critical decisions or equipment to do the necessary tests. All the equipment she needed was in use serving hundreds of other patients with potentially more life-threatening injuries.

"Do we have any information on who he is or where his parents are?" Satarah asked to no one in particular as she removed the curved earpiece end of her stethoscope from her ears and the round metal disk from against the child's chest after again checking his lung function. She suspected that he had a crushed larynx based on the bruising and swelling on his chest, at his thin neck and, as a result, he was not getting enough oxygen into his lungs. It was difficult working around the neck brace that kept his head and shoulders immobile. Although they were forcing air into his nostrils, his lungs were not inflating sufficiently.

"He was on one of the school buses headed to Florida from Richmond, Virginia, is all I know. Some type of school trip," Jennie whined. "Two of the three school buses were totaled in the accidents. One of the other people, a teacher, in the accident said he didn't know everyone on the buses."

"Seventy over forty," Mary Ella reported, casting concerned eyes at Satarah.

Checking his chest again, Satarah heard the decreased breath sounds. She brushed her hand over the boy's tightly knit, curly-haired head. He could not have been more than twelve or thirteen years old, she surmised. About the same age as her own son would be, if she were allowed to keep him. Satarah refused to let herself dwell on her loss and pain at the moment. She was still blessed to have her twins.

"Call the surgical floor, again, Jennie, and get one of the doctors on the line," Satarah said with urgency as she turned to the washbowl at her back and lathered up scrubbing her hands and short nails with a hard-bristled brush. *License be dammed!* She would not stand idly by and watch this young boy's life slip through her fingers. She would do the tracheotomy or the child was going to die. Once she stabilized his breathing, there would be time to deal with his other obvious injuries.

While Jennie dialed, Satarah held up her now sterile hands so Mary Ella could glove her. They made steady eye contact as Mary Ella, also an experienced ER nurse, silently, but swiftly, prepared Satarah for what, she too, knew was necessary. In their silent stare, they understood that if anything went wrong, at best, they could lose their licenses and open the hospital up to a wrongful death suit, or, at worst, be brought up on criminal charges or both. When the time came, she would deal with the consequences of her actions.

"I'm still not getting an answer!" Jennie whined and hung up the telephone. When she turned to the patient, her eyes grew wider darting between Satarah and Mary Ella. Then her mouth flew open. *"What?... what are you doing?"* she screeched.

"What I have to," said Satarah, calmly. "Increase the drip on the sedative, Mary Ella, then get a crash cart and glove up. Jennie, get a tracheotomy kit and four-oh silk. Stat!"

Though her hands wanted to shake, her nerves riding on tender hooks, when Mary Ella began sterilizing the field and then handing the surgical knives to her, Satarah was focused, steady as petrified rock when she made the first incision between the boy's Adam's apple and the Cricoid cartilage.

An hour later, Satarah sat alone in the bay specifically colored to put small children at ease while she monitored the boy's vital signs. He could not appreciate the effort that went into the wall murals and maybe never would.

They almost lost him.

There was still blood on the floor—his blood. Her hands trembled a bit at the thought of what she had done to someone's child. They shocked him when he went into ventricular tachycardia, but they stabilized him, achieved sinus rhythm, and then opened up his airway. As she had suspected, a pinched esophagus prevented normal airflow. She was able to thread the tracheotomy tube through his mouth past the obstruction and into his lung within minutes. While she sutured the incision, Mary Ella started the respirator that steadily pumped oxygen into his lungs. With the tube holding open his airway and the respirator working at full tilt, his vital signs began to return to near normal.

Running on adrenalin, Satarah was beyond tired and she dearly wanted to rest. However, the blizzard and resulting accidents that involved three busloads of junior high school students, four jam-packed inter-state buses, seven tractor-trailers, numerous cars and motor homes and hundreds of people, contrived to bind her to the hospital for the last forty-eight hours with a skeletal nursing staff and no Emergency Room doctors. Satarah and her nurses triaged patients in the halls and waiting room area until the more seriously injured patients could be evaluated and then moved to the surgical theatre. Regrettably, they were not successful in saving everyone, but fortunately, that number was few.

Since there were very few administrators in the hospital, Satarah had taken on the additional responsibility of pressing the available kitchen workers, housekeeping personnel and maintenance crew into service to get less gravely injured people into available beds in the hospital and see to their needs. All available Emergency Room doctors were pressed into surgical duty while part of the nursing staff continued to treat the steady influx of patients in the Emergency Room hallways. Satarah abhorred assembly-line medicine, but during this crisis, everyone in the hospital was forced to operate on a factory mentality.

The snow was still falling heavily, winds were high, the temperature was dropping, and the roads were impossible to travel. Emergency medical personnel or other emergency service organizations could not get to them through the disastrous storm. Yet, area farmers cranked up their harvesting and other heavy farm equipment to help clear the six-mile stretch of road from the hospital and high school campus to the interstate. Neighbors with four-wheel-drive vehicles were making perilous round-trip runs along that road transporting the injured and the stranded to the hospital or the county high school for shelter as their conditions warranted.

Summer County General was not a major hospital, but it was the only one in the county and the closest one to the interstate where the accidents occurred. From what little information Satarah had time to hear, Interstate

95 was a disaster area for miles in both directions. An oil tanker truck was burning out of control and a poultry truck flipped over spilling its load of live chickens. Eighteen-wheelers had jackknifed causing more casualties and injuries. Huge steel girders were stacked like so many pick-up sticks across both the north and southbound highways. South Carolina had experienced hurricanes, tornadoes and even snow before, but this blizzard had to be the worst that Satarah had experienced in her twenty-nine years in the South. The February storm downed trees, telephone and electrical wires throughout Summer County. The hospital was operating on its back-up power systems and the end of this crisis was nowhere in sight.

Satarah turned back to her prize patient. She had set his broken legs and arm. His fingers and toes warmed and pinked satisfactorily to her touch, but he was still very pale. She gave him an antibiotic, a mild sedative, and painkiller along with the saline solution to stave off dehydration. He was resting quietly with his blood pressure hovering around a normal range for a child of his approximate height, weight and age and his heartbeat was steady and even with no arrhythmia. She was still concerned about possible head trauma and internal injuries, but his eyes responded to her penlight stimulation so he was not in a coma, yet, and the bruises, lacerations and contusions seemed more superficial than serious. Nevertheless, she would feel a lot better if one of the doctors, preferably not Dr. Reynard Steward, could come and evaluate the child sometime soon.

Automatically she turned to the shouted vital signs of the fire department medics rushing through the ER sliding glass doors as the volunteer firefighters wheeled in three more gurneys and assisted the walking wounded. She was out of the cubicle and already climbing on top of one of the patients to continue administering CPR as the firefighter climbed off. While riding the gurney, keeping cadence, she issued orders to her exhausted staff. The firefighters were double-timing it back through the electronic doors as her nurses responded to the new crisis—six more patients.

No, Satarah thought silently as her new patient's heart began to beat with a restored sinus rhythm on its own; they weren't going to get any help or relief anytime soon. Still, they were performing small miracles and beating back the Grim Reaper from stalking their heels like a dark shadow.

2

"Hey! Johnson!" Battalion Chief Orson Stovall shouted, irritably, shaking the man out of a deep sleep.

Douglas Johnson, faced down on his bunk, rolled his two hundred fifteen-pound frame part way onto his side and, over his shoulder, looked up through red, sleep deprived eyes at the man standing over him. "Yeah?"

"You're on for another twenty-four hours and I want those incident reports before end of shift today."

Doug bit off a curse at the gleeful malice on the other man's face. Even in his fatigued state, Doug knew that arguing with Battalion Chief Stovall was an exercise in futility and would add credibility to allegations that he was not a team player. It was hard being a team player when he was not considered one of the members in the good old boys' league. He knew the odds were that he would get the worst assignments even before he testified in a wrongful death class action suit filed against the fire department for its failed response times to emergencies in the poorer districts of Richmond, Virginia. He tolerated the snide remarks, being passed over for promotions, even the lack of a back-up partner when fighting fires. Despite whatever the fire department threw at him, he could and would deal with it because he still wanted to make a difference.

And he was just too stubborn to quit.

Underlying that stubbornness, he admitted to himself that he still gave a damn about his career and the people he swore to protect and serve. Doug was proud of his contributions as he had made many changes in fire-safety procedures and helped with school programs that fostered fire prevention. He recognized that not everyone shared his dedication.

Because of Doug's sworn statements, his Battalion Chief and some of his cronies careers were on the line.

Doug sat up, swung his long, strong legs over the edge of the bed, and pressed his feet again the cold floor. According to the clock on the fire station wall, he had slept for two hours. He had been on duty for six days already and had responded to an extraordinary number of fires and other emergencies since his tour of duty started. He had not had three consecutive hours of deep sleep in the past six days. Now he was being ordered to pull another twenty-four-hour shift.

Scrubbing his rough, calloused hands over his face, he felt the scratch of the five-o'clock shadow on his square jaw. He needed a long hot shower and a shave, but when he returned from responding to the last alarm and completing his reports, other firefighters were already in the open shower stalls playing slap and tickle with wet towels. He decided to forgo the shower for a while to get some much-needed sleep.

Doug stood and Battalion Chief Stovall took a jerky, quick, two steps backward and braced as if expecting Doug to attack. Towering over the man, Doug stretched his six-foot-four-inch frame to loosen his large, tensed muscles, picked up his shaving gear and towel, and headed for the showers. "The incident reports are on your desk, Battalion Chief," he said over his shoulder as he walked away. *What? Did the man think that he was going to resort to violence?* He saw more than enough violence in Afghanistan to last him several lifetimes. When he asked to re-enlist, he declined, taking his Marine-furnished college fund and enrolling at Richmond State University. Always wanting a career as a firefighter and fresh out of college, he joined the department. He was trying not to regret his decision.

"Yeah? Well, the reports must have been written in invisible ink, because I didn't see them, Johnson," Stovall said, snidely.

Doug stopped, turned and looked at the man built like a fireplug, and going soft in his middle with thinning hair who was dogging his heals. Battalion Chief Stovall jumped back, his eyes grew wide. Doug knew that with his thick, wooly hair, brown skin and brawny build, he must look like a criminal, but the menace in his dark brown eyes must have convinced Stovall that now was not the time to press his luck or Doug's patience.

When Stovall scurried away, Doug proceeded to the shower room. He snatched the handwritten "out of order" sign off the door and went in. Kneeling in the closet behind the door, he turned on the water and flipped the circuit breaker to the hot water heater. Some firefighters pulled this same crap on him before. He wasn't going for it this time.

While the water tank heated, he pulled his cell phone from his shaving kit and dialed his home. When he got no answer, he hung up. According to his watch, it was nearly 9:00 P.M. and the boy should have answered the telephone. He dialed his neighbors who were his tenants, Mr. and Mrs. Diggs. They looked after twelve-year-old Donovan while he worked. The phone was answered on the third ring.

"Good evening, Mrs. Diggs. This is Douglas Johnson. Is Donovan with you?"

"Donovan? No, he's not with me, Doug. Did you forget?" she said and chuckled. "Donovan went on that spring break school trip to Disney World."

"Disney World?" Doug asked, puzzled. "He couldn't have gone, Mrs. Diggs. Donovan was on restriction for skipping school and because his grades were poor."

"He told me that you gave him permission to go. I helped him pack his clothes."

"When did he leave?" Doug asked his jaw muscles tight.

"Yesterday. I'm not sure what time the buses left the school. Tom took Donovan to school on his way to work. He's not home yet or I would ask him what time the buses left. I sure hope the children didn't have any trouble with that big snow storm on their way to Florida. The weather reports say that the storm is moving this way."

Snowstorm? Doug battled emergencies caused by icy rain and sleet for the past few days, but there was no predicted snowstorm for the Richmond area. At least it hadn't been predicted when he went to sleep more than two hours ago.

He had bigger problems to deal with than snow in February. "Thank you, Mrs. Diggs. I'll contact the school and..."

"Oh, sorry, Doug, but I have another call..."

"That's alright, Mrs. Diggs. Have a good evening." He turned off his cell phone and put it back into his shaving kit. He was sure that he would not be able to contact anyone at the school at this time of night, but, as time permitted tomorrow, he would find out how the school allowed Donovan to go on this trip without his permission. He also would find out how Donovan was able to pay for the trip. It would be a simple matter to find out where the students were staying in Orlando. If he did not have to work this additional shift, he would have time to fly to Florida and bring Donovan back.

Doug braced his large hands on either side of the cold porcelain sink, closed his eyes and hung his head between his massive shoulders. He and the boy were going to have *another* long talk. That seemed like all they did was talk, but nothing ever got resolved. He didn't know what else he could do to reach the child, but he would have to find a way soon. He and Donovan couldn't keep up this silent battle of wills for much longer without serious intervention. After his wife's, Lily's, death everything seemed to go to hell in a hurry.

Lily, he thought with regret and some measure of guilt. If he had known how depressed his wife was, maybe he could have done something to prevent her suicide, but he had not been there when she took her life. Nor had he been there emotionally perhaps for some time. He loved her, but no matter how often he told her or tried to show her, she still demanded more of his time and energy than he could afford to give. He tried to give her everything she wanted, even a child that her body could not produce.

Freshly shaved and showered, feeling somewhat more human, Doug dressed and went to the community kitchen/lounge to find something to eat. As expected the other firefighters had not left anything for him. Even the last frozen meal that Mrs. Diggs prepared for him was MIA. Of course, no one would admit what happened to it, so he did not bother to ask.

Doug did not miss a beat, though he could feel the eyes on every move he made waiting, and perhaps, hoping that he would explode. He grabbed two bottles of water from the refrigerator and checked the caps to insure no one tampered with them. Checking his watch again, he noted he had about half an hour to order Chinese food from the restaurant at the end of the block before it closed. Twisting off the cap of one of the bottles, he downed it in one long swallow.

After he drank his fill, he went to his bunk and fished a jump drive from the lining of his fire-retardant coveralls. There was no use in trying to locate the reports that he had put on Stovall's desk. By now, a person or persons unknown would have shred those reports. When his desk top computer did not boot up, he checked whether it was plugged in. Sure enough, not only was it not plugged in, but the cord was also missing.

Absently, Doug noted the volume on the big, flat screen was particularly low even though there was a highly touted, close-scoring East/West basketball game going on. Not a sound came from the community room as he went to his footlocker and keyed in his electronic code. He dug inside the locker and pulled out his laptop. There was good battery life left on it. After closing and setting the alarm on his locker, he went back to his desk, plugged the computer directly into the printer and reprinted all the reports.

When Doug finished, he documented all the silly, childish pranks that they had subjected him to so far that day, including the fact he had been ordered to work an additional tour of duty while Stovall took his fat rump home and enjoyed another day off. He attached the documentation to an e-mail to his attorney. Several months earlier, Doug filed a harassment suit against his Battalion Chief and the Fire Department. It was a tedious process, but his attorney drilled him on documenting everything that happened.

After he made a back-up copy of his records and secured his laptop, he put on his heavy weather gear to go to the restaurant to pick up his dinner.

"Where do you think you're going, Johnson?" Stovall asked, his face flushed red with temper.

"To get some air," Doug said, as he dumped the reports in his Battalion Chief's lap. "Here is another copy of the incident reports."

"Another copy!" Stovall blustered. "You didn't do them the first time!"

"Really?" Doug said, without a hint of the rage that he actually felt.

"Yes! Really! Are you trying to call me a liar in front of all these witnesses?"

Doug took a moment to look at the other ten faces in the community room. Some wore smirks, agitated anticipation, or others didn't have the decency to look him in the eye. A few even looked embarrassed.

"I wasn't trying, but since Command acknowledged receipt of the original reports three hours ago..." he said, shrugging his massive shoulders, he let the implications speak for themselves.

Not waiting for more abuse, he put on his hat and gloves and walked out. Before the door closed, he heard the steam-kettle like machinations coming from Stovall and the raised voices from other firefighters frustrated that he hadn't responded to their high jinx.

What generally took five minutes to walk to the restaurant took twice as long as Doug carefully picked his way down the icy block. The slick sidewalk was treacherous. Some of the store and shop owners were salting the sidewalks and, as they stopped him to chat, he noted for the first time that the icy pellets were mixed with heavily falling snow.

"Hey, Deputy Battalion Chief, it's a mess out here, ain't it?" a hardy voice called to him.

Doug looked into the near distance to see some of the next shift of firefighters coming toward him. Bob Sweeny, a big man of Irish ancestry with red hair and laughing green eyes, smiled broadly. Sweeny was one of the better firefighters in the squad. He did the job well and kept his nose clean. Doug had written Sweeny up for a couple of spot awards and a commendation for his handling of a tricky situation where someone could have gotten hurt if it was not for Sweeny's alert action. Doug liked the kid's leadership qualities too. Sweeny would do well in any situation.

"Yeah, it's something, alright," Doug said as he swung open the restaurant door and went in. He was followed in by Bob and three other firefighters; all solid workers.

"Didn't go for the Kielbasa and sauerkraut, huh?"

"Something like that," Doug said cryptically.

"Yeah, me neither. When I called the station, Brewster said that Stovall made a huge pot of the stuff; enough to eat off for a week! Frankly, the stuff gives me gas," he said, laughing. "So I called ahead and ordered Chinese."

It did not bother him, Doug mused, but clearly that big pot had been hidden somewhere when he looked for something to eat. Another note would go into his file and to his attorney about the missing meal. Not that he could trust anything Stovall cooked. If Mrs. Diggs did not force her big, home-cooked, frozen meals on him, he generally cooked for himself at the fire house and there were rarely any leftovers. He was a big man who enjoyed good food but he did not gain weight easily. His doctor told him he had a high metabolism rate so the food never turned to fat. However, the fuel did turn to muscle and energy, which he needed to do his job.

Doug paid for his food and was about to leave when Sweeny asked him to wait. Doug was starving and was tempted to ignore the request, but was in no real hurry to get back to the station house, so he waited. As they walked back together silently, Sweeny cleared his throat a few times and then slowed his walk to let the other firefighters pass by. When they slowed to a stop, Doug looked into Sweeny's earnest green eyes.

"Look, Deputy Battalion Chief. I don't hold with all this stuff some of the guys are putting you through," he said, his discomfort evident. "I mean, not everyone thinks you're a rat fink for testifying against... or suing the Department..." he paused, startled by how his words may sound, his eyes grew wide. "I mean," he hastened on, "I don't believe it's fair what's happening to you. You've always been straight up with me. I mean a stand-up kind of guy."

With a dismissive hand gesture, Doug brushed the "rat fink" comment aside and Sweeny visibly relaxed. Then he nervously licked his lips and continued. "Look, Brewster said that some of the guys have been doing stupid stuff to you all week trying to get you to go buck wild. He said, well," Sweeny took a deep breath and released it in a huff, "the Battalion Chief kinda' engineered it." He seemed to hold his breath as he searched Doug's eyes and face for a reaction.

Doug was starving, dog-tired and although he had no reason to disbelieve Sweeny or distrust his motive for giving him the low down, he would keep his own council. He didn't have the energy or inclination to confront Stovall tonight. He also would not betray Sweeny's confidence.

All he wanted to do was eat, sleep, and hope the squad didn't have another hellfire shift before the end of his tour of duty.

Well, he did get one of his wishes. He did eat, but by midnight, they were fully involved in a five-alarm apartment house fire that was not cleared until 4:00 A.M. By the end of his tour, Doug was not sure he could drive to his home safely. They had six alarms of varying intensity during the day and he was up to his calves in snow with underlying ice. When he finally pulled into his block, he could barely see the outline of his driveway. Doug was pulling off his clothes as soon as he entered his house and kept walking to his bedroom. He was butt-naked when he fell face first into his mattress.

Six hours later, he mumbled a "Yeah?" into the telephone. Mere seconds after that, he was up packing a travel bag, snagging his emergency gear and heading south to some place called Summer County, South Carolina.

3

"Chuck?"

Dr. Charles Montgomery was having a wonderfully erotic dream about his wife, Vivian, the judge, and something salacious about her in her black robes wearing nothing underneath. He didn't want to lose the euphoria they were about to reach, but his mother-in-law's quiet, but urgent voice had him coming fully awake almost instantly.

"Mom? What's wrong? Is it Vivian? Is the baby coming?" he asked in a rapid-fire cadence.

"No, no, Chuck. Vivian is fine," Sylvia Alexander said, laying a comforting, restraining hand on his arm.

"Are the children okay? Did something happen?" God knew that his children were a diverse and rambunctious group, all twenty-three of them. All but four were adopted; ten before he married Vivian Alexander Jackson and one, Derrick, Jr., the only baby Vivian and her late husband, Derrick "Dunk & Jam" Jackson, Sr., the basketball icon, and Chuck's best friend since puberty, had before Derrick, Sr., died on April 1; the same day that little DJ, Derrick Jelon Jackson, Jr., was born.

"They are fine, Chuck. The children are fine. Some came in with me to help out because we are short-handed."

"The rest are with Vivian?"

"Yes, and everything was fine when I left them. Bernie and Romelo were taking some of the children to the school campus to help set up an emergency shelter for victims of the snowstorm. Olivia is there at the house and so is Bill. Everyone is keeping an eye on Vivian and the children."

"Okay," Chuck said taking a calming breath while he rubbed his eyes with the heels of his hands and yawned hugely. "So, what's the problem, mom?"

It did her heart good to know that her eldest daughter had found true love and respect twice in her life. Derrick Jackson, her daughter's first husband, was taken so tragically nearly ten years earlier leaving Vivian devastated and their adopted children nearly inconsolable. Derrick give up his superlative basketball career when his heart condition was discovered, then became a noted pediatrician. When he died, he left Vivian Lynn a very wealthy woman; one of the wealthiest in the world.

For years, Sylvia worried that Vivian would never accept the love, honor, and respect that Chuck Montgomery, Derrick's best friend, had harbored for Vivian even before Chuck introduced Vivian to Derrick. For five years after Derrick's death, Vivian was hostile toward Chuck because he knew about Derrick's heart condition, but at Derrick's request, kept it a secret. It devastated Chuck because he and Vivian were good friends even before she met Derrick.

Vivian and six of her friends from Georgetown Law School opened a very successful law practice in Washington, DC. As time passed, Chuck never gave up hope that Vivian would one day turn to him and accept the love he had harbored for her since the first time they met at O'Hare Airport in Chicago.

Sylvia had worried that Chuck's Caucasian skin may have contributed to Vivian's angst toward him. Heaven knew that she and her husband, Bernard, taught Vivian and her other four siblings tolerance and respect; to judge people by the content of their character and not the color of their skin. When Vivian acknowledged Chuck's race was not the issue, but her own feelings of disloyalty to Derrick's memory and her guilt over loving Chuck, Sylvia knew eventually all would work out. She was pleased that Chuck and Vivian found a way to overcome their problems, affirm their deep and abiding love for each other, and marry five years ago. Together they continued to adopt children who had medical or health challenges and were abandoned or unwanted by their respective families. Vivian was also pregnant again. Soon, Sylvia and Bernard would have another grandbaby to love and cherish.

"What is it, Mom? Has something happened to someone else in the family?" Chuck saw the play of emotions over her gamine face. She looked so much like the superstar songstress, Nancy Wilson, and had a beautiful singing voice too. Bernard Alexander had that timeless sophistication and handsomeness reminiscent of the actor Sydney Poirier in his younger days. Although Bernard and Sylvia Alexander were in their fifties and had raised five, well-rounded, stable, and dynamic children, neither of them wore a wrinkle on their smooth, brown complexions.

"Everyone is fine, Chuck, but I do have a situation and I need your help."

Sylvia relayed the events surrounding her chief ER nurse's decision to perform an emergency tracheotomy on a boy who was one of the victims of the numerous accidents. Although the other charge nurses, who were in the room at the time, agreed Satarah Whitfield had no choice but to act or lose the boy, the Chief of Medical Services, Dr. Reynard Steward, wanted to bring Satarah up on charges so severe that, if proven, could land her in jail.

Chuck listened carefully to his mother-in-law and understood why she needed his intervention to forestall any disciplinary action, at least, until their crisis abated and cooler heads could prevail. Although Sylvia Alexander was the Chief of Nursing and the Nursing School Administrator, she couldn't influence the Chief of Medical Services, who was technically her boss, to back off without help. Since Chuck was on the hospital's Board of Directors, made heavy financial contribution to the hospital, and had medical privileges at the hospital, his intervention might prove more influential than hers might be.

"How is the child doing now?" Chuck asked when she finished.

"He's stable, but not alert. Satarah is concerned that he may have had head trauma or that she didn't act quickly enough to avoid brain damage from a loss of oxygen."

Chuck was sliding off the gurney he found in a supply closet when Sylvia delayed him. He looked down at her from his nearly seven-foot height into her concerned expression.

"I should also tell you that Satarah Whitfield is not only a Nurse Practitioner and the Chief ER nurse, she is also my niece."

"Which tells me that you trained her and if you did and support her actions, then she made the right decision to treat this child without a doctor's advice and counsel."

Sylvia released a breath that she didn't realize she was holding. "She's one of my best and brightest, Chuck. She would never act capriciously. She is young, but she is solid. She enjoys the respect of her nurses and deserves it."

"I don't remember meeting her."

"She was working at one of the outreach clinics in the county when the position opened here at the hospital. I begged her to apply. When she did, I suggested that the Chief of Medical Services conduct her interview because of my familial relationship with her and to prevent any allegation of nepotism or impropriety. He hired her and now wants to fire her and bring her up on charges."

"I haven't met her at any of the family reunions, have I?"

"No," Sylvia said sadly. "She doesn't come, but she does let her boys come when we get together."

The sadness was evident on his mother-in-law's face. He didn't want to press her for more information at the moment. He'd talk with his father-in-law later. For now, his primary concern was the boy who had somehow slipped through the cracks and needed to be seen and evaluated. "Come on, Mom. Let's go."

◌❁◌

Satarah sat in the conference room adjacent to the Chief of Medical Services', Dr. Reynard Steward's, office. Now that most of the critically injured patients had been attended to, she had taken time to prepare a full report on the emergency surgery she had performed and the other steps taken to save the boy's life. Even in her deep exhaustion, she knew it was necessary to get the facts down while she could remain vertical. Earlier, she located Rey Steward in the doctors' lounge having coffee with some of the other doctors, including the Chief, Emergency Room Resident, Dr. Garrison St. Clair, who was horizontal and snoring loudly on a too short sofa. Fatigue covered everyone's face as they rested between surgeries, but the crisis was not completely over. Especially not for her.

Earlier, while she was reviewing medical charts, making notes and preparing the daily reports, she was amazed, but pleased to see her Aunt Sylvia come in the ER doors flanked by five of her teenage grandchildren who had offered to help as general dogs bodies. Satarah had not seen her first cousins in years and she was stunned by how astute they were and grateful for their help. When the teens were deployed to help, Satarah pulled her aunt aside to tell her what she had done and gave her a copy of the incident report.

Sylvia went over the report thoroughly, questioned her rigorously, examined the boy herself, and interviewed both Mary Ella Baker and Jennie Jones. Then she told Satarah to go back to work and swiftly marched off on some unknown mission. Satarah had done as her aunt directed.

After reading the report, Rey Steward was called back into surgery. His secretary called Satarah to meet him in his conference room where she now sat trying desperately to fight off the sneaky tug of sleep. Finally, after sitting alone in the quiet for so long, she stretched out on one of the long padded benches by a window and allowed sleep to embrace her.

Reynard Stewart entered his conference room fully prepared to take Satarah Whitfield to task over her actions and then to offer her the comfort of his arms. What he found was a woman who found comfort in her own arms.

He quietly locked the door so that he would not be disturbed while he watched her sleep. If he was lucky and quick enough, he could get her naked. He approached and stood over her reaching out to touch her long, thick, course hair that had come loose from the severe bun she habitually wore at the nape of her neck. When she didn't stir from his gentle caress he became more emboldened and lightly moved the thick strands partially covering her face. Her hair fluttered from her light snoring.

They were all fatigued from four consecutive days and nights of non-stop emergencies, but it did not distract from her earth, sensual beauty. He rushed through an emergency laparotomy so he would have time alone with Satarah. He scanned the length of her wanting desperately to part her muscular thighs that were seemingly so strong enough to crack walnuts.

Satarah was not a beauty in the classical sense as much as she was vital and voluptuous. Everything about her screamed "made for sex."

And he had wanted her for more than a year since the first time he saw her in the rural clinic he visited as a part of his administrative duties as Chief of Summer County's Medical Services. Initially, she discouraged his advances, but after several dates, he had taken her with him to a medical conference in Atlanta on the pretext of expanding her knowledge of the medical field and furthering her services to the rural clinic. After a few bottles of wine and a wonderful dinner, he finally seduced her into his bed. He knew that she was not exactly coherent, but he convinced himself she certainly was not drunk.

When he had finally gotten her naked, he could only stand and stare. From her toes to the top of her head, she was any man's fantasy. He made love to her thoroughly throughout the night. He saw paradise in her arms and wanted to visit there again, but when he awoke the next morning, Satarah Whitfield was gone. By the time he got dressed and to her hotel room, she had checked out, leaving a note at the hotel reception desk that offered her apology for her part in the mistake they made by sleeping together.

He was hurt and then angered when she refused to see him again socially. It had taken months and a lot of patience to maneuver people around until he had her within arm's reach as the head ER nurse.

Though she downplayed her sexiness by wearing loose-fitting uniforms and smocks and no makeup, he was familiar with what was under her clothes.

Every time he thought of her, his member went to half-mast. He damned those smocks to hell now as he stroked lightly over her breast. He could not risk unzipping the damn thing so that he could feast on her nipples. So, he contented himself with stroking himself while he watched her lips part in sleep. Whenever he was in a room with her, he had to button his lab coat to hide his arousal.

He convinced Satarah he had accepted their interlude in the same way she had; as a mistake, a one-night stand brought on by too much wine. An incident that would not be repeated. Yet, nothing could have been further from the truth. He wanted her, and now he had the means to have her. He just had to be patient a little longer and, once again, Satarah's body would soar under his.

Satarah jerked awake at the rapid staccato raps at the door. She blinked owlishly. When her vision began to clear, she noticed Rey Steward fasten his starched white lab coat, shoot this cuffs in his sleeves and straighten his tie. Then he took a deep breath before he opened... no, before he *unlocked* and then opened the door to admit her Aunt Sylvia, her cousin's husband, Dr. Charles Montgomery, and a man she didn't immediately recognize. Satarah sat up straight on the bench and rubbed her hands over her face.

Sylvia came to Satarah and patted her hand. "I know you're tired, Satarah Jo, but we need to talk for a bit."

The quiet urgency in Sylvia's voice put her instantly on alert. "But, what—?" Satarah began, but was shushed by her aunt before she turned to the man who stood at her side. Satarah stood up beside her aunt.

"Satarah Whitfield, I'd like to introduce William Anthony Chandler, attorney at law. Mr. Chandler is a founding partner in Alexander, Carter, Chandler, Charles, Lightfoot and Towson, Vivian's law firm in Washington, DC."

As she extended her hand to accept his, she said, "Mr. Chandler needs no introduction." And, indeed, he didn't. The man was considered one of the best legal minds of his generation, the reincarnation version of William Jennings Bryan. He looked a lot like the actor Tom Selleck, in his younger days, but a much-improved version, Satarah thought as she released his hand and tuned into his voice.

"Thank you. May I call you Satarah?" he asked gesturing her to reseat herself at the conference table.

She sat with her back straight and hands folded on the table. Looking at William Chandler was certainly no hardship. She admired him from afar as much for his mind as for his matinee-idol good looks and had no idea that he was a founding partner in her cousin's law firm. He was a regular contributor on nationally televised, political, talk shows, including, Sweet Justice. He was a male model of choice in world-class high fashion magazines and television advertisements. She saw every movie he had appeared in and, though she did not buy his magazines, "Risqué" or "Stallion," she had seen them prominently displayed on newsstands, in bookstores, and at checkout lines in the grocery stores. The man was multi-talented.

Although she had not heard that William Chandler and her cousin, Vivian, were law partners before Vivian became a judge on the federal bench, Satarah was confused about why he was here and wondered how he had gotten here through the snowstorm that was still raging outside.

"Mr. Chandler is a long-time friend of our family," Sylvia said, as if reading Satarah's thoughts. "In fact, he came down last week with Vivian and Chuck for spring break. I thought that he could chat with you for a bit."

"Sorry, but I don't understand," Satarah said, still confused.

William Chandler rose from his seat and turned toward Sylvia, Chuck, and Dr. Stewart. "If you will excuse us, I'd like a moment with my client."

Satarah startled at the word "client," but remained seated when she felt her Aunt Sylvia's restraining hand on her shoulder. She must have looked dumbfounded when attorney Chandler turned toward her after the others left the conference room.

"Okay, Satarah, the next words I want to hear from your are..." he said, as he began to grill her about the events that began more than three days ago.

Hours later, Satarah put on her inadequate winter coat, signed out of the hospital, and flipped a heavy shawl over her head to protect her from the furious snow and icy wind.

When the electronic doors opened as she approached, she bent her head to exit, fighting the gale force winds. Suddenly she found herself knocked flat on her well-padded butt. Before she could register what had happened, she was being quickly lifted to her feet by what appeared to be a walking mountain.

"Sorry. Excuse me, ma'am," the mountain rumbled as he continued his ground-eating strides to the nurses' station.

Satarah turned in his direction to say something, but the man was already out of earshot. So again, she braced herself and this time kept her bloodshot eyes opened when she went out to tackle the elements.

4

OUG HADN'T MEANT TO KNOCK the woman down, but in his haste to find the boy, he barrowed through the emergency entry doors heedless to anyone or anything in his path.

He had been on the road cutting through barely-plowed countryside of unrelieved white and soot-grey vistas for fifteen hours, ever since he got the call from Mrs. Diggs saying Donovan's school had called many times looking for him to tell him about the bus accident in South Carolina. His gut knotted at the news, but he didn't have time to waste on his own fears. He simply had to get to Donovan as quickly as possible.

The drive from Richmond, Virginia, to Summer County, South Carolina, was long and arduous; blinding whiteouts that, at times, obscured the view to a few feet ahead of his front bumper. He exhausted the deicer in the truck's reservoir and refilled it twice to keep the sleet from freezing to his windshield and wiper blades. He filled his gas tank three times and had a spare can in his truck. Although few other vehicles were on the road, the further south he drove, the more difficult it became for his big, all-wheel-drive truck to get through the snow with underlying ice and battering, near hurricane-strength winds. According to radio reports, North and South Carolina, and Georgia never experienced anything like this storm and were ill-equipped to handle the emergency. Road crews were out, but motorists failed to heed media warnings to stay off the roads. Doug was among them. He stopped several times to help stranded motorists pull their cars out of ditches or tow them to the nearest off ramp.

Equipped with GPS, his CB radio, and cell phone, Doug stayed in contact with fire stations, highway patrols and CB radio operators as he drove. As he crossed into South Carolina, he learned that, due to the accidents, most of the highway ahead was closed and the injured children and adults were taken to Summer County General Hospital. Using his GPS guidance system, he found a secondary route being plowed by a huge piece of farm equipment. It was spreading potash and sand in its wake for traction. After a jug of convenience store coffee and a few day-old deli sandwiches out of a vending machine, Doug was relieved to see the large, blue, glowing Summer County General sign atop the hospital.

When he jogged through the Emergency Room's electronic doors, the woman he upended was just a blur in his peripheral vision. He headed straight for the two nurses who had their heads together whispering at the waist-high semi-circle desk. They discontinued their whispered conversation when he reached them.

"May I help you?" one nurse asked as the other one looked on.

"I'm looking for Donovan Johnson. The highway patrol announced that all of the injured children from the Richmond school buses were brought to this hospital."

"Are you a relative?" one nurse asked while the other keyed into a computer.

"I'm Douglas Johnson, Donovan's father."

He waited as the nurses checked their records. When they looked up blankly, his stomach took a long uncomfortable dive.

"Do you have a picture of your son? We have several boys who have not been identified."

Oh, God, Doug moaned silently, as he shook his head. He didn't carry a picture of Donovan in his wallet. If Donovan could not tell them who he was, then he must be in terrible shape—or dead. The thought had bile rising in his throat chased by fear. A million gut-tightening sharp pains were killing him from the inside out.

"Mr. Johnson? Mr. Johnson?" one of the nurses said again, finally penetrating the black haze that narrowed Doug's vision.

"Yes?" he asked. "Is he...?" He could not quite get the word out.

"He may be at the high school, but, if he was on one of the school buses, we'll find him. Would you have a seat for just a moment?"

Reluctantly, Doug moved to a hard plastic seat and, for the first time, looked around the Emergency Room's waiting area. The place looked as busy as Grand Central Station at rush hour. People were rushing or being rushed in and out in some kind of controlled chaos. He let the hum of voices swirl around him while his eyes scanned the many faces. He thought that parents might have made it through the storm, but he did not know whom they were. He met with Donovan's teachers during parent-teacher conferences, but he didn't socialize with the other parents. He knew some of the parents had come on this trip as chaperones with the seventh grade teachers, but he did not recognize anyone. He desperately wanted answers, but he realized, having dealt with similar situations many times, that his patience was necessary to get through this crisis.

His eyes lit on a group of teenagers, obviously volunteers, who wore blue pullover vests with the hospital's logo emblazed over a heart. He hoped Donovan still had a chance to grow up to volunteer as these kids were doing. The three boys and two girls were consulting small spiral notebooks, talking quietly, but quickly to someone who seemed to be taking notes on a computerized clipboard.

He turned toward the high-pitched screams and giggles of two little kids playing some unknown kind of game around two adults who looked totally exhausted. The man picked up the little Oriental boy and hugged him to his chest while whispering something in his ear. The little girl looked on, her brown complexion aglow, her big, round chocolate eyes watchful.

Little vignettes repeated throughout the waiting area. Some watched the large, overhead, flat-screen televisions tuned to stations covering the news and some reporter hip-deep in blinding snow.

One of the teen-aged aides zipped by and knelt before a man sitting alone in a prayerful position. The man stood and the aide took his arm, guiding him through another set of electronic doors.

Doug didn't notice the aide standing to his right until he touched his shoulder. "Mr. Johnson?"

"Yes?" Doug answered, but the young man stopped him from rising.

"My name is Kenny Alexander. Is there anything I can help you with?"

"Donovan?"

"Uh, no. I mean, do you need food? The cafeteria is open serving sandwiches, soup, coffee or tea and pound cake."

"No. I just want to find out about Donovan."

"The nurses are working on that. You're from Richmond, right?"

"Yes."

"Do you have somewhere to stay in the area?"

Doug hadn't thought that far ahead. He didn't know anyone in the area. "I'll find a motel or something."

Kenny looked sympathetically at him. "Almost everything is booked up for at least fifty miles. The snowstorm," he said gesturing toward the double electronic doors. "Look, Mr. Johnson, why don't I start a search for you while you wait and once you're ready to leave just look for me. Again, my name is Kenny Alexander."

"Thanks," Doug said distractedly while he shook the young man's hand, who then walked away flipping open his little notebook to make a note and to search for the next person on his list to offer aid and comfort.

Too edgy to sit, Doug stood and walked to the big glass windows overlooking the Emergency Room entrance. He needed to stretch his tense muscles and dug his unsteady hands into his pockets. He watched a fire company ambulance pull up outside to off-load more casualties. They moved like a well-choreographed team getting the injured inside to the waiting hands of the medical team. Once vital information was exchanged, the ambulance sped off again.

"Mr. Johnson?" a woman asked; her voice like warm scotch over a cold night.

Doug turned and did an involuntary double take. She was very attractive and looked so much like the songstress Nancy Wilson.

"My name is Sylvia Alexander. I manage the nursing staff here," she said extending her hand. "I understand that you're looking for your son Donovan. He was on one of the school buses from Richmond?"

"That's what I was told by an official from Donovan's school. I told the nurses at the desk, but they didn't have his name—."

"Yes, so I'm told," she said warmly, but efficiently. "Would you follow me please?"

He fell into step with her ground-eating stride as they walked a long, brightly- painted hallway with street murals on the walls and then turned a corner into another wing equally as interesting. He observed other patients and medical staff, but kept his focus straight ahead. When one of the teen aides streaked by, Mrs. Alexander's voice had the girl slowing her jog to a more dignified quick step. The girl turned, walking backward, and gave Mrs. Alexander a wide innocent smile over mischievous dark eyes and then sped off again.

When they made another turn and came to a locked double door, Mrs. Alexander placed her badge over a scanner and the door, labeled "CRITICAL CARE STEP DOWN" opened. Together, they entered a wide, round critical-care ward and she guided him to a bay on the left. The boy lying in the bed looked so battered, bruised, and swollen that he was almost unrecognizable.

Doug must have uttered a sound, before Mrs. Alexander asked, "Is this Donovan?"

"Yes," he spoke barely above a whisper. Then clearing the lump in his throat, he said "yes" again. "What happened to him? I mean is he going to be alright?"

"Please sit down, Mr. Johnson. You look like you're about to collapse."

"I just want to—," Doug started, then plopped down into the chair Mrs. Alexander pushed against the back of his knees.

"Dr. Montgomery is his attending physician. He will be with you shortly and explain Donovan's injuries and course of treatment. In the meantime, would you give information to me about his medical history?"

As Doug struggled through the information, his eyes never left Donovan's face. He didn't readily know a lot of information, he realized. Lily was the one to take care of Donovan's health and dental needs. He was surprised to learn that Mrs. Alexander had certain information from Donovan's school records, but until Doug arrived, she was unable to match the records to the right child. When an extremely tall Johnny Depp look alike entered the bay, both Mrs. Alexander and Doug turned toward the man. Recognition came slowly to Doug, but when they reached to shake hands, Doug said, "You're Chuck Montgomery, aren't you? I followed your career in basketball in college and in the NBA for many years."

"I've been practicing medicine since I left the hardwood."

"I was at your last all-star game in New York." The awesome feeling of meeting one of the legends in basketball passed quickly as Dr. Montgomery explained Donovan's injuries. Mrs. Alexander slipped from the bay to answer a page. Doug and Dr. Montgomery sat for nearly thirty minutes talking, and when the doctor finished answering Doug's questions to his satisfaction, they were on a first-name basis.

Dr. Montgomery cleared his throat. "Doug, we have a situation that I need to discuss with you." At Doug's assent to continue, Chuck began to explain about Donovan's initial treatment in the Emergency Room and his options to take legal action against the nurse and/or the hospital.

"But this nurse saved his life, didn't she?" Doug asked.

"Yes, she did, but she acted without the knowledge or consent of a physician."

"And I should care about this because why?" Doug asked, incredulously. "Donovan is expected to make a full recovery, isn't he?"

"Yes, his prognosis is good, not excellent," he cautioned. "He is not in a comatose state, but the bus he was on flipped over several times before it landed upside down in a ditch. The children were not wearing seatbelts. All of them were knocked around pretty badly. Most of their injuries are like Donovan's. He's young and healthy. I believe that his body will heal, but only time will tell us about the swelling in his spinal cord and brain."

Doug took a deep, shuddering breath. Chuck explained the worst-case scenario and that Donovan would need constant care for at least a month. Afterward he may need physical therapy for as much as six months to a year. Depending on his mental faculties once Donovan woke up, they would have to plot his medical and emotion regimen.

A short time later, Chuck received a page to report to surgery. Before he left, he gave Doug his pager and cell phone numbers and encouraged him to call at any time he needed him. Doug settled in to sit with Donovan in the treatment area filled with patients, beeping machines and medical personnel. Two medical personnel stations, at either end of the circular room and built in the round, contained desks, rolling chairs and monitors. Overhead reader boards reported the patients' names, condition and attending medical team. As Doug sat watching Donovan's vital signs continuously scroll across the reader board, he wondered how he was going to work his unpredictable schedule and manage to take care of Donovan's medical needs for the next year. He couldn't even move Donovan from the hospital until the extent of his spinal-cord injuries could be determined. Not that he wanted to move Donovan from Dr. Montgomery's care, but Doug would have to find a rehabilitation center somewhere here to care for Donovan before he could bring him home to Richmond. At least, if Donovan was at home, Mr. and Mrs. Diggs would watch over him as they did now. Doug resolved to ask Mrs. Alexander for a recommendation. He didn't have experience with hospital administrators, but she seemed very intelligent, competent, and efficient and one of the warmest, most caring individual he had ever met.

A few hours passed as nurses frequently came in and out of the bay to check on Donovan. While they did, Doug would get up to stretch his legs. After one such walk to the Men's Room, he returned to find the teen-aged boy putting a tray containing soup and a sandwich, chips, an orange, coffee and a bottle of water on the adjustable table adjacent to where Doug had been sitting. When Kenny Alexander turned to Doug, he smiled.

"You didn't come to the cafeteria, so I thought I'd bring something for you to snack on."

Doug was astounded at the teenager's compassion and efficiency. Then something occurred to him. "You're Sylvia Alexander's son, aren't you?"

The young man laughed quietly in amusement. "Grandson. One of many."

"The other young people I've seen streaking around here?"

"Guilty," Kenny said, chuckling. "We're first cousins. I live in California most of the year or in Washington, D. C., but I come home to visit my family as often as I can. We all do."

"Your parents are separated?"

"Hardly." Kenny said, wryly. "My dad's Kenneth Alexander, Lieutenant Governor of California, and my mom is Congresswoman JeNelle Towson Alexander, representative to the US House of Representatives from Santa Barbara, California. My brothers, sisters and I usually come home to

Goodwill to visit for spring break. In fact, all of the cousins come for spring break."

"But you're working during your holiday instead of heading to the Florida beaches?"

"Oh, that's nothing new," he said, with a little shrug. "My grandparents always put us to work."

"All five of you?"

Kenny chuckled. "Well, actually there more like thirty of us." At Doug's incredulous look, Kenny hastened on. "Only the five of us came to help at the hospital. Seven, including my twin brother, Kevin, went to the high school campus with our grandfather, uncles, and the rest are at several family homes in Goodwill fixing or cleaning up old toys; gathering clothes and shoes; washing pots and pans," he continued while Doug ate. They had spent a pleasant twenty minutes talking when Kenny rose to take the tray back to the cafeteria. Before he left, he promised Doug that he would return periodically.

For a few moments, Doug sat shaking his head. Never had he encountered any young adult like Kenny Alexander, Jr. This sixteen-year-old kid was, obviously, very proud of his parents and grandparents. His grandfather, Doug learned, was Dr. Bernard Alexander, Sylvia Alexander's husband, a former principal of Goodwill High School, then Superintendent of the Summer County school system, and was now the State Senator representing Summer County in the state capitol in Columbia, South Carolina.

Doug's mother died a few months before he enlisted in the Marine Corp. He had an older brother somewhere and he didn't have a clue where his father was these days. He got a post card from the man every once in a while, but never from the same place. Lily had been his family until she insisted on adopting the infant and naming him Donovan. Lily died nearly four years ago leaving Doug with Donovan, a child he barely knew or understood.

Doug was pretty much on his own since he joined the military and very much a loner during his military career. He met Lily Stone in high school and married her when they were twenty-two years old. Now at thirty-four, Doug was struggling with his single-parenting role while pursuing his career as a firefighter, a career requiring he be away from home most of the week. Mr. and Mrs. Diggs, who lived in the same duplex, watched over Donovan. Mr. Diggs, a retired postal worker, who worked part time at a Super Wal-Mart, and Mrs. Diggs, a retired elementary school teacher, became Donovan's surrogate grandparents. Doug knew that, without the Diggs', he would have been up the proverbial creek without a paddle when it came to taking care of Donovan.

Doug wondered how different his life would be if he had grown up in a supportive and challenging home environment, as Kenny Alexander did. He certainly did not have a frame of reference. Most kids in Doug's inner-city neighborhood were products of broken homes. In his youth, the area had its share of drugs and gangs, but Doug hung out at the fire station down the block from his home. One firefighter, Duke Patterson, spent time with young Douglas helping him with his homework, playing video or board games or just talking about male things. Doug met Duke's sister and his two daughters when Duke took them on outings to the beach or to the Richmond waterfront. Doug and Lily were invited to Duke's home for a few holiday parties or backyard barbeques and Duke and Douglas were still "close," he might say, although Duke was now higher up on the fire department's food chain and nearly ready to retire. They still might get together, now and again, to have a beer or to go to a ball game. Yet, if Doug had to name someone else who he was close to, there would not be anyone else on his list. He didn't have close friends, maybe a few guys he kept in contact with from his Marine Corps days, but they were scattered all over the country. So he had no one except Donovan in his life.

That was a sad commentary for a thirty-four-year-old man and a twelve-year-old kid.

5

Sometime, in the wee hours of the morning, Doug woke stiff from sitting upright in a chair. He yawned, stretched and then got up to check on Donovan. The boy was still asleep. During the night, Doug noticed the changing shifts. Now a new group of medical professionals was checking in and sitting at the nurses' stations. Doug overheard one nurse consoling another one.

"They just can't fire her like that, can they, Mary Ella?" Jennie Jones, whined, anguished, before she noisily blew her nose. "We were in that room when Satarah did the tracheotomy on that boy and set his fractures. But Dr. Steward didn't fire us, did he?"

"At this point, no one knows exactly what's going to happen to Satarah," Mary Ella said, patting the weeping Jennie on the back. "Dr. Steward wanted to fire her, but Mrs. Alexander and Dr. Montgomery stopped him. For now, Satarah has been suspended pending a formal investigation. They reassigned us, but Satarah and Mrs. Alexander both told us to just tell the truth about what happened."

"But what about Satarah? She saved that boy's life?" another nurse asked, disgusted.

"If you ask me," someone else said, "we could all be out of a job if that boy's parents sue the hospital."

"Oh, shut up, Cara. Stop scaring everybody. The hospital has insurance coverage to handle things like that."

"It's Dr. Steward who is ringing all the alarm bells," a male nurse interjected. "Satarah saved more than just Donovan Johnson's life since this storm hit us. She worked like a demon for five straight days with very little staff and no doctors available. If anything, I think they should pin a medal on her for courage above and beyond."

"Yeah, you would think like that, Morgan. You've been trying to date her since high school."

"That's enough. We have work to do," Mary Ella said, and walked away.

Others congregated in little groups from time to time recounting events surrounding Satarah and speculating about what could happen to her. Doug overheard most of the conversations. At least Doug now knew the first name of the woman who saved Donovan's life: Satarah. Mrs. Alexander declined to discuss her with him, but, by 6:30 A.M., Doug had finagled the name Satarah Whitfield out of one of the orderlies in the cafeteria where he went to have breakfast. Using the local county telephone book, he found an address.

When Dr. Montgomery made rounds at 7:00 A.M., he told Doug that he didn't expect Donovan to regain consciousness for, at least, another twenty-four hours, so Doug gave him and the nurses his cell phone number and left the hospital.

◈

Satarah Whitfield was deep in sleep when she heard the front door bell followed by the banging. Last night, when she got home from the hospital, it was after midnight. She waded through snow up to her kneecaps from the county road up the long quarter-mile driveway to her barn at the back of her home. Fortunately, her second-hand bobcat started and she was able to plow a wide enough trench to bring her temperamental old Jeep closer to the house. What the bobcat couldn't clear, she did herself with a shovel. Three hours later, numb with cold and fatigue, she left the lukewarm, stingy, shower spray. The hot water heater was on its last leg, but she would get to that in time. She actually had nothing but time now that she didn't have a job. That was her last coherent thought before she climbed naked under a mountain of homemade quilts

Since whoever was banging on her front door in this storm didn't want to give up and go away, and family knew that the door was never locked,

Satarah crawled out of her warm bed. She put on her old chenille robe and, as an afterthought, tried in vain to tame her long, bushy hair on her way to the front of the house.

Doug prided himself on being a pretty good detective by finding out the woman's name, but was not sure he had the right house after all. When he saw the name WHITFIELD stenciled on the old, battered mailbox and looked up at the monstrosity someone dared to call a house, he was nearly positive no one could possibly live in the derelict place. Oh, it might have been something in its day—the early 1800's—but it now resembled something from a bad Freddy Krueger movie. The big, iron gate at the entrance listed to one side. One brick post was crumbling. Slats, in what someone might laughingly call a white, snaggletooth fence, were missing. Huge elm, oak or maybe sycamore trees that lined the allée on both sides bent dangerously under the heavy ice and snow and could break at any moment in the nearly gale-force wind.

However, someone had plowed a narrow trench up the long, sloping driveway and there was a very old Jeep parked near a dilapidated side portico. As he made the turn into the allée, he noted that the house — perched on a knoll—sported broken, upper-level windows covered with cardboard. Doug didn't know anything about the style of the huge columns or the intricate ironworks that circled the three porches above-ground level of the house. He didn't know the difference between a gargoyle and a griffin. They were both ugly to his way of thinking. When he fought his way through the wind and snow up to the front porch, he wasn't sure it would hold his weight. After he rang the doorbell and banged on the door several times, he turned to look out over the vista and the panoramic view through the grey-white world stole his breath. There weren't any other houses he could see, but through the furious snow, nothing obstructed the scenic view for what seemed like miles of snow-draped trees. So in awe, he didn't immediately register that someone had opened one of the tall, wide, wooden doors with beveled-glass inserts"Come in," a sleep-laden voice called from behind the door.

Cautiously, Doug stepped inside. The door closed and then a figure with wild hair covering most of its face and head, down beyond its shoulders, shuffled off toward the back of the house. It was so cold inside that Doug could see his breath in the still air.

"Uh, excuse me," Doug called out, uncertainly, to the retreating Smurf-like figure. He thought he heard it mumble the words "coffee" and "come on back."

Cautiously he followed. When he entered a huge kitchen with sophisticated appliances and a long, wide, granite-topped, center-post prep station, Doug was genuinely surprised. Beautiful, honey-colored cabinets and closets hung or lined up on two walls; one of the cabinet doors hid the head of the person whose face Doug had yet to see. A quick glimpse to his left took in a family room of sorts with big, colorful pillows on the floor. A big flat-screen television sat on a raised brick hearth beside a glass-enclosed fireplace. On the wall, facing the door where he stood, were two sets of French doors that led outside to a covered porch. Beyond the porch was a field of snow.

Turning again to his right, he said, hopefully, "Excuse me, but I'm trying to locate Satarah Whitfield."

"Okay," was the foggy-voice response as coffee was ground and water dumped into a contraption commonly found in a coffee house. The person then set about pulling big, thick, royal blue mugs from another glass-fronted cabinet and placing them on the center-post island. Finally, turning toward Doug and using both hands, the mass of hair was lifted and pulled away from a woman's face. She blinked owlishly at him, as if she had forgotten he was there. "Oh, I'm sorry. Have a seat. This will be ready in a moment."

Never in Doug's life did he recall a complete stranger open a door to him and then turn their back. Certainly, no woman had. He was a big man and his size alone often intimidated people. Now Doug was sure it was a woman; a very attractive woman.

"Are you going to sit down or stand there staring at me while you drink your coffee?"

Doug blinked a couple of times, but the peek-a-boo glimpse at a long, sturdy, but shapely brown leg and thigh had him, momentarily, speechless. "Uh, are you Satarah Whitfield?"

"Yes. Hold on a minute." She breezed by him leaving a warm scent of woman in her wake.

When she returned, she was wearing old, grey sweats, thick grey socks, and run-down tennis shoes. He was still standing where she had left him. She had almost tamed the wild skein of hair in a scrunchy, but she still looked like someone who had done battle with a hairdryer and lost. She went to the coffee contraption and poured two mugs of something that smelled heavenly, like coffee, mint and chocolate combined. She sat one of the mugs in front of Doug and then took a sip of her own moaning pleasurably.

"Now," she said after another long sip, "I'm almost awake. What can I do for you?" She tilted her head to read the nametag pinned to his work shirt, "Deputy Battalion Chief Douglas E. Johnson?" She raised her mug again, which covered her nose and mouth, but something about her eyes, other than they were intelligent and utterly beguiling, tugged at the edges of his memory.

"I, uh. I understand that I have you to thank for saving Donovan's life." He watched an expression of curiosity cross her face.

"Donovan? I didn't have a patient named Donovan."

"The boy you did the tracheotomy on and—?"

"Is he alright?" she asked, urgently, reaching a hand out across the beautiful granite countertop to him with concern evident on her face. "When I left the hospital, Chuck, I mean, Dr. Montgomery said that your son's surgery to open his airway had gone well and that his vital signs were good." She went on recounting much of the prognosis Chuck had given him.

As they talked, Doug relaxed and was struck by the fact that she didn't seem to have concern for her own fate in the impending investigation, though she mentioned it several times. Her concern centered unerringly on Donovan. She even advised him on the possible legal actions he was entitled to take against her or the hospital, but she defended, vehemently, the actions of the two staff nurses who assisted her.

His admiration for her grew exponentially.

"Have you had breakfast, Douglas E. Johnson?"

Her question took him by surprise. "I had cereal and juice early this morning."

"For lands sake. That's not a breakfast on a day like today. I'll make a real Southern breakfast for you. Do you want to take a bath or shower before we eat?"

Doug chuckled. Southerners were a whole new breed. "I must smell pretty gamey." He ran his hand over his thickly-bristled head and jaw. "I've been wearing these clothes for more than forty hours."

"Get your bag and meet me down the first hall on your left."

When he did as instructed, he found Satarah in a big, combination sitting room and bedroom with high ceilings. A high-rise, four-poster bed dominated the room. An old-fashion chifforobe polished to a high gloss and a matching desk sat near a patterned settee and floor lamp. The walls were royal blue with white trim and brightly-patterned boarder wallpaper. Satarah was sitting on her haunches while lighting the fireplace that was stacked with wood. She turned and motioned him to put his duffel on a long, low, padded table and then yawning, pointed to a door that led into an old-fashioned bathroom, complete with a cast-iron, claw-foot tub. A shower curtain hung from a circular holder suspended from the ceiling. The sink was a pedestal style with a wide, square bowl. A white hutch with a royal-blue, face bowl and matching pitcher sat on top. The bath was painted white with royal-blue accents, thick bath towels with a white SH embroidered on each one. Two, long, thick robes—one white, the other royal blue—hung on hooks behind the door. He noted the perfusion of coordinating silk flowers and eucalyptus that hung on a wall opposite the tub and reflected in the oval mirror trimmed in gold Florentine over the sink.

Surprise, surprise, he thought, as he lathered up for a shave. From the outside, the house looked like it was ready for demolition. On the inside, however, the wide entrance hall had warm tones from dark blue to light with the SH scripted in royal-blue marble in the center. Empty rooms—or what he guessed could be called parlors—jutted off to the right and left. Curving wood banisters led up the wide staircase and looked like a replica of the one in the movie *Gone With The Wind.* Hallways apparently jutted to the right and left from the center staircase before going up to the third level of the house. Clearly, this place had been an old antebellum mansion at one time, Doug surmised.

While he trimmed his hair, he heard Satarah tell him, through the partially open door, to bathe fast. Breakfast would be ready shortly. He did just that, although the water was not plentiful or particularly warm, but when he stepped back into the bedroom to dress, it was melt-into-bed toasty with a hint of some type of fragrant wood smoke in the air.

Before he dropped his gear by the entrance front, glass-paneled door and found his way back to the kitchen, the scent of food hit him like a run-away train. His taste buds were doing a happy dance while his stomach growled a familiar refrain. When he entered the kitchen, he noticed Satarah at the opposite end of what looked like a round sunroom, though all he could see through the tall bank of windows was crazy snow. When he approached the semi-round, dark-blue banquette, the table was beautifully set with wide, white china and large, royal-blue, heavy-crystal glasses. However, the aromas coming from the covered blue and white patterned dishes and the breadbasket with big blueberry and apple cinnamon muffins drew him forward like a fish on a hook.

Satarah turned and smiled at Douglas E. Johnson. He wasn't an overly handsome man by traditional standards. What he had was a definable presence. His nose was a little too long and off centered and didn't quite line up with the cleft in his strong, square chin. His dark brown eyes were alert, but set a tad too far apart under heavy, black eyebrows and lashes. He was clean-shaven and wore no facial hair. His hair was still a little too long and thick, though he seemed to have shorn off a full inch. His wide mouth tended to curve down and she had yet to see those lips curve into a smile.

Of course, he had a son in intensive care at the hospital and facing many months of recuperative therapy so she guessed he had little to smile about at this point. What he lacked in general appearance, however, he more than made up for in size. He was *"a biggun,"* a big one, as her sainted grandmother might have said. Satarah smiled a little broader. She liked men his size. Beyond his less than star quality appearance, he was a bit reserved. Not aloof or snobbish, but not the type to offer an embrace easily or often. He had a definable military bearing that indicated he did not readily trust anyone.

Oh, yes, she had noticed how wary and suspicious he was when she invited him in to her home; a Northerner's reluctance not to be familiar too soon or too deeply. He didn't wear any artificial scent, but the light tang of fire smoke seemed to seep out of his pores and cling to his clothing. Yet, blindfolded, she'd be able to pick him out of a room full of men from touch or scent alone.

Interesting, she mused. She hadn't experienced the yen for a man's touch in quite a while. Still, something about big, strong Deputy Battalion Chief Douglas E. Johnson made her want to take a nice, healthy bite out of him.

"What?" Doug narrowed his gaze on Satarah's face. Something about the shift in her expression had him mentally slowing his pace and wanting to take a giant step back.

"Feel better?" She turned to pour more of the delicious tasting coffee into the fat mugs on the table.

"Uh, I do, yes. Thanks. I needed that."

"Would you like to wash your clothes?"

He would, but he didn't have an iron and board. He liked his clothes starched and pressed and wrinkle free. "I'll find somewhere in town to handle that while I'm here."

Satarah's laugh had his forehead folding into rigid vertical lines, but when he wanted to ask what she found so funny, she had bowed her head to bless the food. He waited until she finished to ask a few questions.

"You don't live here alone, do you?"

"Oh, no. My kids live here too."

"Kids?"

"Uh, yes, Jonathan and Jeffrey. They're nine going on nineteen." She chuckled.

"Then they must be out with their father."

Satarah almost laughed the food right of her mouth. She had to put her hand over it so she wouldn't embarrass herself.

"Not likely. He left nine years ago with Jonathan's and Jeffrey's mother."

For a moment, Doug was confused and sat back staring at Satarah. When nothing made sense, he said, "Come again?"

Satarah plopped a forkful of warm, sautéed apples into her mouth and chewed thoughtfully washing it down with a sip of orange juice before she spoke. Doug waited patiently for her to continue.

"It's a little complicated. You see, I married Jonathan Jeffrey Whitfield when we were much younger. We lived in a little, two-room place back of my parents' home for a while. My older sister, Carlotta, was still living at home and working at Miz Minnie Mae's beauty shop in Summerville. When she got pregnant,—my sister, not Miz Minnie Mae—without benefit of husband, our father kicked her out of the house. JoJeff and I took her in, since she said that she had no place else to go. She lived with us during her pregnancy; I helped deliver her twin boys and took care of her and the babies for about six weeks.

"One morning," she continued, while cutting into a fat, hot sausage, "I woke up late because JoJeff had been a sex maniac before I went to work and I had worked the night shift at the clinic. The boys were screaming at the top of their little lungs. I dragged myself out of bed and went to see what was wrong. No one else was home, so I got the boys changed, and fed, and went back to bed. The next time I got up the boys were making a racket. So, I changed them and fed them again. I didn't think about the fact that no one was home, but I stayed up to play with them, get some housework done because the diapers and baby clothes were piling up, and to get ready to go on duty at 11:00 P.M.

"When neither Carlotta nor JoJeff were home by dinner time, I wasn't worried, but by the time I needed to leave for work neither one had called or come home. I was going to take the boys to my father and ask him to watch them until Carlotta came home. That's when I noticed that my car was missing, but JoJeff's Harley was in the yard.

"My father was at home, but refused to keep the boys. So there I was stuck with two six-week-old boys and no transportation. If Carlotta were home, I would have taken JoJeff's Harley to work. I had to call the clinic where I worked to ask for the night off. I put the boys to bed and started calling around looking for Carlotta, but no one had seen her. Then I called Jinx's Juke Joint where JoJeff hung out with his friends to ask him to come home and stay with the boys so I could go to work, but he wasn't there and no one knew where he was. His parents own the garage over in Summerville where he worked as a mechanic, but he hadn't come to work that day.

"That's when I started to get worried, so I called the sheriff and asked if he would try to find JoJeff or Carlotta. Two weeks later, I got a post card from Carlotta saying that JoJeff was the twins' father and that she and JoJeff had run off together. They took the house money I kept in a cookie jar and the little savings JoJeff and I had in the bank. I haven't heard from either of them since." She rose from the table and picked up Douglas' plate. "Let me heat that up for you." She moved to the microwave oven, put the plate inside, and set it to reheat. While it did, she topped off their coffee. "Little did I know that my sister wasn't down at Miz Minnie Mae's salon curling hair all the time. Instead, she was curling my husband's toes often and continuously while I was in nursing school and working nights."

Doug sat in stupefied silence until his reheated food was placed before him. Satarah had delivered the story as if she were reading it from the newspaper.

When Doug tucked into his now piping hot meal, he asked, "So, was it a really good car?"

After a moment, Satarah burst out laughing. When she calmed, she said, "It had four wheels and a motor. I got more for the Harley when I sold it on eBay than the car was worth."

Doug could not hold back his laughter. Satarah noticed how his nice smile shifted the plains and angles of his face pleasantly and made his eyes dance with merriment.

"You have a nice smile."

He looked at her over the rim of the coffee cup. "And you're a great cook and have a great sense of humor."

"And two great kids who keep me cooking and laughing," she said around a warm smile.

There was a palpable, but comfortable, silence between them until Satarah rose to clear the table.

Doug got up to help. "Why don't I do that?"

Satarah looked over her shoulder briefly before she began rinsing the dishes and putting them in the industrial-sized washer. Deputy Battalion

Chief Douglas E. Johnson looked about ready to drop in his tracks, she thought.

"This won't take but a moment. Why don't you knock out for a few hours before you go back to the hospital?"

He was weary, more so than he realized before the meal. He had worked a seven-day shift, been awaken after only a few hours of sleep, driven for hours to get to the hospital and sat upright by Donovan's bed all night. It was now 8:30 A.M. The tension over Donovan, the long tedious drive through the storm, hours of restlessness, semi-conscious sleep beside the boy's bed finally coalesced into a deep exhaustion. "I don't want to impose."

"Take the room where you showered and dressed. I'll contact the hospital and let them know you're here if they need you."

"Thanks." He was humbled by her hospitality and left to take what he thought would be a short nap.

6

welve hours later, Doug woke in darkness and a bit disoriented. He knew he was not at the fire station house in Richmond and certainly not in his own bed at home, but it took him a moment to recall where he was and why he was there. The warm glow in the room came from the cheerfully burning logs in the fireplace. When he swung his legs out from under the heavy quilts, he rested his elbows on his knees, and dug the heels of his hands in his eye sockets to clear away the sleep. He had to admit that he felt very rested, renewed; better than he had felt in a long time. He also had to admit that the mattress was like sleeping on a cloud. After all the coffee he drank at breakfast, he should have been wired, but he wasn't. Stretching, he noted his neck and shoulders were devoid of tension. Pleased, he headed into the bathroom.

Doug was surprised his stomach grumbled while he brushed his teeth. He had eaten a lot only hours ago. He looked out the window and noted that snow was still falling on what looked like a good twelve to fourteen inches of snow. He didn't believe how much time had passed when he looked at his watch—twelve hours—half a day. While he dressed, he heard what sounded like pipes banging together. He also noted that his clothes from the thirty hours of wearing were cleaned and pressed; even his underwear gleamed in the bedroom glow. He picked them up and brought them to his nose. They smelled as clean and as fresh as a spring day.

When he stepped out of the bedroom, the clanging of metal against metal grew louder, but he could not determine where the noise was coming from so he called out for Satarah.

"Down here. The door is under the steps," she yelled back.

He went down the winding staircase, through a huge unfinished cinderblock area and followed the sound of the music she had playing on a small radio beside the area where she worked. She had on what could only be termed an old, washed-out, red rag tied around her perfusion of hair. Cobwebs stretched over her grungy sweats, and she had a couple of black streaks of what looked like tar on her face, hands and clothes. She was using a monkey wrench to tighten a water line leading from an ancient boiler. A couple of work lights hung from hooks in the ceiling illuminating her work area. Putting protective goggles over her eyes, she began soldering the joints of metal together. When she finished, she sat back on the ladder and looked at him critically.

"Sorry I woke you. You were sleeping pretty good when I went in to check on you. You look much better now; well rested."

It embarrassed him that he had slept so soundly that he did not even know that she was in the room. That big, comfortable bed and warm comforter were lethal.

"I've checked on your son several times while you slept, but there has been no change in his condition. He's resting comfortably, in stable condition." She resumed her work. Then she stopped and huffed out a frustrated breath. "Well, that's that until I can get replacement parts."

"What, may I ask, are you doing?"

"Changing out a few valves on the output water line." She went on to explain that the valves were corroded nearly shut, which accounted for the thin trickle of water. She proceeded to show him how she had wrapped the water pipes in insulation to keep them from freezing up. She relit the boiler and it pinged and hissed before it finally turned over. They watched the gauge as it began to register the increase in water pressure and temperature. "Well, no leaks. That's got it for a while. I soaked the valves in a solution of white vinegar and water while you were sleeping, and then cleaned out most of the corrosion with a wire brush, but I need new valves." She disconnected the spotlights and rolled the cords between her left hand and elbow. She put everything into a toolbox.

Doug took the ladder from her and then trailed her to another room. When she flipped on the florescence lights, he just stood inside the door and gawked. The workspace would have made Bob Vila envious.

Two sides of the wide, deep room contained peg-board walls that held an impressive array of woodworking tools, many of which he could not identify. There were long lengths of copper pipes arranged along the walls with extension ladders hanging lengthwise above. Nearly completed boxes, which looked suspiciously like the ones hanging in her kitchen, stood grouped together near a pair of sawhorses. A few opened boxes of floor tiles that were identical to those he saw in the vestibule were stacked on the concrete floor. Cans of paint, varnishes, and stains were neatly lined up on shelves. On a vinyl-top table were electronic saws, woodworking tools and laves. In wire baskets on shelves were electrical wiring in large bolts, switches, junction boxes, plugs and electrical faceplates. As she stepped further into the room, he saw a remarkable array of hand tools-hammers, augers, power drills, *ad infinitum.*

Noticing his silent gaze around the room, Satarah said with a little shrug, "So I'm a fan of HGTV."

"This is all yours?" Doug asked, incredulously.

"Some people can't resist The Shopping Channel, but I can't seem to pass up a sale at Home Depot."

"I'll say. You must have paid their light bill."

"And then some."

Doug picked up a tool belt that hung on a wall, and looked at Satarah's waist to her hips and then back at the well-used belt in his hand.

Satarah chuckled at his expression. "Some women wear jewelry around their necks and arms. Me? For some reason I prefer rawhide around my hips."

All Doug could do, without making a complete idiot out of himself by saying something about her impressive hips, was give a low hum in his throat.

He spent a good hour going through her workspace. She knew the names and uses of all of her tools and everything was well organized. She told him how she rewired the entire house using the secret passages that servants used back in the early 1800s when the house was first built. She had nearly completed all of the plumbing, too, using PEX tubing instead of copper. She let him work on one of her kitchen cabinet boxes while she instructed and looked on. He thoroughly enjoyed her stories about the nooks and crannies that honeycombed the house and the workroom. He was itching to do more, but it was getting late.

As they climbed the stairs, extinguished the lights, and closed the door, Satarah suddenly sprinted toward the back of the house, but veered off opposite the kitchen. Alarmed, Doug followed and found her in what looked like a large broom closet. It turned out to be a very cluttered office space with one skinny window.

"This is Satarah, over," she announced into a microphone.

"Oh, thank The Creator you're there, Sara Jo. We have a situation. Vivian Lynn has gone into labor, and we can't shake loose anyone at the hospital. Chuck's in surgery, but Kenny said you might—."

"How far apart are the contractions? Over."

"About fifteen minutes. Over."

"Okay. It's early yet. Keep timing Vivian's contractions. I'll be there as soon as I can. Over and out."

She turned to Doug who stood expectantly. "I need your help. Would you drop me off about six miles from here? It's on your way to the hospital. It would take too long to dig my car out."

"Sure, I'll dig mine out and be ready when you are."

"Unnecessary. I dug you out about two hours ago." She rushed out of the little office pulling her rag off her head. "But if you would load up that food packed in boxes on the kitchen counter, I'd appreciate it."

She was gone before he could comment. So he went to the kitchen still awed and a bit miffed that she'd dug his truck out while he'd slept. Not only that, she'd washed, starched, and ironed his clothes, pulled off a minor miracle with the water system and, he thought as he pried up Tupperware lids containing a huge, cooked turkey, a whole, fully-dressed ham, and what looked like the hind quarter of a cow covered with cooked onions and button mushrooms. Other equally-large containers held boiled potatoes and string beans, a large, deep aluminum pan of golden macaroni and cheese, collard greens, boiled brisket and cabbage, sweet potatoes swimming happily in a buttery cinnamon and lemon sauce, corn pudding with finely-diced green and red peppers, and dirty brown rice with a tub of giblet gravy. Five rows of biscuits and three rows of sponge cake with a chocolate sauce were in other containers. It took five trips to get everything loaded up. He was closing the back door of his truck when Satarah tore out of the house carrying a black medical bag and buttoning her hooded parker.

"I don't know how you expect me to ride in a car loaded with all those good smells."

"Did you get the shopping bag?"

"Shopping bag?"

"Oh, never mind. Here, catch." She tossed her medical bag to him and streaked back into the house.

He noted that her front doors were not locked and she was out of his view for a moment before she streaked out again carrying a shopping bag that appeared to be pretty weighty.

"What's that?" he asked when she placed the bag on the floor then climbed up into the front seat.

"Your supper or, as they say up North, your dinner."

"What's in it?" he asked, foolishly grinning as he drove down the long drive that now resembled a canyon.

"Oh, a little of this and a little of that," she said, flippantly, as she got comfortable. "Turn right at the fork in the road." A moment later, she said, "Hot damn, heated seats!"

He didn't want to think about what those seats were heating. Oh, to be a piece of leather that was heating her up.

"Thank God for Bigger. I absolutely love that man!"

"Bigger?" he asked and didn't want to think about why Satarah's mention of some man she loved caused his gut to seize up.

"Yeah, Bigger Thenham. He has better farm equipment than I do. He must have plowed my road for me."

"Uh huh," was all he could contribute while Satarah directed him through a series of what looked like single-lane back roads. His headlights flashed on a sign on the side of the road that read WELCOME HOME.

"Turn down this lane to your right."

He was tracking his route via GPS, but even as he zeroed in, the scene just showed a large patch of nothing. No roads or streets, but sure enough there were roads or "lanes", as Satarah called them, and glimpses of big, impressive homes the likes of which he never expected to see in the rural South.

She directed him up into a huge yard with a mansion nearly the size of hers, except this one was built in this century with fieldstone and glass; an absolute architectural wonder. The house was lit from inside and out. As they scrambled out and up to the double glass front doors, one opened and a small woman stood framed in the light.

"Hey, Aunt Oliver," Satarah called out simultaneous with a big bear hug. "Where's Uncle Romeo?"

"Mind yourself, Satarah James Whitfield. You know I'm miffed with you. Can't come visit a body or even show up at family dos."

"You know I've been working."

"Too hard I hear tell," she said and then turned a 1000-megawatt smile on Doug. "And you must be Douglas Johnson, the fireman from up North in Richmond. I'm Olivia Alexander Dixon, Mayor of Goodwill. Welcome."

Small towns, Doug mused, but was caught off guard when Satarah's Aunt Olivia hugged him like a son returning home a hero.

"Nice to meet you, Mayor Dixon. Uh, I can't stay. I have food in my truck to deliver to the hospital and check on my boy."

"Hello, Mr. Johnson," Kenny Alexander interrupted as he came in, from what must have been the kitchen, wearing a smudged, white-bibbed apron that read, *"I'm the King of the Kitchen and I've got the spatula to prove it."* "I checked on Donovan a little while ago. He's still not awake, but he's resting comfortably. Let me take your coat. My cousin, Linda and I have to go back to the hospital. We'll take the food with us. You can help Satarah Jo a lot better than I can."

That was when Doug noticed that Satarah was nowhere in sight.

Kenny must have noted his bewilderment, because he said, "Satarah is in with the monsters. I'll show you where."

Doug followed Kenny and as they got deeper into the cavernous house, the noise level grew. It sounded like a schoolyard at recess. When he stepped into what must be a playroom, Satarah was sitting cross-legged on the floor with about thirty children hanging off every conceivable part of her body. He imagined that one of the sets of twin boys was hers, but there were so many sets of twins that he couldn't determine which ones might possibly be her kids.

She seemed to be leading a very earnest discussion about birth. Hands flew up to ask or answer questions. Then they would quiet down to listen before hands flew up again.

"This might go on for a while," Kenny said, as he took off his apron. "I need to head back to the hospital. I drew KP duty for the monsters."

"I'm not a monster," a small voice said from below.

Doug looked down at the most adorable little girl he had ever seen. Kenny swooped up the child and looked into her big, earnest, hazel eyes.

"You're my lollipop, Shannon Rose," he said while the girl took his face in her small hands and puckered up for a kiss, which Kenny delivered with lip-smacking noises.

"You said I was your lollipop, Kenny James," an identical twin said fervently.

"Me three, Kenny James," another replica chimed in.

Again, Doug looked down to see identical upturned faces. He looked at Shannon Rose in Kenny's arm and then the two girls looking up. *Triplets?*

"Did you notice that we have a visitor?" Satarah asked the horde of children suddenly standing around him. To her question, the children chorused, "Hello, Mr. Johnson."

After he acknowledged them, he answered a barraged of questions about being a firefighter. Thankfully, Satarah rescued him and took him through a series of tastefully decorated rooms and hallways to a room that might have been in a hospital.

"So, how has your day been so far?" Satarah asked a very pregnant woman in the throes of labor.

"Oh, just like a day at the beach," she said, cheekily, and then held out a hand to Doug. "Vivian," she said by way of introduction. "You're Douglas Johnson from Richmond."

He took her hand to shake and something in her eyes caused recognition to light.

"Yes, and you're Mrs. Alexander's daughter. You have her looks." And, indeed, she did. She was a younger version of her mother except that Mrs.

Alexander had thick gun-medal gray hair, while her daughter wore her hair shorter than Doug's and plastered to her scalp in curly ringlets and waves. She had the look of Jada Pinkett Smith.

Vivian smiled brilliantly. "Thanks, Doug. I hope I have her constitution," she said around a grimace.

Satarah exited a wash area. "Scrub up, Douglas. It's almost show time."

If he was surprised or panicked, he didn't show it. Satarah gave him points for that.

"You're about to see parts of me unknown except to my most recent husband." When he didn't laugh, Vivian said, "Oh, lighten up, Doug. I promise to do all the work."

"And bless Eve in The Garden for it, too," he said, earnestly, and had both Satarah and Vivian snorting out a laugh.

"So, read any good books lately?" Satarah casually asked Vivian.

It didn't seem possible for such language to come out of the mouth of such a lovely woman, Doug thought.

$$7$$

Nearly an hour later, Satarah and Vivian were still wise cracking at each other.

"So what's it going to be this time, Viv? A boy or a girl?"

"How the Sam Hill am I supposed to know? I didn't put it up in there, did I? Ask my husband. He did it, for crissake!"

Shortly, thereafter a supremely pissed off baby girl pushed her way into the world. Chuck Montgomery strode in moments later and immediately went to wash his hands, and to gown and glove up.

"Can't leave you alone for a second before you have to steal the show," Chuck wisecracked.

"The fact that you *won't* leave me alone is the reason *for* this show," Vivian deadpanned.

"Never could and never will leave you alone," Chuck said around a salacious grin before delivering a kiss to Vivian's mouth that had Satarah's toes curling involuntarily and Doug swiping sweaty hands over his equally sweaty face and hair.

"Hush up, woman. I was talking to the newbie."

Everyone laughed while Chuck smiled at the new baby girl with a moist shine in his eyes. He reached a hand out palm up to receive the surgical scissors that Satarah slapped into his palm. Chuck cut the cord, tied off the parts, then raised his baby daughter up to inspect her universe as if he had taught Kunta Kinte's father the move. He then passed the baby off to Satarah who weighed and measured her, then cleaned her up while Chuck dealt with his wife. Doug was supremely happy that he had not eaten since breakfast as he watched Chuck work. Chuck and Vivian, though tired, carried on a running commentary the entire time.

Doug had a few minutes to himself to digest his dinner and the fact that the great basketball player, cum doctor, Charles Patrick Montgomery, was not just a local doctor, but Vivian's husband and that Vivian was a judge on the DC Circuit Court of Appeals; one step away from the U.S. Supreme Court. It also surprised him that Vivian was once married to one of the few true basketball icons, Derrick "Dunk and Jam" Jackson, a Black man and Chuck's best friend.

A Caucasian man married to a Black woman in the Deep South and this house, with its built in medical facility, *duh*, was their home. He shook his head, amused while he continued to wash up after dinner. Then a thought had him springing erect. He tried to recall his conversation with Kenny Alexander. Something about his family, but when there was a knock on the door, his thoughts dimmed and shifted to his need to get to the hospital to check on Donovan. It was going on forty hours since his arrival and he needed to work things out before he had to return to Richmond for his next shift.

When he walked out of the small bathroom, a tall, older man, who could have been Sidney Poitier's double, was sitting in what Doug could only describe as another parlor. The man rose and offered his hand.

"Hello, Mr. Johnson. I'm Bernard Alexander. I wanted to shake your hand and thank you for helping to deliver my grandbaby."

It took Doug a moment to connect the dots. This man was Vivian's father, the State Senator, who Kenny Alexander mentioned, and Mrs. Sylvia Alexander's husband. "You're welcome, sir, but I really didn't do that much. Satarah Whitfield did most of the work and Dr. Montgomery did the rest."

"Nonsense, Mr. Johnson. Vivian Lynn told me how you kept her distracted by joking with her and Satarah through the hardiest part of her labor."

What could he say to that? Just then, Chuck Montgomery strolled into the room, hands deep in his pockets, and wearing a silly grin. He walked into Bernard Alexander's open arms. Much to Doug's embarrassment, they hugged each other rocking back and forth, for what seemed like an inordinate period, and then held each other at arm's length staring into each other's moist eyes.

The three of them sat for a while, drinking a couple of excellent beers and smoking fat, aromatic cigars, before Mrs. Alexander and Satarah joined them.

"So, where's my cigar?" Satarah cracked when she plopped down in a big, forest green, leather, easy chair, leaning forward with elbows on her knees dangling her hands between her widely spread legs.

Satarah's behavior gave Doug something to focus on instead of the way Sylvia Alexander sat on the arm of her husband's chair, crossing her very impressive legs and delivering a very salacious kiss to her husband's waiting mouth while his big hand squeezed her knee. Focusing on Satarah, as she lit the cigar and took a long swig of beer straight from the bottle, had Doug nearly gaping. In a million years, he could not imagine his wife, Lily, ever behaving in that manner or looking half as sexy doing it.

Regrettably, she was wearing trousers when she crossed one ankle over the opposite knee, leaned her head back, took a very impressive pull on the cigar and blew perfect smoke rings into the air.

When he could take his eyes away from Satarah, he tuned back into Chuck's voice.

"We talked with Kenneth and JeNelle, Benny and Stacy, Gregory, and Aretha. We haven't caught up with Donald and Cecil, but we did get James and Janice. Mom and Dad will come down as soon as they can."

"When is the family coming?" Bernard asked.

"Easter. Everyone will be here then."

"Good. Good," Bernard Alexander said, pleased. "You'll be there, Sara Jo."

Doug watched the interesting array of emotions that played across Satarah's face while she contemplated Bernard's pointed stare; because it truly was a statement and not a question. When she simply nodded once, everyone seemed to release an easing breath that in the ensuing silence everyone, including Doug, seemed to have been holding.

They sat together for another little while drinking beer in the cozy parlor, with a roaring fire cheerfully licking logs, the underlying scent of something lemony, and enjoying a lively conversation. Sylvia Alexander looked at her watch.

"Okay, it's time we were all in bed. It's very late."

Doug, reluctantly, rose from his very comfortable chair. "I'd better get going to the hospital—."

"Not tonight," Chuck said, as he rose and stretched his tall, bulky, toned frame and yawned expressively. "I'll ride in with you in the morning. I have to make rounds at 6:30 A.M."

"But—." Doug sputtered.

"I'll show you and Satarah to your rooms," Sylvia said, as if the fact that he was spending the rest of the night there was a foregone conclusion.

"Don't bother to argue," Satarah said in a stage whisper. "It would be an exercise in futility."

So he didn't argue, since the expression on Sylvia Alexander's face didn't bode too well for his success. He followed Mrs. Alexander through hallways until they came to rooms across from each other.

"You're in here, Douglas, and Sara Jo, you're across the hall." Much to his surprise, Mrs. Alexander hugged and kissed them both on the cheek before sauntering away.

It was difficult for Doug to adjust to this demonstrative show of comfort, affection, and warmth, but when he turned to make a comment to Satarah, she was closing her bedroom door with a simple "Goodnight." He stood in the long hallway alone for a moment before going into his own bedroom. He was too tired to wonder how his duffle got into the room ahead of him. He shrugged out of his clothes, climbed into bed and was instantly asleep.

In the morning, Doug had just finished stowing his shaving kit in his duffle when a knock sounded on his door. He called out a "Come in," and Kenny stuck his head in.

"Good morning, Mr. Johnson."

"Good morning, Kenny. Did you have a long night?"

"Very long, but I checked on Donovan every few hours. No change yet."

Doug was genuinely appreciative of the young man's conscientiousness and expressed his appreciation.

"If you'll follow me, I'll take you to the breakfast room. Uncle Chuck will join you shortly."

"Thanks, Kenny. I wasn't sure that I'd be able to find my way alone."

Kenny chuckled and led the way. "If you think of the house as a giant letter H, it's not too hard to find your way around. You're in the guest wing, like the left inside leg of the H on the front of the house."

That made sense to Doug. He had a good sense of direction. "And we're moving up the left leg to the bridge between the two wings."

"See? Easy, right?"

Doug simply nodded. It was easy. When they turned left at the corridor intersection, they were having an easy conversation.

"So how long did it take to build this place?" Doug asked.

"Two years," Kenny said. "The house was designed by JaiHonnah Baylor and built by her husband, Roderick Baylor."

Doug stopped walking and stared at Kenny before he asked, "J. Rock Baylor?"

Kenny grinned and said, "Yeah," as if he tasted something delicious before they continued walking. "I actually dunked on JRock last year at the family reunion," he said with relish.

This family was replete with great basketball icons, so Doug asked, "You're related to JRock?"

"Not by blood, no. His wife, JaiHonnah, and Aunt Vivian were in undergrad together at Spelman. They're as close as sisters. My Uncle Derrick Jackson played ball in the NBA at the same time that JRock did. They were good friends, but Uncle Derrick died before I got to know him."

"Yes, I remember him. He was one of the greatest basketball talents. He and your Uncle Chuck."

Kenny acknowledged the sentiment and went on. "Anyway, JaiHonnah and JRock will probably be here for Easter with their children."

"Your grandmother mentioned something last night about family coming for Easter."

"Oh, yeah," Kenny said around a sigh. "Everybody comes home when there is a baby-naming ceremony."

Doug wanted to ask more, but they arrived at what could only be described as a cozy cafeteria. Buffet tables were lined up the center of the large breakfast room with steam puffing out of the long array of chaffing dishes. Round tables of eight ranged around the room that had three straight walls and one huge, floor-to-ceiling, curved-glass wall. Though the limited early morning light outside, Doug could see that snow still fell and the wind was still brisk. Somehow, surveying this room, that seemed to invite you in to relax and enjoy your leisure, the outside world seemed only a backdrop strictly for your entertainment.

One of the pretty, young women, who Doug saw streaking through the hospital was putting low-cut flowers at the center of each table. She stopped her task and moved toward Doug, with her hand extended toward him.

"Hello, Mr. Johnson. I'm Linda Jackson-Montgomery, Chuck's and Vivian's daughter. We didn't get a chance to meet at the hospital when you arrived."

"A pleasure to meet you, Linda," Doug said, shaking her hand. She was a pretty girl, but she didn't resemble Chuck or Vivian. Since she said that her name was Jackson, she must have been Derrick's and Vivian's daughter. "I noticed how busy you must have been when your grandmother stopped you from running in the hall."

"Yes, my grandmother knows how to rock and roll right over everyone." She chuckled. "Please, help yourself to the buffet. Dad will join you shortly."

Dad? Now he was really confused, but it would be inappropriate to ask so he simply said, "Thank you," and marveled at the poise and sophistication of yet another one of the Alexander grandchildren.

"Well, I'm out," Kenny said while he and Linda exchanged kisses on the cheek. "I'm going to crash for the next eight to ten hours, but I'll see you later, Mr. Johnson," he said shaking Doug's hand before disappearing through a door.

Doug stowed his duffel out of the way and then helped himself to the buffet. Just as the day before, at Satarah's home, the array of delectable breakfast entrées was irresistible. Doug could feel his arteries snapping shut before he took his first bite of fried catfish and then cutting into a big, hot, fluffy waffle with butter, blueberry syrup and warm strawberries dripping from the edges.

Doug was enjoying his meal so thoroughly and watching the panoramic view through the window wall that he didn't immediately sense that someone else was standing near him until he spoke.

"Uh, excuse me, Mr. Johnson. Do you mind if I join you? My name is—."

"William Chandler, attorney at law," Doug said, as he rose from his seat and shook the attorney's hand. He recognized the man he had seen on many Sunday magazine television shows and political networks. He was a regular guest on *Sweet Justice* and had filled in for the host, Constantina "Tina" Justice from time to time.

"My friends call me Bill," he said as he put his plate in front of him and sat. "I wanted a moment to speak with you. I should let you know that I will be representing Satarah Whitfield in the incident involving your son."

"Mr. Chandler—Bill, I am not going to take legal action against Mrs. Whitfield. She saved Donovan's life."

"I'm pleased to hear that, but if you change your mind, have your attorney call me at this number." He produced a business card.

"I'll accept your card, but I won't change my mind. In fact, if there is anything that I can do to assist Mrs. Whitfield, please don't hesitate to contact me in Richmond."

"You're leaving?"

"Not for a few days. I need to make arrangements for Donovan's care, but I have to get back to Richmond."

Before Bill could comment, Linda leaned in to pour more coffee.

"Well, good morning, beautiful."

"Hi, Uncle Bill," she said before giving him a kiss on the forehead.

"You pulling KP duty today?"

"Only the morning shift. Donald, Jr. has the lunchtime and Petra has the dinner shift. I have to be at the hospital around 11:00 A.M."

"You trying to hit on another one of my women, Bill?" Chuck interrupted, as he kissed his daughter's cheek. He placed two full plates on the table and took a seat.

"Since you stole the only woman I could ever love out from under me, you're damn straight I'm hitting on Linda."

"You still singing that same old sad song, Chandler?"

"Vivian and I did live together first."

"Yeah," Chuck said and laughed, "but she married me."

Doug's head swiveled between the two joshing Caucasian men until Mr. Alexander sat down with his plate of food and said, "Don't believe a word either of them say, Douglas. I am the man Vivian Lynn loved first and she still loves me best of all."

"Actually, I am the first *person* Vivian loved," Sylvia Alexander said, casting stern eyes around the table, as she sat down with her plate of food.

"Morning, Mom," Chuck and Bill contritely chorused before they commenced a silent prayer.

It was clear to Doug who ruled around here and she looked so lovely doing it, too. He almost felt like saying "Yes, my queen," and genuflecting to kiss Mrs. Sylvia Alexander's ring.

The conversation shifted to Vivian and the new baby when Satarah joined them at the table. She was wearing loose fitting white sweats and had almost tamed that wild a la Diana Ross mane of hers. She had it pulled away from her face, but it glistened with health and vitality in the subdued light. He had been staring at her for so long that when she looked up from her food and winked at him, embarrassment crept into his belly.

8

It was 6:15 A.M. when Doug and Chuck walked into the hospital, headed for Donovan's room. A man, not five-feet even, swaggered, in a hip-rolling, gun-fighter-cowpoke gait, up to Chuck.

"Howsit going, Bigger?" Chuck asked.

"Fair to middlin'," the small man said around an engaging, gold-toothed smile. "Had to bring old Rick Morrow in. Heart attack."

"How is he doing?" Chuck asked, concerned.

"Doc says how he'd be out drinking corn liquor and chasin' loose women soon enough." He beetled his brow around a serious thought, then said, "Don't know is how his misses is gonna' take too kindly to that though. Mz. Lula Mae, she don't take no tea for the fever, ya know?"

Doug could sense that Chuck was doing an admirable job of holding in a laugh considering the seriousness of Bigger's expressive statement. Besides, Doug didn't want to examine the glee he felt over seeing the man who Satarah said she loved. The top of Bigger's head might not reach much above Satarah's navel. On second thought, that, too, was a scary thought.

Chuck and Doug walked into the hospital ward labeled STEP DOWN INTENSIVE CARE together. While Chuck stopped at one of the round nurses' stations to review charts before he began his rounds, Doug went into Donovan's bay. He had to admit the boy looked somewhat better than he had the preceding morning. His skin wasn't quite as ashen, though the angry bruising around his face and upper body was clearly evident. The swelling had receded some, too. He seemed to be sleeping, but as Doug bent closer to the boy, he noted eye movement behind Donovan's closed eyelids.

In an uncharacteristic move, Doug reached out and touched Donovan's hand, careful not to disturb the intravenous feeding tube. He didn't recall ever physically touching the boy. He may have at some point, but couldn't remember when. Clearly, nowhere near the extent that he had witnessed over the past few days around the Alexander family. Touching each other seemed to be casual, but mandatory, even hugging was expected. Doug had never hugged another man, not even his counterparts in the Marine Corps and certainly none of the firefighters. He had shaken Duke Patterson's hand many times, but had never hugged him.

Of course, Doug acknowledged, he had touched women intimately both before his marriage and after Lily died. He hadn't formed committed relationships with any woman except Lily. Recreational sex was all that he wanted or expected from other women. Occasionally, it took a few dates to get to the sex, but after the few dates, the contact was only about mutually satisfying sex.

Doug never witnessed the blatant love, respect and honor displayed between Mr. and Mrs. Alexander or between Chuck and Vivian Montgomery. Certainly not in his own household. When his father and mother were together, they moved around each other much like two strangers. Doug never saw them kiss or hug each other. He couldn't recall whether either of his parents had ever been demonstrative to him or to his older brother.

Odd, he mused while holding Donovan's hand, how a few days of living in other people's homes brought up thoughts that he never examined before. He needed to think more about this issue. He had no real frame of reference, but, if Donovan survived, they were going to have to find a new way to communicate. Something that would not have Donovan sneaking off, disobeying direct orders or misbehaving in school. Doug silently vowed to make the effort and hoped that Donovan would respond better to a different approach. Maybe Donovan wouldn't grow up the way he did, without parental support, or grow to be as confident as Kenny Alexander or Linda Jackson-Montgomery, but, Doug wanted a chance to try and help Donovan achieve whatever goals he did have for himself.

Something moved, or lifted or changed inside him when he felt the slight pressure from Donovan's hand in his. Noting the rapid eye movement, he squeezed Donovan's hand, and whispered, "Come on back, Donovan. You can do it, kid. Everything is okay. Just open your eyes and look at me."

It was like swimming through molasses. He couldn't see anything, but he could hear something like buzzing in his ears. No, not buzzing—a voice. Someone was talking. It wasn't like what he heard walking through that long, dark tunnel toward that bright light at the end. The closer he got to the light, the brighter it got. The light wasn't like anything he had ever seen before. It pulsed like a living thing. When he reached out to touch it, to hug the light to him, to rub his face against it for warmth, his hands passed right through it.

Suddenly, the light was moving away from him, but he couldn't run fast enough to get back to the light. He was in that long dark tunnel again. Then he couldn't breathe. Something was stealing his breath until something else sharp opened him up and he could breathe under the molasses. He could swim and drift in the molasses like floating on a calm pool.

But the voice was there somewhere. He looked for the voice, but he couldn't see it. He knew it was there. If he could just see the voice. Touch it. Touch? Was he touching the voice? Yes, he was looking for the voice, but he was touching something. He squeezed the voice and it squeezed back. Then the voice was lifting him up. He held on to the voice as the molasses seemed to thin; getting lighter until what once was black was now brown. The voice was still pulling him up through the red, through the gold to the silver to the light.

"Open your eyes, Donovan," Doug said, when Donovan seemed to be searching for something, responding to his voice. Doug held on to

Donovan's hand and stroked his left hand over the boy's head. "That's right, Donovan. It's time to wake up."

Slowly, Donovan's eyes opened, but seemed unfocused or confused. Doug kept talking to him, as the boy's eyes followed the sound of his voice.

Chuck stood on the other side of Donovan's bed watching him try to connect, to plug into the world again. The monitors showed Donovan's vitals were coming up again, but this was only the beginning, Chuck knew. Next would be the hard part; testing and monitoring to determine whether the swelling in his brain and spinal cord would need surgical repair. And determining whether Donovan would live to be in a vegetative state for the rest of his life.

⁊

It was after 11:00 A. M. when Satarah's cell phone rang. She was surprised when she read Douglas Johnson's name on the caller I.D. When she answered and they talked about Donovan's progress, something seemed different about Doug's voice. What that something was she couldn't put her finger on it, exactly, but it was palpable. If she had to put it into words, she would say that some invisible hand was reaching out in his voice to touch her. *Silly thought*, she mused when they ended their conversation.

Douglas Johnson was the loneliest person she had ever met. Not in a sad way, particularly. Just that he was a loner. Unaccustomed to offers of help or support or affection. Not once since they met had he called anyone in Richmond to talk to about Donovan or what he was going through. No wife or other female companion accompanied him to South Carolina to give him moral support or comfort. His behavior was such that he didn't seem to want emotional help. In fact, he seemed surprised when that support came from her family.

Satarah had met self-sufficient people. In fact, she prided herself on being such a person. Yet, when she wanted or needed moral support, she knew how to reach for it. That was a difference between them. Douglas Johnson didn't know how to reach out for comfort or support. Or didn't have anyone to reach out to.

"Problem?" Vivian asked.

Satarah shook her head and turned on the ottoman to watch Vivian while she nursed her daughter. "That was Douglas Johnson on the phone. His son woke up this morning. He wasn't awake for very long, but Chuck has scheduled neurological tests for later today. Do you think that Chuck will be able to follow up on Donovan's care?"

Vivian nodded in the affirmative. "This little girl was either a little early or Chuck and I were wrong about when she was conceived. He planned to take a six-week leave of absence once our baby was born. Chuck's already rescheduled or reassigned patients at his hospital and office back in Maryland. He and I plan to stick around here until after Easter."

"What about you? Your work?"

"My close friend from undergrad at Spelman, Kristin Bryant Marshall is taking my place on the bench. She and her husband, Thomas, are living in DC now. Well, I should say that they are working in the city, but JaiHonnah and her husband, Roderick, built a nice home for Kristin and her husband, Thomas, not far from our farm in Prince George's County, Maryland. It is great to have close friends nearby."

"What about your other children? You're not going to keep them out of school until after Easter, are you?"

"I couldn't do it even if I wanted to. They wouldn't let me. They have their own schedules: school and outside activities." She went on to list what each child was involved in and then finished by saying, "And last but not least, Linda, my oldest, will start training again for the Alvin Ailey summer tour. Chuck and I will keep the little ones here with us, but Chuck's father, Steven Montgomery, and my mother-in-law, Harriet Jackson, will fly down as soon as the weather clears to take the other children back to Washington. We'll shuttle the children who don't have planned activities or events back and forth on weekends until after Easter."

"Good thing you own an airline, Viv. All that shuttling could get expensive."

"Ha! Remind me to explain how much it costs to keep one aircraft flying."

They talked a while longer until the baby was finished nursing and put to bed in a cradle next to Vivian's and Chuck's bed. Then Satarah insisted that Vivian stretch out for a nap before lunch.

"You like him, don't you?"

Satarah didn't pretend that she didn't know that Vivian was referring to Douglas Johnson.

"Jeez, Vivian. Who are you now? Our sainted grandmother?" Satarah laughed. "You're only, what, six or eight years older than I am?"

Vivian laughed too. "And if you think that you can get away with that little diversionary tactic, think again."

Satarah sobered somewhat. "Like him?" she questioned with a little shoulder shrug. "I don't know if it's that kind of party, Viv. He's an interesting study."

"For crissake, Satarah Jo, he's not a science project. He's a healthy male—."

"Uh huh, with a twelve-year-old son. And, perhaps, a mother for that son who Douglas Johnson calls a wife or a significant other somewhere in Richmond. Even if he is free, single and disengaged, he's carrying some heavy emotional baggage. I don't think I want to take that on right now."

"You don't look intimidated to me."

"I don't look crazy most of the time either, but I am. I want to help Douglas Johnson in small ways to get him back on an even keel by offering him friendship and moral support. I like a good roll in the hay every once in a while, like any other healthy twenty-nine-year-old female, but I don't want to buy the farm to get to the hay. Besides, I have almost enough sanity to raise my boys."

"I understand," Vivian said around a huge yawn, "but I'm not Sylvia Benson Alexander."

Satarah visibly shuddered at the thought of her *Steel Magnolia* aunt. "Geez, Vivian, why don't you just shoot me now?"

9

"The answer is no," Battalion Chief Stovall growled into the telephone. "All requests for a leave of absence must be submitted and approved ten days before——."

"This is an emergency leave request, Battalion Chief," Doug interrupted. "Not a request for vacation time. Emergency requests can be granted without prior notice. All I need is a doctor's statement for a medical emergency."

"You're not sick or disabled and you're not a freaking doctor, Johnson! The City of Richmond is not paying you to sit on your butt all day and look at your kid! So, if you're not back here by tomorrow to start your tour of duty, I will write you up as absent without leave!"

When Stovall slammed the phone in Doug's ear, he reluctantly resolved to get back on the road and make the drive to Richmond. It was either that or let Stovall put him on report. Doug had half a mind to let Stovall put him on AWOL and fight it out later in court. Going over Stovall's head to the Senior Battalion Chief might net some results, but it would take months to clean up the mess. Stovall would pile on extra duty, which meant Doug would not be able to get back to Donovan for another six-or-seven days.

"Ah, just the person I was looking for," Sylvia Alexander said, brightly, as she strode toward Doug. "I have a situation that I need your help with."

Doug automatically rose from his seat outside the radiology lab where Donovan was undergoing tests. "Sure," Doug said, shrugging. "Do you need more blood for the Blood Bank?"

"Oh, no. I know that you've already given blood today. I need help with a different situation."

"All right. Do you want to talk about it here and now?"

Sylvia checked her watch. "Have you had lunch yet?"

"No, not yet."

"Good. Let's go eat."

"Actually, I was waiting for Donovan's test results," he said, hooking his thumb over his shoulder toward the radiology lab. "He's been in there for about two hours."

"Oh, then you have plenty of time for lunch. The technicians have to read the data, do a report on each test, and then discuss the results with the primary physician and specialists. We will be finished with lunch before Chuck is prepared to speak with you about what the tests show.

"Chuck is in surgery now and he's going home to have lunch with Vivian and the children when he comes out. He's been busy since he got to the hospital this morning. I don't know how he keeps up his stamina, but he has always been that way. Dedicated to his family and his patients. He's very pleased that Donovan woke up."

It took a moment for Doug to realize that while Mrs. Alexander was talking, she had tucked her arm through his, guided him through the hallways, and they were now standing in line ordering lunch. So intent on her conversation, he didn't even remember the stroll through the halls and into the crowded hospital cafeteria. They talked through lunch, but it wasn't until they finished eating that she got around to discussing what she wanted him to do.

"Early this morning," she began, "our Summer County fire chief suffered a heart attack. He has been scheduled for a triple bypass tomorrow. His prognosis is good, but he will be off the job for some time and we need someone to step in to hold down the fort until Rick Morrow is back on his feet. So, we thought that, since you were going to be here anyway to monitor Donovan's progress, that you would be willing to help us out."

Usually, Doug was a quick study, but Mrs. Alexander made it difficult to keep up.

"Let me see if I understand what you're asking. You want me to step into your fire chief's position indefinitely while he is recuperating?"

She nodded and smiled at him. "See, that wasn't too difficult, was it? I knew you were a quick study."

"I want to help, Mrs. Alexander, but I'm only a Deputy Battalion Chief in Richmond. That's a long way down the chain of command from Fire Chief and Director of the Fire Department. I don't have the credentials to step into a Fire Chief's job.

"Second, if the roads are passable, I have to leave later this evening and get back to Richmond before my tour of duty starts tomorrow morning.

"Finally, there must be other officers in your fire department who can step in while your chief is recuperating." He waited a beat before saying, "Why are you smiling like that?" He felt more than a little suspicious about the way she was looking at him.

"Oh, nothing, really. I noticed that you didn't mention any personal reason for not being available to help us."

Doug stared a hard moment at her before he said, cautiously. "Personal reasons? Do you mean a wife or female friend?"

"Yes, that's what I'm referring to or any other familial relationships. For example, your parents or elderly relations who you're caring for."

Doug's suspicions grew. "Donovan's mother died four years ago. There is no one else who I'm responsible for except him."

Interesting how he phrased that statement, Sylvia mused. Not that his wife died, but that Donovan's mother died. Also interesting that he did not mention any other familial or committed relationship. "I'm sorry that you lost your wife, Douglas, but as to the other concerns, let me address them in the same order in which you raised them.

"First, you are more than qualified to handle our Fire Chief's position. You're a decorated Marine Corps veteran, which says that you know how to lead in a critical situation, a graduate of Richmond State University with thirty hours toward your master's degree, and a published author of several fire safety and training manuals. You've lectured on the subjects of proper training and procedures at conferences and firefighters' conventions. You're a bright young man, a smart man. What you do not know about this job, you will figure it out in no time. Our current Fire Chief is a retired dentist. He started with far less skill and knowledge than you. He was appointed to organize our fire department and used your published manuals to do it.

"Next, your Battalion Chief simply hasn't been made aware of his duty to help other struggling communities and to share information on new or emerging firefighting techniques. I'm sure that once he's approached on the need to share your talents with Summer County, he'll consent to letting you remain with us.

"Finally, our department is sixteen months old and mostly staffed with volunteers. There are no officers qualified to take over for Rick. My husband got funding from the state and other sources to buy the equipment, build the station houses, and outfit the firefighters. My husband is a bright, energetic man, but even he can't handle being our representatives to the state senate and run the fire department simultaneously. Now we could start a search for a temporary chief, but that takes time and we're in a crisis mode right now. The firefighters are a young group of men and women; their average age is twenty-four. None of them have prior experience." She sat forward, bracing her forearms on the table and gave him one of her bright, beguiling Cheshire cat grins that had Doug mesmerized. "So, as you can see, Douglas, you're our man. A bird in the hand, so to speak."

When her beeper sounded, she excused herself and went to one of the blue telephones to answer her page.

Doug sat back in his chair to consider her offer. People, who stopped by the table where he sat to introduce themselves or just to say hello, interrupted him a few times, but he still had time to contemplate Mrs. Alexander's offer. Strangely, he didn't question whether she, a nursing school administrator and the Chief of Nursing at the hospital, had the authority to make such an important offer.

Frankly, he was a little stunned that she knew so much about his background and had an uncomfortable feeling that she knew more about him than she had revealed. Not that he had anything to hide or to be ashamed of. There weren't many mysteries in his growth and development. He was an inner-city, street kid who managed to dodge the pitfalls that swallowed others in his neighborhood. He wasn't a particularly gifted student, just curious enough to stay in school through high school. He wasn't particularly athletic either, never had an opportunity to play organized sports. Well, he did like baseball and joined in impromptu games while he was in the Marine Corps.

He wanted to be a firefighter, so he subjected himself to the discipline, academic and rigorous physical training required by the job. Because there wasn't much to do between alarms, he read novels for relaxation and newspapers and magazines to keep up on current events. He used his computer mostly to do research, but occasionally he'd log-on to one of those game sites to play Backgammon or chess. He did things that he could do alone. That was pretty much his life's story.

Doug looked up when Mrs. Alexander resumed her seat. She was again grinning at him.

"Sorry for the interruption. That took a little longer than I expected. So, are you going to help us?"

"I want to, but you don't know my Battalion Chief. He is adamant that I report for my tour. I can't afford not to go. It's a bread and butter issue, you understand. My health insurance covers eighty percent of Donovan's care. I'll have to cover the rest out of pocket. I need to stay employed, so that means I have to work."

"Oh, I forgot to mention that the Fire Chief's job is salaried, with both full medical and dental coverage. We have several other positions budgeted, but not yet filled. We'd hoped you'd be able to bring in experienced firefighters and investigators to fill those positions." She went on to discuss other plans that the county had in the works that involved the fire department. Summer County was particularly keen to have county homes and businesses inspected for potential safety problems and then corrected to avoid disasters. "So, you see, we really need your help, Douglas."

He had a growing interest, bordering on excitement, when he decided to lay out certain facts.

"I need to tell you about something that may change your mind about me." He went on to discuss the court case that had put him in disfavor with the Richmond Fire Department and the harassment suit he had pending.

When he finished, she asked, "Did you tell the truth about what your research revealed?"

"Yes, but——."

She held up a finger to forestall his interruption. "Given what you know now, would you do the same thing again?"

He had to think about that for no more than a moment. "Yes. Given the same set of circumstances, I would do exactly the same thing."

"Yes, I know that you would, Douglas. You have the courage of your convictions to sustain you, even in the face of adversity from your peers. You're exactly who we need to head the Summer County Fire Department."

"Mrs. Alexander, there is still the problem of my station chief—," he started, but then his cell phone rang. He was surprised since he rarely received calls except from Mrs. Diggs or Donovan. Without looking at the number, he took the call. When he heard Battalion Chief Stovall's voice on the line, his eyes landed on Mrs. Alexander like a ton of bricks. Stovall's voice was so conciliatory, so solicitous and supportive that Doug wasn't sure that it was the same man he had spoken with a scant few hours earlier, but when Stovall ordered Doug to stay and help the Summer County Fire Department, Doug knew that Stovall's body must have been invaded by aliens or that someone had given him a come-to-Jesus lecture.

Doug had a sneaking suspicion of who that person was: The Steel Magnolia sitting across from him holding his stare with a completely innocent expression on her lovely face. Her eyes, however, held a devilish gleam.

He ended his call and sat for a long moment while they stared at each other.

"How did you *do* that?" he asked, bewildered.

Sylvia didn't pretend that she didn't know what he was talking about. She just shrugged her shoulders elegantly and grinned at him. "Well," she said on a long breath. "Now that that's settled, I have to get back to work. Why don't you meet me at 6:00 P.M. in the employees lounge? You can take me home. We'll have dinner at my home so we can talk a little more."

Doug had a feeling that any attempt at protest was futile. "Yes, ma'am."

She winked at him, causing something to stir in his memory, but before he could capture the thought, she was off and running, her wonders to perform.

⸎

It was 6:15 when Doug, behind the wheel of his truck with Mrs. Alexander in the passenger seat, entered what he considered a "dead zone" on his GPS system. Briefly taking his eyes off the road, he tapped the glass-covered system again, but still it did not register the road they were on. The screen had gone blank shortly after they left the hospital.

"Something wrong?" Mrs. Alexander asked.

"Nothing much. The GPS program has been malfunctioning. The software probably just needs to be updated."

"Turn left into the lane up ahead."

Doug did as directed and soon a snow-covered farmhouse with a barn and outbuildings, that looked like they should be in a Currier and Ives painting, came into view. The lane had been cleared of snow and veered off to the right and left. As he followed her directions, he could see lights from other homes that seemed to circle the one they were approaching. Before they pulled close, lights flicked on, illuminating the SUV with state senatorial tags parked under a *Porte cohere* at a side entrance to the farmhouse. Snow topped the roof, attesting to the extraordinary depth that had fallen.

"We're here," Mrs. Alexander announced.

Doug climbed out and opened her door. She took his hand as she stepped down from the high carriage of his big SUV. The side door to the house opened and Dr. Bernard Alexander waved a cheerful greeting before he took his wife into his arms for a welcome home kiss. The aroma of food and warmth wrapped around Doug like a willing woman's embrace and his salivary glands did a familiar happy dance.

"Come in, Douglas, and welcome to our home," Dr. Alexander said with a hardy handshake. "According to the reports, this weather system isn't done with us yet. There is still a lot of moisture in the air and it's supposed to be in the single digits tonight." He patted Doug's shoulder. "Come back to the kitchen. Dinner will be ready shortly."

Doug took off his coat, hat and gloves, which Mrs. Alexander took to hang up. He followed Dr. Alexander into a very cozy area that must be a family room. Family pictures covered nearly every wall.

"Make yourself to home, Douglas. I need to check my pots."

"Thank you," Doug said, before Dr. Alexander went to the big, country kitchen that overlooked the family room. "Is there something that I can do to help?"

Dr. Alexander waved him off.

"He wants the kitchen all to himself," Mrs. Alexander said and chuckled. She handed a glass of ruby-colored wine to Douglas. "Bernie fancies himself a cook."

"I heard that, Silvy, and I am a chef, not just a cook. You just wait and see."

"Yes, honey," she said, patiently, and as an aside to Doug, said. "Don't worry. I know how to pump your stomach," and chuckled at his horrified expression. "I have to change out of these clothes. Relax. I'll join you shortly."

Doug turned and walked toward a raised hearth fireplace that pumped out heat from the roaring fire and was immediately intrigued by the long, panoramic photograph hanging above that easily could have been ten feet long and two feet high. He drew closer and looked at what must have been hundreds of smiling faces at some type of gathering. He walked along it and easily picked out Dr. and Mrs. Alexander and then Chuck and Vivian Montgomery.

Dr. Alexander flipped on spotlights, which enhanced and illuminated the picture and then came to stand beside Doug. "Last year's family reunion."

Doug nearly goggled. "These people are all related?" he asked.

"Everyone one of them," Bernard said, proudly. "Not everyone can get home for the July 4th family reunion, so about half are missing. We're spread out all over the globe."

"Missing?" Doug couldn't imagine it. That many people related to one another. "This many people come together for one day?"

Bernard chuckled. "Oh, no. The annual reunion is up to five days now. The family council wants to extend it to seven days next year. Goodwill's population swells substantially for the holiday."

"Goodwill is not a big community. Where do they all stay?"

"RVs, tents, pop-ups. We bring in doublewides, too. Housing isn't a problem with all the farm land in the family and the families who live or have homes here. Food or facilities either. My nephew, James Dixon, my sister's son, manages our families' hydroponics' farm. We grow fruits, vegetables, and flowers year round. My brothers, Edgar, Alvin, and I have a herd of cattle and a poultry farm. We raise pigs, too, and sheep." He turned to look at Doug. "You'll be here for the next family get-together. You'll meet many of Sylvia's relatives, too. We've got some great things planned, and, as Fire Chief, you'll be able to make sure everyone has a safe holiday. Of course, we would like it if you would do a seminar at the reunion and consider teaching our prep school students about careers in Public Safety."

Obviously, word of his temporary assignment had gotten around. Doug agreed to put it on his schedule, which delighted Dr. Alexander.

"This is our eldest son, Kenneth James, our daughter-in-law, JeNelle, and seven of our grandchildren," Bernard was saying as they turned to look at a wall filled with family group portraits.

"There's Kenny," Doug said, spotting the young man among his very handsome family.

"No, that's Kevin. Kenny's the other twin sitting on the floor beside his mother. This is their younger twin brothers, Jarrett and Justin, their twin sisters, Marcella and Michelle, and then Kendra, and their younger brother, Kirk, and sister, Kristine." He went on to give the name, age and interests of each one. "And this is our next son, Benjamin Staten, who is an Air Force Colonel, and our daughter-in-law, Stacy, who is a Naval Officer, and another seven of our grandchildren."

"I met these three little girls at Chuck's and Vivian's house." Doug leaned closer. "They have two sets of triplets?"

"Mmm," Bernard hummed around a grin. "The eldest daughter is Whitney Ivy, then the girls, Shannon, Sierra, and Sharon and the boys, Benson, Bernard, and Bradford."

They moved on to a very large portrait. "Chuck and Vivian you've already met."

"Yes, I recognize their daughter, Linda, but I didn't know they had this many children."

"There are a lot of children who need a loving home," Bernard said proudly. "Chuck and Vivian live on a farm in Maryland outside of Washington, DC. They have plenty of space in their hearts and in their homes for children, so they adopt children who need them. Most of their adopted children had health challenges at one time or another. People are sometimes reluctant to adopt a child who may have excessive medical bills, but that doesn't concern Vivian and Chuck." He went on to name each of Chuck's and Vivian's children without delineating which were natural or adopted. He listed them only by age.

"Next is Gregory Clayton, our youngest son. He lives in New York City. He's a stockbroker, but he's not married yet. And our baby is Aretha Grace. She's in her final year at Harvard. You'll meet them at Easter time."

"You have quite a family, Dr. Alexander."

"Thank you, Douglas, but, please, call me Bernard. We don't stand on ceremony here."

Somehow the honor touched something inside Doug, so he simply nodded. Bernard continued to introduce Douglas to the faces and families on the walls, his brothers and sisters and those of his wife and all of their offspring. Mayor Olivia Alexander Dixon and her husband, Romelo, Doug learned was Bernard's sister. They had two sons, twins, Donald and James. They were married to very intelligent and attractive women, Cecil and Janice, respectively, both of whom held PhDs. The resemblance between Donald's and James' eldest ten-year-old sons was strong and uncanny, Doug thought. Even Kenny and Kevin could have passed for twins. Most of them seemed like recent photographs until he got to some that didn't look recent.

"My parents and grandparents," Bernard said, with warm reverence and then pointed to Sylvia's parents' and grandparents' pictures. Something about Sylvia's grandmother had Doug drawing closer. Though it was an old portrait, strangely enough, the grin on Sylvia's grandmother's face, the hip-shot stance, and the voluptuous body, reminded him of Satarah Whitfield.

"Your grandmother-in-law looks like an interesting woman, Bernard."

"Singer, dancer, actress," Sylvia said, as she joined them. "She and my grandfather were in show business. My grandfather played any instrument he could get his hands on. In their youth, they toured America and Europe with the big bands; Count Basie, Dizzy Gillespie. They were top headliners in France and other European countries and traveled with the great Josephine Baker. They lived in Paris until the war started, then came home to raise a family."

"Uh, your grandmother didn't do that—." Doug hesitated.

Sylvia chuckled and her eyes lit with merriment. "The Banana Dance? *The Danse Sauvage?* Yes, she did, quite well, actually, according to the show reviews. She was often a stand-in for Ms. Baker."

"Quite an experience for a young couple," Doug commented, embarrassed, recalling that Ms. Baker's signature dance was very provocative at the time, and then pointed to a sepia-toned picture. "This woman resembles Satarah Whitfield."

Sylvia chuckled. "My older sister, Mariah, Satarah's mother."

Doug turned his head toward Sylvia. "Then Satarah is your niece. I knew there was something about the two of you that was familiar. You have similar mannerisms."

Sylvia beamed, her appreciation evident. "Mariah named Satarah after Ms. Baker, Satarah Josephine. That made our parents and grandparents very happy. Sometimes we call her Sara Jo."

"Does she live here? Your sister, I mean."

Sylvia shook her head. "No, Mariah lives in Paris, France. She is the only one of my sisters and brothers who followed in our great grandparents' and grandparents' footsteps. She's an actress and songstress. She doesn't tour as much anymore and only occasionally accepts a movie or television role. She owns a jazz club that is quite popular in Paris. She hasn't been home since Satarah graduated high school."

"What? Wait! You don't mean The French Mariah, do you?"

She nodded, her smile sweet, but a little sad, Doug thought.

The way Bernard touched his wife, drew her to his side and pressed a kiss to her hair spoke volumes to Doug. There was a story there that neither Bernard nor Sylvia seemed willing to tell, so Doug moved on and got little bits and pieces of the rest of their family trees.

When they sat down to eat, the Alexanders were chatting amusingly with him about their families' antics. The meal was delicious—chunky beef stew chocked full of fresh vegetables and new potatoes, crusty homemade cracked wheat bread with a tossed field greens salad, smooth vinaigrette dressing, and a full-bodied red wine. After his second helping, Doug thought he had died and gone to heaven, but when Bernard brought a hot-from-the-oven pineapple upside-down cake to the table with homemade pineapple ice cream, Doug found space somewhere for two slices and three scoops of ice cream.

"Bernard, you missed your calling. You should have been a gourmet chef," Doug said, laughing while he patted his full, flat stomach.

"See?" Bernard boasted, gleefully, to Sylvia. "What did I tell you? Douglas knows good food when he eats it. I think you should let me cook more often."

Sylvia looked at her husband, and spoke to Doug. "He races home so that he can fool around in my kitchen, but I'll admit this has been one of his better experiments." She rose from the table to collect their dishes. "There's a method to his madness, though. He hates to do the cleanup. Especially since our children aren't here to do the dirty work for him."

Bernard looked suitably contrite until Sylvia planted a noisy kiss on his pursed mouth and then winked at him. Bernard watched the sway of his wife's hips as she sashayed to the sink to begin the cleanup. He wasn't a bit chagrin when he turned back toward Doug grinning. They laughed the way men would wont to do. They went into the family room to prop their feet up on ottomans and downed after-dinner coffee and cognac while they solved the world's problems.

Doug was pleasantly surprised at how much he had enjoyed the evening and the Alexanders' company. "It's been a wonderful evening and I thank you for having me."

"We're glad you enjoyed it. We certainly did and we'll expect you to come back often."

"Thank you. I'd be happy to," Doug said, as he rose to shake Bernard's hand.

"Let me get our coats," Bernard said. "We'd appreciate it if you'd give us a lift to Chuck's and Vivian's before you take Satarah back to Summerville."

Doug was taken aback. "Sure, but does Satarah know that I'm coming?" Doug asked Sylvia.

"Of course, she does. You'll be staying with her while you're here," Sylvia said, brightly.

"But, but, I don't want to impose—."

"Psshaw!" Sylvia scoffed, mildly, as Bernard helped her into her coat. "You're doing a favor for us and for Satarah Josephine. In fact, for the whole community. You can keep her company while her boys are visiting with their cousins at Chuck's and Vivian's. Tomorrow, Satarah can take you to the Fire Department headquarters in Centerville to meet your crew. I think the meeting is set for nine o'clock."

Doug stared. "And if I asked how you set all of this up since we talked at lunchtime today, you probably wouldn't tell me, would you?"

She rose on her toes and kissed his cheek, then smiled gamely. "See, I told you that you've got smarts."

There was that little wink again so reminiscent of Satarah.

When they arrived at the Montgomery's mansion, the Alexanders insisted that he come inside for a visit and to see the baby girl he helped deliver. He was a smart man or he had a healthy fear of what Sylvia Alexander was capable of if he refused.

An hour later, he had not only seen the "newbie" as Chuck dubbed his and Vivian's new daughter, but he had also met all of their children, their cousins and Satarah's boys, Jonathan and Jeffrey. Mayor Olivia Dixon was there and introduced him to her husband, Romelo, a real comical character nicknamed Romeo, and one of their son's, James and his wife Janice Atterly Dixon, both of whom held PhDs. The other son, Donald and his wife, Cecil Jordon Dixon, were out of town. Donald was an attorney and his wife held a PhD in Oceanography. She was also a Nobel Prize winner and held post doctorate credentials. Their children as well as James' and Janice's were present and accounted for. The adults watched a new *Star Wars* movie in the in-home theater with the children complete with hot buttered popcorn and iced fruit drinks.

Doug sighed. He hadn't felt this good in he didn't know how long— probably ever. Chuck discussed Donovan's progress with him, the results of the tests, and a course of treatment he planned for Donovan's recovery. Talking with Chuck about Donovan was a load-lifting experience. Even more energizing was watching him and Vivian interact with their children. They were very natural and comfortable with their multiracial, multicultural brood crawling all over them and it was clearly apparent that the children loved their parents and each other. The older ones took special care of the younger ones. The cousins, Kenny and Kevin, and Linda, worked and played, as if they were brothers and sisters. There was teasing and horseplay, but all of it good-natured and based on a bedrock of mutual love and respect. And then there was Bill Chandler stretched out on the floor with Chuck's and Vivian's children snuggling up close to him as if this legal icon was their teddy bear. Doug found himself in the midst of it all enjoying himself just like the kids.

When all of the children had been washed and bedded, Doug and Satarah waved goodnight and drove away, headed to her home. The night was very cold, but the storm was slowly passing, leaving a pristine winter wonderland and a deep-blue sky with few snowflakes and bright twinkling stars.

"Take the next right," Satarah said, bringing Doug out of his thoughts. He did as she instructed, then decided to tackle the next hurdle.

"Satarah, I know that the Alexanders arranged for me to stay at your home while I'm here. If you're uncomfortable with the arrangement, I could find somewhere else to stay."

"You don't like my home?"

"No, no," he sputtered, "I mean, I like your home very much, especially your workroom. It's just that—."

"If you don't like my cooking, I'll understand."

"Your cooking? Are you kidding me? Satarah, you're a great cook!"

"Then you don't like me."

"Tarnation, woman! Of course, I like you! You saved Donovan's life and you've been nothing but gracious and supportive since I landed on your doorstep!"

"Well, then, enough said. The next turn is up ahead on the right and then we're home."

Home. She said it as if he truly belonged there. And he had to admit that everyone he met since he arrived made him feel like he was returning home. He liked the feelings he was having. A lot. He was looking forward to his new professional challenge, even though the Fire Chief's position was temporary. At least, so far, he felt he wouldn't have to watch his back every minute he was on duty. And he would try not to be so suspicious of everyone. Examining and dissecting everything anyone said to him, looking for a hidden agenda. He'd keep his guard up, for the next little while, but he would do his job; the best job he was capable of for the people who had given so much of themselves to and for him and Donovan and asked for his help.

10

Satarah sat cross-legged on the padded seat in the kitchen waiting for the sunrise and sipping her first cup of coffee of the day. She needed something good to happen today and watching the sunrise was about as good as it got after the blizzard. Though she regretted not going in to the hospital and working with her staff and patients, she felt content that Mary Ella Baker would keep up a high standard of care in the ER until she could return to work. And, after talking with William Chandler—Bill, she corrected, and Vivian yesterday, she wasn't concerned overmuch that she wouldn't be permitted to pursue her nursing career or return to her position at the hospital.

Though Aunt Sylvia, Chuck and Bill argued in her defense when they all met with Dr. Reynard Steward, he was adamant that she be suspended— without pay. That put a hitch in her step, all right. She had to have an income during the winter months until the spring. The little nest egg she had from the sale of Christmas trees from her tree farm would hold her over for a month or two. Just enough until she could sell her lumber and maybe some of her seedlings. But she was afraid that she would have to delay further work on her prize project: renovating, restoring and remodeling her bed and breakfast. She had only completed a few necessary rooms on the main level mostly to accommodate her family, but she hadn't begun any work on the west wing of the house or the second or third floors and nothing in the basement except her workroom. Her roof leaked, the boiler would not last another season, the windows needed repair or replacement, and the outside work would take her far longer to complete and more money than she had originally budgeted. The Summer House would not open for business for more years than she could contemplate.

She was a practical woman, she reminded herself. She would have to focus on the necessities: food, clothing and shelter for her and her boys. Food wasn't a big problem yet. She had canned plenty of food when she harvested her garden last year. Her freezer was well stocked with meat and her pantry filled with dry goods. She would barter for eggs and milk. She might even talk with Bigger about selling a few of his setting hens to her and a milk cow. She and her boys would not eat grandly, but they would eat.

As for clothing, she wasn't sure her boys were too hyped up about the clothes she made for them; after all, she wasn't a great seamstress. Nor were they crazy about the clothes she bought from the dry goods store in Goodwill. Wal-Mart or Target over in Richmond County offered some cost-conscience options. Shoes were another concern. Every other month the boys seemed to grow right out of every pair of footwear they owned. If they grew as fast and big as their father and her sister, Jonathan and Jeffrey were going to need more than Wal-Mart to keep up.

She, on the other hand, could live with the clothes she had. Sacrificing had been her middle name since JoJeff and Carlotta left her destitute. She let her hair go natural rather than pay to have it done by Miz Minnie Mae down at the beauty shop. She also did her own manicures and pedicures. And not a bad job of it, if she had to say so herself.

Her Jeep's engine needed an overhaul, but if she continued to do her own maintenance, the car may catch its second wind. If not, she would cross that bridge when she got to it.

Finally, the question of shelter. The mansion had good bones, but it was expensive to maintain especially without an income. If she had to move out to one of the two-bedroom cottages at the back of the property, it wouldn't be as difficult to maintain. Though the boys were happy in the big, old house with its secret nooks, crannies, and hidden back stairs, they weren't selfish or demanding. Her little family would survive this little setback. And, bless her aunt's maneuvering, little heart for conjuring up a way to help her through the tough times without loss of her dignity. "Boarding Douglas Johnson wasn't a hand out," Aunt Olivia had argued. Satarah was "doing the community a favor by providing room and board for the Fire Chief."

When Aunt Sylvia asked for a favor, she knew Satarah wouldn't say no. So Satarah regarded this situation as doing something to help out the community and a stranded visitor to their county. The Fire Department was picking up the tab for Douglas Johnson's room and board. There was any number of other places where Aunt Olivia could have arranged for him to stay, Satarah knew. Her aunt and uncle had empty bedrooms in their home, since their children were away. Vivian and Chuck had more than a few guest rooms and they would be going back to Maryland after Easter, leaving their home in Goodwill empty except for the household and ranch staff. Douglas could have stayed there. Her cousins, Kenneth and Benjamin Alexander, built homes in Summer County, too, but they lived elsewhere most of the year so their homes were empty. Other relatives, such as Donald or James, would have easily accommodated Douglas Johnson, but Aunt Sylvia asked her, and Satarah was loathed to refuse. Truth be told, the additional income was more than adequate to sustain her and would be appreciated. Having the Chief there would help her gain experience as an innkeeper. It would be a good deal all around.

As the sun rose over the snow turning it to a soft bed of sparking gems, Satarah sighed, wrapped her arms around her knees and mused how terribly beautiful Mother Nature could be.

It was going to be a beautiful day.

⊙✲☽

Doug was usually an early riser, but the comfort he felt when he woke caused him to linger and enjoy the quiet and beautiful sunrise through his bedroom windows. He turned onto his side to watch as the sky in the east went from shades of deep blue to mauves and golden as the top crest of the sun come up over the horizon.

After Satarah went to bed the previous night, he went back to his truck to get his gear and duffel. In the stillness of the night, he took a moment to enjoy the crisp night air. The moon cast its clean, white light over the snow and complemented the stars that seemed so large and tangible that he felt he could reach out and caress them. Before he went to his room he stopped in the kitchen for a bottle of water and discovered that one of the doors wasn't a cabinet, but the entrance to the butler's pantry that led to a dining room. He wasn't snooping, but he stepped through the opening and flicked on the ceiling light. The room was very cold and large, and a complete disaster area. Wallpaper was pealing from the walls; the wainscoting was dirty with parts missing. Water spots blotched the ceiling where there was a ceiling, and the floor was scarred and marred. Apparently, Satarah hadn't gotten to this room yet, but wallboard was stacked in a far corner and tools were arranged on an old, paint-splattered table. He stepped toward a large cardboard box that held an old, ornate chandelier with gold fitting and glass teardrops. The windows and doors were boarded up, but pieces of old, crown molding sat next to long lengths of new lumber. Satarah was apparently going to match the missing pieces with new woodwork. Doug spent another twenty minutes divining Satarah's strategy before he closed the double doors, got his water, and went to his room.

After a shower and shave, he had set a fire in the grate and sat in the big comfortable lounger to watch the red and gold flames lick the slowly burning wood. Reflecting on the day, he felt so much. So many good things were happening out of what could have been a completely devastating disaster. Donovan's prognosis was cautiously improving. The anxiety over his career was diminishing and he may have time to work on a hobby of his: carpentry. That is if Satarah would let him work with her.

Now, with more of the sun breaching the horizon, Doug could not deny that life was fragile, but good and well worth living. Especially if he could get a cup of Satarah's excellent coffee.

When he went to the kitchen, Satarah was sitting with her arms hugging her legs and her chin on her knees apparently enjoying the sunrise that he had admired. Her hair was loose and in the sunlight shown dark brown with natural red highlights. It flowed over her shoulders and down to midway her back. He had never met a woman with so much real hair, and not have it be some kind of weave or wig. She could not contain it under the baseball cap she habitually wore turned backward on her head, but he liked the way it looked and smelled. He'd hate to see it tied up or tamed, much like the woman who wore it.

"Coffee's ready or do you plan to stand and stare at me all day?"

Doug shook his head in amusement. "I didn't want to disturb you."

"Nonsense. Get your coffee and come share this beautiful dawn with me before it gets away from us."

Doug filled a cup and sat next Satarah in silent agreement, as the sun cleared the horizon. She patted his knee as she rose and said, "Was that as good for you as it was for me?"

Doug barked a laugh and shook his head at the sexual innuendo. "Made me want to smoke afterwards and I haven't had a cigarette since I was sixteen years old."

"Yeah, me too. When I found out I was pregnant with JoJeff's baby, I gave up the smokes."

"You had a baby at sixteen?" he asked, surprised.

"Mmm," she hummed in her throat. "Actually, I was fifteen when I got pregnant. JoJeff was eighteen, Carlotta's age." She poured batter onto a hot griddle.

"You didn't mention your child, only your sister's twins."

"I gave him up for adoption. According to the Right Reverent Obadiah Baker James, no decent girl got herself pregnant. As if I did it on purpose," she muttered with angst.

"What happened?"

"The condom broke."

"Not that. I mean, why would your minister force you to give up your child?"

"The Right Reverent isn't my minister," she said, finally turning to look at Doug, "he's my father."

Stunned, Doug stared. "Your father forced you to give his own grandchild away? Didn't JoJeff say anything to try to stop him?"

"As soon as JoJeff got the word about his impending fatherhood, he enlisted in the Army."

"JoJeff is a real piece of work."

"And as handsome as sin, got a body you could bounce a quarter off of, and he's as slick as an Exxon oil spill."

"Why do you call him 'The Reverent'?"

"Actually, most of the time, I call him The Irreverent because that's how I think of him. Although he attended a seminary school for a hot minute, he never gained a degree. He's little more than a smooth-talking, jackleg preacher. As you might guess, I don't hold him in high esteem."

"What about your mother? She couldn't influence your father?"

"See, that's what I mean. My father waited until Mama went on a trip with the choir to drive me to Pittsburg to stay with a minister friend and his wife. On the drive, he told me that Mama was ashamed of me, didn't want to hear from me, and didn't want me under her roof anymore. That her family was embarrassed and didn't want me around my cousins. He told me that mama agreed with him that I should be sent away until after the baby was born and then give it up for adoption." She shrugged her shoulders and expelled a quick breath. "Needless to say, I was crushed. So I did what I was told and stayed in Pittsburg trying to keep Reverend Miles hands off me until after the baby was born and given up for adoption. When I got tired of fighting off the Good Reverend Miles, I came back, but Mama was gone. She had moved to France. I found out later that my father lied and told my mother that I ran away with some bum passing through town. I also found out that she was heartbroken that I left and tried to find me. Everyone believed my father's story, but it was clear that he is a liar.

"When JoJeff came back from the Army, he told me that my father had the sheriff in the next county over put him in jail for statutory rape. They offered JoJeff the option of enlisting in the military and never contacting me again or staying in jail. Of course, JoJeff chose the Army, so my father drove JoJeff over to Columbia that very day to enlist. My father let me believe that JoJeff had abandoned me. Another lie.

"I tried to find my baby, but Reverend Miles said that he was adopted by a good family who lived somewhere in Illinois. Of course, if I would become his mistress he would see what he could do to help me find my boy. I turned the Reverend down, but I haven't given up looking for my son.

"Right after I finished high school, JoJeff and I got married. While on our honeymoon in Myrtle Beach, my mother came to see me. She told me that she couldn't live with my father after I left; that she loved me and was never embarrassed by my pregnancy.

"Later, when I divorced JoJeff, Mama and her family gave me the deed to this property. My great grandparents bought it at auction and passed it on to their children with the stipulation that it could never be sold; just passed down, generation to generation. So here we are," she said, as she placed a platter of light fluffy pancakes and a rasher of crisp bacon on the table. "More coffee?"

Doug just stared at her. "You are the most amazing person I've ever met."

"So far," she said, laconically. "Your life's not over. You'll meet plenty of people who you will consider 'amazing', but none of them will be as good a cook," she said and grinned. "So eat up and let the games begin. I intend to hold the title of the best cook you've ever met."

❧

It was 8:35 A.M. when Doug and Satarah pulled into the Fire Chief's assigned parking spot in front of the Summer County office building in Centerville. The building was a long, modern, single-level, red brick structure with a dark green standing-seam roof. It housed the county services and offices, including the headquarters of the County Fire Chief. As they approached the big, glass doors, people were coming and going, but everyone, to a person, smiled and spoke as they walked by. Most called Satarah by name. Many, complete strangers of every type and description, shook Doug's hand and welcomed him to Summer County. The people were so open and friendly, Doug was beginning to believe he had stepped into a parallel universe. A feeling that multiplied when he stepped into a conference room and fifty or so young men and women stood and applauded.

A young woman stepped forward and said, "On behalf of the Summer County firefighters and our community, we welcome you aboard, Chief Johnson."

She stepped back and a young man stepped forward and handed a beautifully- carved wooden box to Douglas. The box contained the Fire

Chief's hat, a badge, credentials and keys to the fire stations; one located in each village in the county. The young man stepped back and the group simultaneous executed a parade-rest stance.

Doug felt the lump in his throat bob dangerous. He placed the box on the desk at his back, took out the Fire Chief's cap and placed it on his head. He looked up at the bright, expectant faces and said, "In a few minutes, this hat is going to be too small for my rapidly swelling head."

The group laughed and applauded.

"I want everyone to pick up a seat and form a circle so that you can educate me on who you are and how I can learn to be a good Summer County firefighter."

As Doug positioned a chair to join the group, he noticed Satarah slipping from the conference room. From the hallway, she gave him one of her quick, cocky grins and winks.

This time he grinned and winked back.

⚜

"In the next few days, I will review your incident reports and prepare comments for the county council. In addition, I will visit each station house to determine what, if anything, I can do to support your efforts to provide public safety. I will also want to know what your individual goals and objectives are in your short and long-term master plan, so that I can help you through your program and achieve your goals.

"I've reviewed your training program and believe you are ready for the advanced training level. A training team of specialists will be brought in to work with you and, as time and budget permit, you will be asked to rotate through certain specialty training schools in other parts of the country.

Doug closed his notebook and looked up and around the circle. "I want to acknowledge the professionalism I witnessed during the recent snow emergency and crisis. One or more of you saved Donovan Johnson's life by your quick, decisive action. I won't ask who specifically, because all of you performed admirably and saved many lives for which you will be commended.

"If there is nothing else on this morning's agenda," he said and waited a beat. When no one raised a hand, he said, "*Semper Fi*, ladies and gentlemen. It's a Marine Corps term that means——."

"Always faithful," a bright-eyed, female spoke up.

"Exactly correct, Laureleen, and thank all of you for a very warm welcome and productive session."

The accolades, loud and boisterous, took Douglas by surprise. The assembled formed a line to shake Doug's hand as they filed out of the conference room. When the last one left, Doug leaned against the desk, crossed his ankles and his powerful arms. He shook his head in amused amazement. In his years in the public safety industry, he never worked with a more energetic, eager, and intelligent group of firefighters. They were young, but very focused on doing the best job possible. He wasn't entirely sure that he would be able to keep up with them.

"Really got your juices going, huh?" Satarah commented from her position, leaning a shoulder against the door jam.

Doug turned his head to look at her. "I'll say, and then some."

She pushed away from the door. He certainly had a command of his subject and a commanding presence. From what she had heard and seen, the group was thoroughly enjoying him. Questions, comments and critiques had bounced around the room like balls in a Lotto game.

"The whole group has Type A personalities, especially, Jeff Logan."

"Mmm," she hummed in her throat. "Ambassador Jefferson Logan's son. Jeff, Jr. comes by it naturally. His stepmother, Dakota Sinclair Jefferson, is a very interesting woman in her own right. She's the daughter of Ambassador Jacob Hawkins."

Doug gave up goggling at the number of high-profile people who lived in Summer County, South Carolina. "I remember the story. Dakota was kidnapped as a baby and grew up in a Native American orphanage in North Dakota. When she went to Spelman, she actually met her biological sister in college, but they didn't recognize the resemblance. It was years later that they ran into each other again at an Embassy reception in Africa that Jake Hawkins hosted. When Dakota was standing in the receiving line talking with JaiHonnah, Jake Hawkins immediately recognized the resemblance between Dakota and his deceased wife. He realized that she was his kidnapped daughter, LaiLoni Skye."

"You have a good memory."

"I read a lot and it was such a compelling story."

"Ready for your next magic trick?" Satarah asked.

"Lead on, Macduff," he said, as he picked up his notes, briefcase and the beautiful box. He stood a moment, fingering the box and trying desperately to get the adrenalin rush he absorbed from the group—*his firefighters*—under control.

Doug followed Satarah to the reception desk where a beautiful painted mural depicted a summer scene of what could have been The Garden of Eden. People were shown working together to harvest the bounty and build a community. It was the most pastoral, peaceful, yet lively painting Doug had ever seen. "This mural was painted by Russell Greene."

"The artist? I've seen his work in magazines. He's very young, isn't he?"

"Hmmm," Satarah hummed. "Early twenties."

"Don't tell me. Let me guess. He's a member of your family," Doug said, amused.

Satarah shrugged. "Well, actually, yes, in an in-law sort of way. He's Stacy Greene Alexander's brother, Benny Alexander's brother-in-law."

Doug stared. "Why am I not surprised?"

Satarah giggled at his deadpan expression.

Doug snapped his finger, remembering. "I've seen murals similar to this on the walls at the hospital. Did Russell Greene do those too?"

"His mother, Helen Greene, did the hospital murals with her art students from Summer County Academy. She does commission work just as Russell does, but she prefers teaching. Russell likes to travel and paint what he sees. He's in Brazil now, somewhere in the Rain Forest." She turned from the mural they were studying and noticed that Doug was looking at her strangely. "What?"

"You know so much about your family, yet you hold yourself back from them. You're very proud of them."

Satarah shrugged, but didn't comment. She took him on a tour of the county office building and then to a door marked **FIRE CHIEF** in gold filigree. Above the title was his name, **DOUGLAS E. JOHNSON** on a block plaque. He was tempted to add "temporary" to the title, but easily restrained himself.

Satarah opened the door and bade him to enter ahead of her. The county crest on the wall behind the big, oak desk above a credenza was similar to the mural in reception. To the left were windows that span the room and, interestingly, a glass door that led outside to a patio. A table and four chairs were covered with mounds of snow. Inside, a round conference table with chairs sat before the window. To the right was a dark-green, leather sofa with contrasting occasional chairs in gold around a squat, round, coffee table. A Spathiphyllum or Peace Lily sat in the middle. The floors were a golden hardwood with throw rugs that looked suspiciously like Berber. Taken together, the office was bright, attractive, functional, and comfortable.

Doug turned toward Satarah. "Where are the Fire Chief's things?"

Satarah stepped away from the door to reveal two boxes that appeared to hold personal items. When Doug refocused on Satarah, she shrugged nonchalantly.

"Lula Mae, Rick Morrow's wife, knows that you're taking her husband's place, but she doesn't want him to come back to work when he recovers from his heart attack. She asked whether I would clean out his office for her."

He looked at the plant on the coffee table. "Did you forget his plant?"

"No. That's a little gift from me to you. My way of saying welcome aboard."

He was genuinely touched by her gesture, but wasn't sure how to express his appreciation. Should he shake her hand, pat her on the shoulder, kiss her on the cheek, . . or, what he preferred, on that mobile mouth of hers? Shifting uncomfortably, he settled on a simple, "Thank you." No touching, he told himself. There was entirely too much of her that he wanted to touch. He had a healthy fear that if he ever touched her, he wouldn't stop there. So he distracted himself by putting the box at the head of the desk and his notes from the meeting and tour inside his briefcase.

When a knock sounded on the opened door, Doug looked up and smiled. He extended his hand. "Hello, Mrs. Dixon."

"Douglas, Satarah," she acknowledged warmly.

"Aunt—."

"Something wrong with your arms, Satarah Josephine?"

"No, ma'am," she said and moved awkwardly to embrace her aunt-in-law, her Uncle Bernard's sister, Olivia Alexander Dixon.

"That's better," she said, and then did something strange to Doug's way of thinking when she moved Satarah's collar aside as if looking for something. Olivia Dixon and Satarah held each other's stare before Satarah dropped her eyes, in what Doug thought looked like embarrassment. In the days that he had known Satarah Whitfield and listened to her many challenges, he had not seen her display a lack of self-esteem, but, clearly, whatever was contained in the visual battle between the two women was profound and potent.

"I'm going to catch a ride to Chuck's and Vivian's," Satarah said, hastily.

"That's not necessary. Why don't you take my truck? If I need a ride, I'll use the Fire Chief's vehicle." He handed his keys to her.

She took the keys, nodded goodbye and was gone.

Olivia Dixon stared after Satarah's retreating figure for a long moment. She seemed to be in somewhat of a quandary before she shook herself from her thoughts and then regarded Doug, as if the little tabloid had never happened. Still, if Olivia Dixon wasn't going to explain, though he was curious, Doug wasn't going to ask.

"Well, I see you've settled in," Olivia said, looking directly into Doug's eyes. He appreciated people who could look you in the eye when they spoke with you, engendering a level of trust.

"Yes, I have. I met with the firefighters this morning and toured the building."

"Good. The County Council is holding an informal grip-and-grin for you and then we'll feed you some good, country cooking for lunch before the afternoon session at 2:00 P.M."

"Afternoon session?"

"Oh, I forgot that you haven't been through orientation yet." At his nod, they settled on the sofa before Olivia continued. "The mayors of each of our six incorporated villages, the Chiefs of Summer County

Security, Health, Education, Fire and Welfare Departments and County Attorney make up the County Council. We meet one day a week, unless there is a reason to meet more frequently. We discuss the needs of the county residents, organize plans to address the issues, implement a plan of action, execute the plan, and then evaluate the results. We have a county administrative staff too."

"Twelve people do all that?"

"Well, actually, in terms of population, we're not a very large county. In terms of land mass, we're one of the largest in the state."

"I had no idea."

"Come on, Douglas. Let us go get you indoctrinated. We've got a helluva lot of work to do."

Doug came in the front door of The Summer House and turned to see Satarah's grinning face so full of anticipation.

"So? So?" she quizzed, bouncing from one foot to the other. "Tell me," she insisted.

She looked so cute that he wanted to enjoy her eagerness a while longer. So he made a production of taking off his hat and gloves, hanging up his coat. Then he heaved a heavy sigh. The wonderful aroma of food and wood smoke enveloped him pleasantly. "I think I'll have a shower before dinner."

Satarah slapped both hands against his chest pushing him back against the closed closet door. Doug wanted to laugh at her antics, but instead he yanked her vertically by her waist until they could look at each other at eye level, and reversed their positions. Satarah's feet dangled a foot off the floor.

"Well?" she still prompted, searching his eyes, his expression. When he only gave her a blank stare, she managed to grab his lapels in a death grip and yanked him forward until they were nearly nose-to-nose. "Tell me!" she demanded through gritted teeth.

Doug could not hold his excitement a second longer; a hardy laugh bubbled up and out. They sat in the kitchen alcove while they had dinner and a lively discussion about the County Council's agreement that Doug should bring in an experienced training team to get the fledgling county fire department on the right course; how he had exactly the right men and woman in mind. He already had the plan in the works and would complete the details over the next few days.

"And I met Ambassador, I mean, Jefferson Logan, Dean Logan. He talked with me about the school system. How the students attend classes year-round. They study only one subject every day all day for six weeks. Then they have a two-week break, before they start on the next subject. That's a very different set up from the system I grew up with in Richmond."

"There are only a few other schools in this country that have this type of system. It gives each student an in-depth study of each topic. All age levels rise to their individual achievement goals during the six weeks. Since Summer County is predominately agricultural, the young people work on their family farms. The school system allows them to do that without missing class time."

"Jefferson told me that the campus never closes. They even have a boarding school for out of county or out of state students. Student schedules are arranged so that they can have flexibility in attendance."

"That's why there's no truancy. Children start going to the campus as babies and by the time they are walking and talking, they are in classes. It is much like the Japanese system of education all the way up through prep school levels. Adult classes are held all day and in the evening, too. That's how I was able to take my nurses' training after I returned from Pennsylvania and work part-time in a clinic."

"Dean Logan started the stranded children from the storm in classes, everyone who can't go home yet because they or their parents are still under medical care. And he wants to include Donovan and the other injured students as soon as possible. He even started collecting school records."

"That's a good thing, don't you think? He doesn't want them to be idle and worry about themselves, their families or friends."

"It's a great plan."

When dinner was over, Doug went to his room to shower before dessert. He was anticipating the warm peach cobbler when he opened the bedroom door and just stared. Six wardrobe boxes stood in the middle of his room. They contained his and Donovan's clothes, shoes and other personal effects from his home in Richmond. His footlocker and gear from the fire station was also there. He had talked with Mr. and Mrs. Diggs that day about this temporary assignment in South Carolina. They had asked about Donovan and, near the end of their conversation, asked whether he would consider subletting his home. He said he would and planned to go to Richmond to pack up these same items and lease his home to Mr. and Mrs. Diggs' nieces who were students at Richmond State University. Shaking his head in disbelief, he said aloud, "How does she do that?"

Sylvia Alexander had struck again without warning, saving him precious time and aggravation. Now he could put his energy into the awesome tasks ahead of him. He didn't know how he was ever going to thank her, but he vowed to find a way.

Satarah knew that Doug was standing in the butler's pantry doorway leading to the dining room. She knew that it wasn't his first visit either. She saw his shoe prints on the dusty wood floor. She didn't mind that he had taken a look around. In fact, she was planning to give him the grand tour now that he would be a guest in her home. Using a wide bristled paintbrush, she slapped more of the hot water and vinegar solution on the old wallpaper as she moved down the jury-rigged scaffolding. She had a wide wooden board leveled between two folding ladders. Layers of old paper were peeling nicely away from the solid plaster walls. It wouldn't take her long before she could start on the ceiling. That was going to take a bit of ingenuity though. She couldn't work overhead on the nine foot ceiling with her jury-rigged scaffolding. She would need the real thing, but that wasn't in her budget right now.

Doug climbed the ladder on Satarah's right and began stripping layers of old wallpaper away. With a wide spackling knife, he gingerly eased stubborn paper away, careful not to damage the plaster walls. As he proceeded toward the end, pulling away what he could, Satarah climbed up to the area he vacated and began the process of wetting the walls again. Together without talking, but completely in sync, they worked their way around the large room.

At some point, Satarah brought a radio into the room and a portable oil heater. They worked in companionable silence or humming to the old school sounds on the radio until all the old wallpaper was removed down to the chair rail and wainscoting. Clean up was a messy ordeal, but together they got the gooey paper into a trash drum lined with large green bags.

When they finished, they sat on the plank of wood scaffolding drinking ice-cold beers and critically inspecting their handiwork.

"I stumbled in here one night," Doug told Satarah. "I thought it was a pantry because the doors looked like the rest of the kitchen cabinets you built. I was looking for a bottle of water."

"Mmm," Satarah hummed while looking up at the high ceiling.

Doug followed her line of vision up to the ceiling. "We've got a cherry picker down at one of the station houses. I figured I could jury-rig a ramp and drive it right through the front door."

He could feel Satarah's eyes on him before he looked into them.

"You don't have to do that," she said, her expression unreadable.

"I know, but if I don't do something with all this extra time and energy on my hands, I'm going to get very fat and then where will I be? Besides, there's thirty inches of snow outside."

Satarah had a very devilish thought wedged in her mind. The man was solidly built without an ounce of excess fat on him, but she could suggest something they could do together—but for now she was keeping her wayward thoughts to herself. So she looked up at the damaged ceiling. "I'll talk to the Fire Chief first opportunity I get and see whether he'll let me rent that cherry picker for a day or two."

"It's likely going to cost you, but it's worth a try," Doug deadpanned.

11

oug stood by the window in Donovan's hospital room. He was silently praying, though he would never knowingly acknowledge what he was thinking was a prayer. He wasn't a particularly religious man. He had never been indoctrinated in any religious dogma. He couldn't deny that there was a Creator, but he shunned any acceptance of the many religions with which he had come in contact. He was so deep in thought that he barely heard Donovan's voice. He turned and went to the boy's bedside.

"You're awake. How are you feeling?"

"Am I really in a hospital?" Donovan asked just above whisper.

"Yes, Donovan. Do you remember being in an accident on your way to Disney World?"

Donovan looked confused for a moment, casting his eyes around the room. Then he looked back at Doug with a steady gaze. "And you came to the hospital to see me?"

What did the boy think I would do? Doug wondered, but said, "I came as soon as I got the word about the accident."

"Am I dying?"

"No, no, Donovan," he said, hastily. "You were seriously injured, but your doctor, Chuck Montgomery, said that–."

"He's that big man, right? He made you come? He's bigger than you—."

Doug didn't know what to answer first. So he settled on something neutral. "How do you feel?"

"Feel? I dunno know. My throat hurts."

"That's because you had surgery. You can have some ice chips if you like."

"I want my mommy. Can you tell my mommy to come and get me and take me home?"

Doug stared in stunned silence. He didn't know what to do or what to think. He stared at Donovan and asked, "Do you know my name, Donovan?"

The boy looked at him curiously for a moment, and then asked, "Is my mommy here? Is Satarah here?"

⚘

Satarah tore through the Emergency Room doors on a dead run. When Douglas called her, he was talking so fast and urgently that she was out her front door and in Doug's truck before the call ended. She could hear the underlying fear in his voice. When she turned a corner, she slammed into Reynard Steward, knocking him backward. "Sorry," she muttered, as she bounced off him, spun around, and kept running. She could hear Rey shouting at her to stop and his foot falls as he gave chase. Up ahead, she could see Doug's agitated pacing outside of Donovan's room. She dodged other people, food carts and medical equipment, as if she was running an obstacle course. The shouts she heard from behind must have alerted Doug because, just then, he looked up and was rapidly closing the distance between them. He caught her on the fly.

"It's okay, Doug. I'm here," she said, in a rush, her breaths coming fast, but even.

"Satarah, he doesn't know who I am, where he is or what he's been through. He looked at me as if I'm a complete stranger. Then he asked me—." He took a deep breath, trying to calm himself. "He asked me to go find his mommy and to tell her to come and get him to take him home. He sounded so lost and scared, like a terrified little boy who couldn't find his home or family. I didn't—."

"What is the meaning of this?" Reynard Steward angrily interrupted, demanded. "Satarah, you have no right to be here. I want you off this—."

"Hush, Rey!" she shot back, sternly, not even sparing him, or anyone else who had gathered around to listen and observe, a single glance. Her attention was riveted on Doug's face and his on her. They were clutching each other's arms.

"—know what to tell him, about his mother, I mean. Lily's been dead for four years, but then he said he wanted his mommy—."

"Satarah, if you don't leave this instant—."

Reynard's voice was like a gnat bugging in her ear, but when he roughly jerked her away from Doug, she swatted him like the pest that he was. That stunned him and everyone gasped, moved back from the woman with the wild mane of dark flowing hair and deadly menace in her eyes.

When Reynard started toward her with blood in his eyes, the red haze around the edges of Satarah's vision closed in as if ready for battle.

Doug stepped between the two combatants, put a heavy hand to Rey's heaving chest, and issued a deathly quiet, but forceful order to Rey, to back the hell off. Something in Doug's demeanor must have convinced Reynard Steward that his self-preservation was at stake. He stepped back and regarded everyone gawking at them. He nervously straightened his neck in his tie, smoothed his starched white lab coat with an agitated snap of his wrists, shot his sleeves and marched away.

Satarah had been trying to get around Doug to get at Rey, but Doug was so big and strong, he was immovable. He had his big hand hooked inside the front waistband of her jeans, keeping her in place at his back like a fly pinned to a wall. No matter how she tried to wring and twist away from him, he held her still. When he turned back to her, the red haze was edging away from her vision. She grabbed Doug's tie and yanked. His head came down until they were eye to eye and she growled, "I fight my own battles, Johnson. I don't need you to protect me. I was about to kick his skinny, pompous butt!"

"I wasn't protecting you, Whitfield. I was protecting the other guy," he said, hooking his thumb over his shoulder in the direction of Rey Steward's departure.

She looked down between their bodies where he still held her fast, then back up to where their eyes met. "Unless you're into some type of kinky, exhibitionist sex, I suggest you get your hand out of my pants." When he slowly removed his hand, his knuckles brushed against her warm skin. She would think about the tingling sensation that erupted in her nether region later, but, for the moment, she still had his tie firmly in her grip. "Now, tell me about Donovan."

Calmer, Doug repeated the story. "Then he said he wanted his mommy and asked if you were here."

It was a jolt to her nervous system. She let go of his tie and glanced around, but most people had moved along since they could not hear the whispered conversation without standing nearly on top of her and Doug.

Vertical lines grew between her eyebrows. She plowed her fingers through her dense hair and worried her bottom lip nervously as she thought about the possible reasons for Donovan's behavior. She knew that Donovan Johnson was not her long lost son; he looked nothing like anyone in her or JoJeff's families. Besides, the birthdates were wrong. Raking her fingers through her hair again, she said. "Look, sometime people can hear what's going on around them, even though they're not fully conscious. I was with Donovan for a long time. Jennie Jones, one of the other nurses, kept calling my name and yapping at me like a frisky puppy. I kept talking to Donovan so that he wouldn't feel afraid or like he was alone. I don't remember exactly what I said to him because my brain was fried and I was so tired, but I do remember saying something like, I don't know, stay with me baby boy. Stay with Mama, but I don't remember. I was running low on brain cells." She looked up at Doug.

"If Donovan's experiencing a bout of amnesia, that's to be expected considering what he's been through or he could just be a bit disoriented. The important thing to focus on is that he spoke to you and his speech pattern wasn't impaired, which means that his brain is functioning and healing. That's a good sign.

"Is any of what I said making any sense?"

"More than," he said, as he rested his head back against the wall. "He woke up and started talking, but things went from bad to worse. I went into melt down." Doug looked down into Satarah's up-turned face, her wide dark eyes, and slightly parted mouth. He had never had anyone come to comfort him, to give him moral support. Since the day he met her, she was a safe haven in a violent storm, and he thought, uncomfortably, that he liked the fact that she was there for him even though she was not supposed to be on the hospital grounds. "I apologize for dragging you back into this mess with the hospital, but I have to tell you, Satarah, I never want to have you angry with me. What's with that guy anyway?"

"He's not important. I have to go see whether I even turned off your truck engine or put it in park. It may be half way to I-95 by now. Then we can go see Donovan."

Doug paled.

⸎

"And then she hauled off and clocked him," Sylvia Alexander said between boughs of laughter so hard that tears were trickled down her cheeks.

"I did not," Satarah muttered, morosely. Then she looked at Mary Ella who sat on the opposite side of Vivian holding the baby. "I didn't, right?"

It was hard for Mary Ella to hold in her merriment. She didn't want to frighten the sweet, sleeping baby girl in her arms, so she steeled her features and spoke as calmly as she could. "I have no idea. I heard the gossip from so many sources. I have no clue what the truth is. You either slapped him or punched his lights out or anything in between."

"I think you should enter the next Olympics because you apparently broke Flo Jo's record getting to Donovan and Douglas." Sylvia hooted out a laugh while wiping away her tears and holding her side to keep it from splitting open.

Satarah hunched her shoulders and looked up at her Aunt Sylvia, Vivian, and Mary Ella through lowered lashes.

"To be a fly on the wall during that little episode," Vivian said, at length holding back her need to laugh.

Satarah, sitting cross-legged on a big, cushy chair, hunched further inward. "Okay, okay. I've heard more than enough from everyone, including Bill Chandler." She looked at Vivian. "How does he speak so quietly when he's so angry?"

"Practice," Vivian offered. "He may look like a boy toy, but the man does not play!"

"Someone else doesn't play either," Mary Ella added with tongue planted firmly in cheek. "Elsie told me that George told her that Ginger said that Douglas Johnson stalked into Rey Steward's office to tell him that if he *ever* put his hands on one Satarah Josephine Whitfield again, he could kiss his ass goodbye."

"Oh, God," Satarah lamented and slapped her palms to her face.

"Mmm, humm, and told the good Dr. Steward that if he tried to stop one Satarah Josephine Whitfield from seeing Donovan Johnson again, he'd sue him personally and the hospital for everything he could, right down to the last Q-tip."

"Interesting, isn't it?" Sylvia interjected, casting a decidedly curious glance at the rapidly shrinking Satarah, "that most reports indicated that Satarah Josephine and Douglas Johnson were playing out some kind of love fest in the middle of the hospital corridor. Curious minds want to know whether Douglas actually had his big—strong—hands down your—."

"Hold it! Stop right there!" Satarah begged, holding up both hands, but her Aunt Sylvia continued.

"And you had him in a lip lock that could melt both polar ice caps."

Satarah cursed a blue streak, palmed her face and fell face forward onto the chaise lounge while her family and friend laughed like loons.

Sylvia Alexander was delighted at the progress made to bring Satarah back into the fold, home to her family. It had been more than twelve years, since Satarah came to her family openly and to share. Sylvia would not speak ill of the emotionally challenged, but what her former brother-in-law, the Reverend Obadiah Baker James had done to her sister and their daughters bordered on criminal behavior. Sylvia desperately wanted Mariah to come home to, at least, visit during family holidays, but understood that it had to be her sister's decision. In the meantime, she had Mariah's baby girl almost back in the fold. And wasn't she delighted that her niece was doing what she had been taught by her grandparents: to extend a helping hand to anyone in need. And Douglas Johnson was one who needed one. Sylvia decided to keep an eye on that friendship as spring approached. All kinds of things blossomed in the springtime. Maybe a little romance between two healthy, young people, who needed each other, whether they knew it or not, would set everything to right.

"Mom?" Vivian said. "Why do you have that devilish little look on your face?"

"Ah," Sylvia said at length. "Springtime is just around the corner and I think it's going to be a wonderful year."

❦

"Springtime!" Satarah spat like it was a dirty word. She had work to do on the grounds, didn't she? Flowers to plant, gardens to tend, leaves to rake, but, oh no! Aunt Sylvia, with her sweet-as-syrup voice, had to have her way—and everyone else's plans be damned. And then to make sure her mercurial plots were followed to the letter, she had sent sixteen—count them, thank you very much—sixteen of her male cousins to Satarah's bed and breakfast to work on getting The Summer House in order before summertime. Sylvia Benson Alexander had decided—no, no, correction, she had ordained that this year, part of the family reunion would be held on the grounds of The Summer House! The sneaky woman!

Satarah had her own plans, didn't she? So what, if her plans for opening her business had to be delayed for a year or two? Okay maybe it would take four or five years at the rate she was going. She wanted to work on the house at her leisure, didn't she? To make sure everything was up to her own standards! And the worst of it was that Aunt Sylvia, the Wicca, had Satarah's pal, Douglas E. Johnson, twisted around her little pinky. There was nothing that Doug wouldn't do for her aunt and uncle. So now that the first floor of the house was finished, he spent much of his free time helping Satarah complete the second floor bedrooms and bathrooms, for crissake!

And, Satarah fumed, that Doug loved to get his big, grimy hands on her power tools! He even bought more and a tool belt to boot. The Neanderthal!

And what was she doing on this bright, Saturday morning when she had plans to get her hands dirty in her gardens? She was hauling a ladder up the steps so she could install light bulbs in the freaking ceiling fans! How demoralizing was that? It was her house, wasn't it? But had she been permitted to work on it the way she wanted? *Hell no!* She had been *ordered* around all morning like a lackey. Go get this! Fetch that! Make a run to the hardware store! Take something somewhere. Now she had been told to get the ladder to install light bulbs for crissake! Absolutely mortifying!

She marched into the first bedroom on the right and slammed the ladder into a standing position under the fan.

"Hey, Doug," James Dixon yelled out. "Sara Jo has a pretty good mad on. You may want to take a look at the woman you're living with."

Doug stuck his head out of the bathroom door, his big hands full of wet wall grout. "Nah, that's not her most impressive mad," he chided. "You should have seen her when she cold-cocked Dr. Steward. Now that was impressive," Doug said with relish.

"So I've heard. I can top that one though," Donald Dixon, James' twin brother, said, as he put the finishing touches on the wood trim around the new windows. "She body slammed Little Willie in eighth grade for feeling her up. Nearly ruptured his family jewels."

"Ouch! Little Willie? Bigger's brother?" Doug asked, impressed. "The man has a body mass of an eighteen wheeler!"

"Yeah, and went down like a redwood. The crash was heard far and wide. We thought it was an earthquake," Kenneth Alexander added, as he put a faceplate on a new electrical outlet. "He crosses the street if he sees her coming."

"You forgot the time Sara Jo faced down Baby Betty over a contested baseball call," Benjamin Alexander recalled, fondly, as he finished hanging a door on the closet. "Baby Betty in a wet T-shirt after Sara Jo tossed her into the swimming pool at school." He patted his heart dramatically. "I had a boner for three days after that. Peace be still!"

"You always had a boner, Benny," Gregory Alexander, Kenneth's and Benjamin's youngest brother, said, then laughed with everyone else, as he screwed the lock set into the bedroom door. "But I remember when Satarah Jo was babysitting me and Aretha and this guy—." he continued.

"You children may want to remember that I'm cooking lunch. I may mistake the rat poison for seasoning!" Satarah said, climbing down the ladder and closing it with a loud, satisfying snap.

Silence reigned.

Her cousins and Doug didn't have to see the little grin that hitched up the right side of her mouth. With less starch in her walk, she crossed the hall into another bedroom to put bulbs in the next light fixture. And she took more abuse from her other family members assembled to work on renovating The Summer House.

⁂

Springtime. Doug sat on an old, rocking chair that he needed to paint with his feet propped up on the banister and watched as the heat consumed the remaining snow. He had finished repairing the porch deck and sat to rest before putting stain on the deck and paint on the old rockers. Water dripped off the eaves of the mansion like a peaceful waterfall and created puddles that the birds converted in to community mud baths, unperturbed by the statue-still human who sat a few feet away.

A herd of deer appeared in Doug's peripheral vision to the north of Satarah's land, not a hundred yards from where he sat, and leisurely strolled toward the fence line. They slowed, scenting the air, scenting him and stood, majestically, watching him, watching them. When they looked their fill and judged him non-threatening, one by one they leaped up and over the fence line down at the lane; their thin legs tucked under their streamlined bodies as graceful as dancers and continued their morning constitutional into the tree farm.

Something shifted inside him, as he watched nature watch him. This was what life on this planet was supposed to be—equal parts hard work and pleasure.

He liked the rhythm of his days, the pace and the ability to do more fire safety and prevention than emergency. He liked knowing the people he was there to protect and serve by their names and now familiar faces. They weren't anonymous groups of strangers in some multilevel structure, but someone in a farmhouse he visited or small business establishment where he was usually a customer more often than not. So he had a vested interest in ensuring that the place was protected.

Though he had more responsibility on his shoulders and a much larger area to cover, he liked having more time to spend with Donovan and pursue his hobbies, something that he had precious little time for when he was in Richmond. It seemed like a lifetime ago that he was battling to save his career and his self-respect. Here in Summer County, he was given respect without having to demand it.

He had more time to take stock of his life and where he was going. And, he realized that he wasn't complete because he didn't know who he was. It is not only who you are, he mused, but *whose* you are. His family was an enigma to him. He was not connected to the ancestry that had come together to form him. And he recognized that Donovan must have felt just as alone in the world as he did.

He had gotten to know people in Summer County, particularly the Alexanders and their extended family and hordes of friends. People would stop by his office or his home to visit or invite him out for a beer or to dinner. He joined a group of men about his age who had formed a baseball league and played once a week. It was good exercise and camaraderie.

He and his son both needed to connect; to plug into each other and those around them.

$\mathcal{12}$

$\mathcal{S}$atarah headed down the stairs dragging a big, drop cloth behind her. The painting was finished on the third level of the house and the beautifully-restored, polyurethane-protected, wood floors had dried to a soft, golden brown patina. When the front door opened, Satarah expected to see any number of her cousins enter. They had been in and out of her house for weeks, whether she was at home or not.

But when Bigger Thenham backed into the house, carrying one end of a long sofa and, his younger brother, Little Willie, the other end, Satarah just stood and gawped. "What the—?"

"Oh, hello, Satarah Josephine," Sylvia Alexander greeted, cheerfully, flowing into the house after the two men. "Just set that in the second pallor," she directed, then turned to her niece. "Are the boys still here?"

Dazed, Satarah nodded. "Upstairs on the third floor. They're just finishing up the punch work. Aunt Sylvia, where did that sofa come from?"

"That? Oh, it was your great grandparents. Bigger did a wonderful job restoring and reupholstering it, didn't he?"

They trailed the sofa into the empty parlor. "Facing the window, I think," Sylvia said, her hands on her slim hips, assessing the room. "Yes, I think it's prefect there. The walls match the sofa exactly. You should call this room The Rose Parlor after your great grandmother Rose."

Satarah sat on the nine-foot, Heppelwhite sofa, fingered the fine fabric with it cottage roses, and caught just a hint of beeswax and lemon oil. "This is so beautiful, Aunt Sylvia." Satarah stood and embraced her aunt. "Thank you so much, but I want to pay Bigger and Little Willie for doing the work. How—?" she started, but her voice trailed off when Bigger returned carrying a sofa table followed by Little Willie, who carried a summer-green, high-back, barrel chair. Her legs failed her when Doug and her cousins joined the parade of furniture quickly filling the room. Her head swiveled from side to side as if she were watching a tennis match. She looked up at her aunt who was directing the placement of each piece of beautiful furniture.

"Aunt Sylvia?"

"Yes, dear?"

"Is all this from my great grandparents' homes?"

"Oh, this is just a few pieces of it. There is more in the moving van outside, but we couldn't get everything in one load. The rest will arrive during the week. Of course, Kenneth James built or rebuilt some of the furniture himself."

"But where has the furniture been all this time?" Satarah asked, awestruck.

"In storage here and there. Such a shame to let it go to waste, don't you think? Your mother shipped home what was stored in France. Your grandparents were avid collectors, too. So you have maybe three generations of family antiques and heirlooms represented. You have so many rooms that we thought that The Summer House would be the perfect place to display a part of our family's history. We'll hold the tours here during the reunion so that the family can see and touch an important piece of our ancestry.

"Now," she said with pep in her step, "Douglas said that you two finished the main dining room. Let's go see how that will work with—," Sylvia stopped talking and walking when Satarah touched her arm.

Moisture glistened in Satarah's eyes. She fell into her aunt's opened arms.

Four days later, the last of her great grandparents' and grandparents' furniture collections from the Benson side of the family were in place. Other family members emptied their attics and garages contributing fine china, crystal and silverware heirlooms to the collection. She displayed the delicate treasures in glass-fronted cabinets she and Douglas built in the basement workroom. Her cousin, Kenneth Alexander, loved woodworking, too. He shipped furniture he made or restored in his home garage in California to her. Her mother also shipped beautiful carpets from the foreign countries she visited. Russell Greene sent paintings and fine art pieces from countries where he traveled. There was more coming in it seemed every day.

Satarah glided from room to room not quite able to take it all in at once. She sat in each room for a while and nearly skipped to the next room to repeat the same gleeful visit.

The dining rooms on the main level and sitting parlors, all twelve bedrooms and sitting parlors on the second level were furnished. She made notes on the linens, towels and accessories needed to complete each suite of rooms. Of course, she would have to order mattresses, pillows and throws, but she could find little knickknacks to add a nice touch to each room at the thrift stores in the area. There were also flea markets everywhere in the South.

She had given every room a name, something reminiscent of her great grandparents and grandparents and their taste in furnishings. The bedroom with the Louis XV furniture was of course, the Parisian Suite. The suite with the American Drew Artisans' Guild furniture was the Americana. The Schnadig furniture was now in the Palazzo Suite. The Egyptian furniture, the Arabian Nights Suite, of course; and the Chinese furniture, the Oriental Suite, etc.

She still had the third floor, to dress. The ballroom on the first floor needed ceiling high curtains and draperies, but the chairs and small round tables were in place on the gleaming, hardwood floors. The double doors off the ballroom opened to a stone patio that still needed work before she could set up the outdoor furniture. She wanted to erect a trellis over the patio covered with honeysuckle as it may have been back in her great grandparents' time.

The feeling of reaching back three generations, a hundred years or more to touch something of her great grandparents, gave Satarah a warm excitement. Aunt Sylvia was right. It was criminal to keep this beauty and ancestry hidden away in storage bins, attics and garages.

"You win the Lotto or something?"

"Better," Satarah said, smiling brightly at Doug, who leaned a shoulder against the door jam. "More important than money. I gained a part of my history, my ancestry." She patted the spot next to her on the sofa. Doug sat, spreading his arms along the back of the settee and his long legs out in front of him crossed at the ankles.

"You're right. It is better than winning the Lotto." He looked about the bedroom suite thoughtfully. "I barely knew my father. My mother worked long hours, so I didn't know much about her. I didn't know either set of my grandparents at all. I probably have cousins somewhere." He looked at her. "I've never known what family was. Or any families like yours."

"We're like a tapestry. You pull one string and you can ruin the picture."

"From what I've seen, your family is made of a tighter weave than that, Satarah. It would take a lot more than one strand to ruin it."

Satarah folded her legs under her, rested her elbows on her knees and interlocked her fingers. "I know my mother's family loves me, Doug. They have shown me in so many ways all of my life. I just don't want to let them down again."

"How do you think you let them down?"

"By not adhering to the family creed and by not wearing the symbol of family unity." She pulled a gold chain from her pocket and dropped it into Doug's hand. The gold letter spelled **FAMILY.** It had no beginning and no end.

"This is very beautiful, Satarah. Do all of your family members wear this chain?"

"And their spouses. You'll hear more about my family's creed at the Easter Reunion."

"Will you wear this chain then?"

Satarah stood, dug her hands in her pockets and paced. Doug let her have her space. She was obviously grappling with something she was not yet ready to share. She turned toward Doug.

"Why are you home in the middle of the day? Did something happen with Donovan?"

"I wanted to bum a hot roast beef sandwich out of you."

"And what else?" she asked, with one arched eyebrow.

"Well, my training team will be here later this week. Funds have been allocated for their rooms and board. I wanted to ask whether you would permit them to stay here at The Summer House. I know it's a lot to ask, especially since you're not open for business yet. You've got the boys to consider, it's a lot of extra work—."

"Come on, Doug," Satarah interrupted. She smiled, extended her hand, and pulled him to his feet. "Let's fix those roast beef sandwiches." She tucked her arm through his as they walked. "The truth is that you didn't want me having fun all day by myself."

"Well, I did want to get a band saw so that I could build a ramp before Donovan is released from the hospital," he said, as they walked down the steps, "and I hoped that the apple pie and ice cream wasn't all gone."

"Liar," she scolded, mildly. "You don't need a band saw to build a ramp. You've been itching to get your hands on one for weeks."

"It seemed like a plausible explanation when I practiced it on the way home."

Satarah's laugh was deep and knowing. "It worked, but if I grant you all these favors, you have to go with me to buy mattresses and linens and things."

Doug stopped and stared at Satarah. "Shopping?" Doug asked, incredulously. "With a woman?"

"How badly do you want that sandwich?"

"You're a wicked woman, Satarah Jo."

She giggled. "Why, thank you, Douglas."

⚬❦⚬

Thank Christ! Doug thought as he lugged the last of Shopping Queen Satarah's loot into the entrance of The Summer House. He dropped the bags on the floor with the others and braced an arm on the newel post. They had spent the afternoon in Columbia. Not in malls or chic couture shops. Oh, no, the Shopping Queen dragged him in and out of a mattress manufacturer in a huge warehouse, linen and towel outlets as large as football fields, and flea markets that took up many city blocks. He watched her wheel and deal until she got exactly what she wanted at below market prices.

The maven wasn't above using subterfuge to get the mattress factory manager to bargain and barter for the best product, and God help him, Doug lamented, he had helped her. In the parking lot, Satarah insisted that he wear his Fire Chief's hat inside and look official. She even straightened his tie and inspected him as if she was getting a child ready for Sunday go-to-meeting. And when he walked in and asked for the manager, the receptionist had the poor man pulled out of a meeting and come on the run. Then Satarah stepped forward and took over. Doug feared that Satarah had criminal tendencies. What she couldn't achieve with hard bargaining, she accomplished by batting her big, brown eyes and going all Southern Belle on the unsuspecting.

He had to put his foot down when she batted those lethal eyes of hers at the owner of a Creole-style restaurant. Doug paid for their very expensive meals over the owner's objections. Then the owner, Jacque St. Clair, kissed both of Satarah's knuckles and asked her out on *another* date. The vixen was wearing sweats and ratty tennis shoes, for Pete's sake! Not a bit of makeup and her hair barely contained. Still, she had St. Clair's tongue hanging out.

Doug didn't examine why he felt it necessary to take Satarah's arm and literally haul her away from St. Clair's admiring gaze before she could agree to the date. He decided to tuck that little bit of insanity away for the mean time. He wasn't going to consider whether his actions were the result of jealousy. After all, he and Satarah were just friends, so to speak. He didn't have any right to be jealous and dismissed the thought as an aberration.

When they left Columbia with Satarah's ill-gotten gains piled in and on top of his truck, they went to the hospital to visit Donovan. The boy's face lit up when Satarah came into the game room, though he seemed a little leery of Doug, but not hostile. The three of them passed time playing a board game, though most of the time was spent teaching Doug how the game was played. A task left to Donovan to explain and teach. Doug won the game, to Donovan's and Satarah's consternation.

The entire day was hectic, but Doug admitted, it was a helluva lot of fun.

"So, are you just going to stand there like a big, contented Tom cat licking the last of the cream from his bowl or are you going to help me haul this stuff upstairs?"

Doug looked up as Satarah came down the wide, central stairs. She looked like a returning warrior woman from the shopping wars. He reached out a hand to her. She put hers in his and there was something comfortable and familiar in their touch. Too comfortable in the way they focused on each other. He needed to think about what he was beginning to feel for Satarah; somewhere private, sometime soon, but for now he had other things on his mind.

He took both of her hands in his and bowed over them. "Oh, Great Shopping Queen Satarah Josephine, may I beg a favor?"

Satarah hooted a laugh, and then sobered into a regal pose. "Yes, what is it, peasant? State your business and be quick about it. I have kingdoms to conquer."

"I beg your Highness to never take me on her shopping wars again. I will be your slave forever if you will but grant this one request."

"You are my slave, peasant. Now get ye to the kitchen and make my coffee, cut my cake, and be quick about it. Then," she spread her arms to encompass all of the bags in the foyer, "haul my bounty to my treasured rooms."

Doug grinned. "Your wish, your High Ass, is my command."

Satarah raised one imperial eyebrow. "And don't ever forget it."

13

When the receptionist, Mabel Longwood, announced Bob Sweeny's arrival, Doug got up from his desk to greet him at his door. Mabel led the way. Doug extended his hand and Bob embraced it with a smile.

"Good to see you, Bob."

"Likewise, Deputy Battalion Chief." He looked at Doug's amused expression, "Did I say something funny?"

"No, Bob. It just seems so long ago that someone called me Deputy Battalion Chief, that I had forgotten what the title sounds like."

"I got the same reaction from Ms. Longwood when I asked to see you."

"Around here we call him Douglas or Chief," Mabel said, then turned to Doug. "Would you like something to eat or drink?"

"Thanks, but no, Mabel. I still have refreshments in my office. I will be leaving for the day to take Bob to The Summer House. I'll see you next week."

"Fine, Chief. Say hello to Sara Jo for me." She turned to Bob again and extended her hand. "And welcome aboard. I hope you'll enjoy your stay with us."

"Thank you," he said and watched her retreat for a moment. "You know, Chief, when I got out of my car, complete strangers walked up to me to shake my hand. What gives around here?" he asked perplexed.

"Get used to it. It's the way things are done in Summer County," Doug said, leading Bob to the sofa. Doug pulled a couple of bottles of water from a small refrigerator and handed one to Bob. They sat across from one another. "I didn't expect to see you this soon."

"I have to admit that I was eager to get here. After you offered the Tactical Training Officer's job to me, word came down an hour later that I was to report to you by Friday. The Fire Chief, himself, actually called me on the telephone. I couldn't believe it or how fast it happened. I did not want them to have time to change their minds. I went straight home, packed and hit the road."

"You made good time. The rest of the training team, Dr. Mark Anthony Brooks and Louise McCrary, are scheduled to arrive on Friday."

"I don't think I know them. Are they with the Richmond Fire Department?"

"Mark Brooks is a doctor on sabbatical from the organization, Doctors Without Borders. He and I were in the Marine Corp together. Louise McCrary is a private, independent fire investigator. We met at a convention several years ago."

"Sounds like you're recruiting some top-notch people."

"All of you are, Bob. That's why you're on the team. I have other specialists that I'm negotiating with for either short-term or long-term positions."

"I don't know what to say, but I'm glad you asked me to come. Everything went to-hell-in-a-hand-basket after you left. It's gotten so bad that some of the guys asked to be transferred. I was about to do the same thing."

"I'm sorry to hear that. By and large, Battalion Company 4 has some of the best firefighters in the city."

"I'm not trying to suck up or anything, but we were good because you trained us. You didn't tolerate sloppiness or slackers. You were a hard ass, but you demanded professionalism. Although the guys didn't show it, they certainly appreciated it. Your training saved a lot of lives."

"I'm still a hard ass, Bob." Doug chuckled.

"Sir, may I ask how your son is doing?"

"He's improving, but he's not out of the woods yet."

"I was in the station house when Battalion Chief Stovall was yelling at you about reporting to duty. We were in the middle of a freaking blizzard and the school bus accident was all over the news. So were your picture and other parents. Most of the guys were pissed off about how Stovall acted. No matter what, you don't mess with a firefighter's family like that. End of tour we went down to the Blood Bank and donated blood in Donovan's name."

"I appreciate that. I didn't know about it, but I'll send a letter to the squad. We're just coming out of that crisis here. So many of the accident victims are still too seriously injured to be moved. When this community was declared a disaster area, federal and state funds were made available. The Summer County Council created an emergency rehabilitation center in an aircraft hangar. It went operational five days after the blizzard started."

"Damn! That was fast!"

"I've never seen anything like it, even in the Marine Corps. As less critical patients were released to rehabilitation, the county's Chief of Medical Services cleared out a wing of the hospital. He set up a specialized medical team to deal with critical care rehabilitation patients. Donovan is in the children's center there. He's receiving excellent care. I can go by the center several times a day and night to visit with him.

"The Chief of the Nursing staff arranged housing for parents and relatives who have to stay in the area."

"How did she do that?"

"I think she's a magician. Initially, the county high school, it's called Summer County Academy, was used to house those who needed emergency food, shelter and clothing, but as soon as the storm broke, mobile homes were rolled in and set up like a camp on farmland within walking distance of the hospital. A number of parents and relatives from Richmond were finally able to travel here. Accommodations were ready for them when they arrived. The county emergency services have been excellent in handling the overwhelming influx of people. The mobile homes are fully equipped with kitchen and bath facilities, but meals are served in the hospital cafeteria around the clock, and in return, the families donate time to the hospital or at the academy with the overflow of uninjured children who have a relative under medical care. There were many families traveling during spring break and ended up in that massive pile-up on I-95. The county got the families into as normal a situation as they could and as quickly as possible."

"Sounds like a lot of work for a Chief of Nurses."

"I think she just twitched her nose and made everything happen," Doug deadpanned, "but you'll meet Sylvia Alexander. Count on it! Let's get you fed and settled in."

"Good. I'm starving."

"Satarah, may I have another slice of peach pie?" Bob Sweeny asked, pleadingly.

"As long as I don't have to get up to get it, you're welcome to it," Satarah said, laughed.

"Uh, I'll get the peach ice cream," Doug said, rising from the kitchen table where they were finishing dinner.

"Real, homemade, peach pie and peach ice cream made with real peaches and cream," Bob said returning to the table carrying the deep-dish pie. "I must have died and gone to heaven. I have never tasted food so fresh and good."

"Wait until breakfast. The hot sausages in gravy with onions and peppers will break your heart."

"I ate so much at dinner, I don't know whether I'll be hungry in the morning. I damn near embarrassed myself."

"More pancakes for me then," Doug said.

"Uh, what time did you say breakfast would be served, Satarah?"

She and Doug laughed at Bob's expression. "Breakfast is served between six and nine o'clock. My boys usually eat at 6:30, or earlier if they know they have to beat Doug to the breakfast table."

"True that," Doug said, expressively.

Everyone laughed.

When Bob sobered, he said to Satarah, "You have a great place here. The Chief mentioned that you're still working on getting it ready to open. I'm a pretty good handyman. I'd like to help if you'd let me."

"Doug showed you the workroom, did he?"

"Briefly. He wouldn't let me touch anything. I'll tell you the truth, when I went in to your workroom, I was as happy as a pig in slop."

"It used to be my workroom. Now, I can't get inside when Doug is around."

"So, it's okay with you if I help out?"

"I'm planning to get started on the game room next. You are welcome to help me with it."

"Hey! You didn't mention that to me," Doug interjected, miffed.

"You were hell bent on building the gazebos."

"How did you know?"

"Doug, every day Tonya delivers the mail and there is always some building catalog in the mail for you. You and Kenneth are always on the computer designing something you two want to build. How would I not know what you're up to?"

"Wait a minute. I wasn't the one who had to be dragged out of the hardware store," he proclaimed, incensed without heat.

"Oh yeah? Who started salivating over at the lumber yard, huh? A grown man tearing up over sticks of mahogany wood."

"I did not," he argued, only for form.

"Hold up. This sounds like it could turn into a domestic situation. So, if you'll excuse me, I'll go to my room and crash." He kissed Satarah's knuckles. "Thanks for the great meal, warm welcome, and fantastic suite. G'night, Chief."

When Bob went to his room, an uneasy silence hung in the air between Doug and Satarah. They would have been surprised that they each had similar thoughts: they did sound like a married couple. They were very easy with each other and often attuned to each other's thoughts. They certainly talked to each other a lot, and always had plenty to talk about. They started calling each other during the day or leaving messages about their plans. Usually, they went to visit Donovan together and Doug went with Satarah to a parent-teacher conference and the boys' baseball practice together. They worked on the house together, making plans, buying supplies and coordinating tasks. Somewhere along the way, they had fallen into a comfortable pattern of being together. Watching a movie in the Media Room or playing cards or a board game with the boys or sitting in the library reading books.

The realization snuck up on them so swiftly that when they finished clearing up the dessert dishes, they said a quick good night and scurried off to their bedrooms.

⚬

"Okay," Satarah said aloud and huffed out a breath. "What's going on here?" She leaned back against the vinyl pillow and let the warm, sudsy water envelop her body. Okay, so she was a little spooked at what seemed to have slipped up on her—on them—in the last six weeks or so, but they were in each other's company every day since they met. Still, she had to admit, at least to herself, that they developed some type of rhythm—chemistry—that seemed to flow easily between them. They were alike in many ways; both loners. So they had that in common and they were both raising children alone—boys at that.

She also had to admit that something about Douglas made her want to reach out to him, not in a sexual way, she promised herself, but to offer support and friendship.

Okay, okay, maybe something in her, some space that hadn't been filled in many a year, had opened. She was a realist, a practical woman, the operative word being woman. She did want him to reach out to her, to touch her, but did she want him to bed her?

He wasn't a handsome man—okay, he wasn't *suavely* handsome, not like Jacque St. Clair, the all-the-way-live woman's Creole wet dream. She wanted to bed Jacque the moment he brought one of his employees to her clinic to have his hand stitched three years ago. All that wavy, black hair and dark good looks with blue-grey eyes had her glands salivating. His brother, Garrison, was no slouch either, but, technically, Dr. Garrison St. Clair was her boss; Chief of the Emergency Room. Yet, of course, she had Jacque in a hot romance for two months before her passion for him burned itself out. She hadn't seen the man in several years and had actually forgotten that he owned the restaurant she took Doug to. When she saw Jacque again, no flame ignited. The embers were cold.

However, there was a helluva spark a few weeks ago when Doug dragged her out of Jacque's restaurant. She hadn't mistaken that green-eyed monster when it invaded Doug's body.

Truth be told—and she'd never admit this to another living soul—she felt that same spark of interest when Doug prevented her and Reynard Steward from going at each other in the hospital hallway. His knuckles had brushed her abdomen and made her wet.

She dearly hoped that her ancestors weren't listening to her private thoughts now. Maybe they were tuned into another branch of the family or *Jeopardy* or *Burn Notice* or something. Anything other than her feeble attempts to sort out sensations that seemed to be present, whether she was with Douglas E. Johnson or not. Still, there was a look in his eyes every once in a while that had her juices flowing.

What kept her grounded was a healthy fear that she would muck up a budding friendship with sweaty, greedy sex that might insult and disappoint him or her family.

Yet, she wondered, not for the first time, what kept Douglas Johnson grounded. What kept him from touching her? Was she not his type? She admitted she wasn't a raving beauty like JeNelle or Stacy or Janice or Cecil, the Alexander and Dixon spouses, or like her own mother, Mariah. Men hadn't kicked her out of bed either. Maybe Doug was still in love with his deceased wife. Or maybe it was very simple: Doug just wasn't into her.

Too much to think about, she decided, as she slid down in the tub and let the warm water cascade over her head.

❧

Doug let the warm water cascade over him. He turned his face up to the warm ample spray so that it beat down on his face and hair. He left the kitchen, less than fifteen minutes ago like a scarred Jackrabbit going to ground. Absently, he rubbed at the burning sensation just under his heart. Lately, he got that same feeling every time he thought of her, of Satarah. He had been thinking a lot of her; finding excuses to be with her. It really didn't matter what they did, where she wanted to go or asking her to come with him while he ran errands. Just that he wanted to spend time with her. He liked that she expected him home for breakfast, lunch and dinner. She would have something new and different that she wanted him to sample. She was working on menus and a cookbook so that when she opened the B&B, her meals would not be boring or bland.

Of course, he felt it his duty to nix the idea of making an authentic Creole dinner. He didn't want Satarah thinking about or consulting with Jacque St. Clair or anywhere near that man. Oh, yes, he had seen, clearly, that there had been something between them, something in St. Clair's eyes. Men knew, instinctively, what another man was thinking when he looked at a woman; when St. Clair looked at Satarah. She had, wisely, agreed that a Louisiana Creole addition to her South Carolina Low County Southern Cuisine wouldn't be advantageous. Though he didn't like the little knowing grin she gave him when he agreed with her.

Sex. That was the problem, Doug decided. He hadn't had any in far too long. How could he when his life had been flipped upside down on him? If he were back in Richmond, he could have some sex. He had sources for satisfying his needs. But here, in Summer County? He didn't think so. Not that a few women hadn't expressed their interest since his arrival. One of the radiology lab technicians offered to cook for him and help relieve his tension. She made no secret of what type of tension relief she was willing to offer. As needy as he was, he hadn't given her offer serious consideration.

There was, of course, Jinx's Juke Joint out near the county line. When Jeff Logan took him and Bob Sweeny there for a public safety inspection, Doug knew immediately the place didn't just serve drinks and provide live music. One look at Sassafras, the on-call receptionist, and the flush on Jeff Logan's high yellow skin told Doug that Sassafras had more than biblical knowledge of the ambassador's son. Though the club owner didn't look like a stereo-typical madam. Her hair was cut New York City slick, as well as her tailored attire. She had a cultured voice with a New England nasal accent. She was about his age, but he feared that if she ever got her hands on him, he would age considerably in one session.

Though the all-woman workforce didn't parade around in skimpy outfits or wear ostentatious hair or makeup, the place had an air of sensual pleasures. Something that Summer County Court Judge Malcolm Galloway must have enjoyed, Doug decided, from the sappy grin on the judge's face when he stopped a moment to chat and wish them a good day before he whistled his way out the establishment's front door.

Jinx's Juke Joint was as clean and neat as the South Carolina Board of Health, but Doug feared being seen coming or going for any reason other than official fire department business. No, if he were going to have sex, it would have to be somewhere like Columbia. He was scheduled to go there for a three-day conference with other South Carolina county fire chiefs and the state Fire Marshall. All he had to do was hold out for a couple of weeks and he would find a woman willing to have no-strings-attached sex.

Damn hard to do with Satarah Whitfield firing his libido every minute of every day, but hold out he would even if it meant resorting to self-gratification like some randy teenager.

Doug shut off the water and stepped out of the tub.

God, he hadn't been this hard for a woman even when he was a teenager and Lily was young and nubile. She was a virgin the first time they made love and dependent on him to show her how to become a woman. She was so small and fragile that it drew out his protective instincts; not like Satarah. Lily needed him to do everything for her. She wouldn't learn to drive or go to the grocery store alone. She didn't want him going anywhere without her. She wanted him to pick her clothes for her and to buy her damn tampons!

He couldn't imagine Satarah asking him to do any of that for her and if he offered, she'd probably spit in his eye. Satarah did her own carpentry, electrical wiring, plumbing and landscaping—and cooked like a gourmet. She even did her own auto maintenance, for Pete's sake! And she was a seasoned Nurse Practitioner. Satarah Josephine Whitfield was the epitome of the phenomenal woman.

Lily and Satarah were as different as a Quaker woman and a Las Vegas showgirl. The problem as he saw it was that he wanted Satarah more than he ever wanted Lily. Still, he was not willing to risk his friendship with Satarah to slake his raging need. He knew many of her family members now and liked the whole lot of them. He would get a serious beat down if he sat down at the poker game, like the one he attended last Friday at her Uncle Bernard's house, and let slip that he wanted to jump Satarah's bones. So, he would look forward to his trip to Columbia; invest in a few drinks and maybe dinner, then talk a willing woman into getting naked with him.

When Doug stomped back into The Summer House, grumbling something unintelligible to Satarah, Bob Sweeney, Mark Brooks and Louise McCrary, curiosity shot back and forth between the four of them.

It was Sunday afternoon. The foursome had an early dinner and was sitting in the front parlor in shorts and T-shirts. Doug had been in Columbia since Friday morning. It was a particularly warm day, so all the windows were opened and the ceiling fans were going at a good clip to catch the breeze. The CD player was loaded with eight CDs programmed to play at random. They were playing a lively game of Uno and sipping on Mint Juleps when Doug stomped into the house. Given his uncharacteristically surly demeanor, no one wanted to be anywhere near the big, angry bear. Plus, it was too hot to argue with him. By silent agreement, they resumed their card game.

Doug stood under the shower cursing a blue streak and it was all Satarah Josephine Whitfield's fault. His plan had worked—well almost. He found a woman, a computer contractor, offering a software program to the fire chiefs at the Columbia conference. Although the place was packed with fire chiefs, she walked up to him in the hotel bar on Saturday night and asked whether he would like to have a drink with her. He excused himself from a group of men to a chorus of good-natured ribbing. He followed her observing the enticing sway of her hips, the skinny high heels, the long tapered legs that went up to her earlobes and the short skirt that didn't. They had talked about fire safety over drinks and then dinner at a nice restaurant a block away from their hotel. After dinner, they listened to a good jazz band at a club, danced slowly cheek to cheek, and then walked back to the hotel. When they entered the hotel elevator, he pushed the button for his floor and waited for her to call the shots. When the elevator doors opened, they were in a lip lock so intense they almost missed his floor. They were nearly naked before his hotel room door closed. She was rubbing, licking and kissing him in all the right places; she even rolled the condom on him with her mouth.

Fifteen minutes later, she dressed, kissed him on the forehead and said, "Maybe next year."

He was mortified. He had never had a "performance problem" before and shouldn't have had one now. But when he looked up at her, as she prepared to mount him, her skin wasn't the right complexion. She was a light-skinned, Black female, with hazel eyes and short dusty-blond colored hair. Not cinnamon brown with reddish undertones in her skin or a wild mane of dark hair so thick and unruly it couldn't be contained. With those characteristics missing, he suddenly wondered, what was the friggin' point? Then he had no point; just a soft, flaccid member. Though she tried mightily to resurrect, rejuvenate and restore his passion, he literally couldn't get it up.

So Sunday, after the Wrap-up Luncheon, he beat a hasty retreat to Summer County more frustrated than he'd been when he left.

And what greeted him on his return? A barefoot Satarah wearing a form-fitting, sleeveless T-shirt, with a scoop neckline and tied up under her breasts and a pair of shorts that should be declared illegal inside the great State of South Carolina! She had more skin showing than was clothed. So now, he stood under a cold shower wondering why his well-laid plan to get *laid* had gone astray.

14

atarah flew in the house nearly bowling Doug over.

"Hey! What's your hurry?" Doug asked as he righted himself and caught Satarah's upper forearms.

"Gotta date. I almost forgot. Got to get ready," she panted between each statement.

"You've got a what?"

"A date. You've heard of dating, haven't you, Johnson?"

"Well, yeah, I've even been on a few myself."

"Gotta go," she stated, but was held in place by a pair of big, strong hands. "Come on, Doug," she whined. "I don't have time now," she said extricating herself from his hold on her. "I'll see you at the Spring Dance," she called over her shoulder as she sprinted to her room.

He didn't have time either. He had to get to the start of the parade route. His firefighters were going to help with crowd control, and, God help him, he was riding in the parade. The parade would start in Centerville and travel through each village until they reached Goodwill to the Summer County Academy campus, circle the baseball and the football fields and then disperse. The County All-star baseball games would begin at two o'clock.

Then the spring dance would begin at five o'clock under a big, white tent that spanned one of the football playing fields.

Doug wanted to see Donovan for a few minutes before all the festivities started. The nursing staff, namely Mrs. Sylvia Alexander, arranged for the young ambulatory patients from the hospital to ride on hay wagons in the parade, representing the new children's Rehabilitation Center. The children, organized by Satarah Whitfield and Helen Greene, painted big, long banners to put on the sides of the wagons. It was a big secret what the banners would say, but Doug knew it would be creative. Jonathan and Jeffrey would march with the Summerville Boys and Girls Club baseball team. All in all, it would be a very busy day, and a very warm one.

Nevertheless, Doug decided he would make time to find out about Satarah and her big date.

⁂

"Whew! That was fun, wasn't it?" Sylvia Alexander said when she joined a group of firefighters at the beer barrel.

"I thought we would have people fainting from heat stroke during the parade," Bob Sweeney interjected, wiping sweat from his brow.

"Psshaw! It's not that hot out here. It's only springtime. Can't you feel that breeze?"

"Mrs. A, if there's a breeze around here, it's hiding from me."

"Your blood will thin out in no time. You've only been here a few months," but Sylvia noticed that someone else had captured Bob's attention. She followed his line of sight and saw perky Jennie Jones wearing a pretty, pale-yellow frock, a shade darker than her sunny golden hair.

Bob quickly excused himself and headed in Jennie's direction. Sylvia returned to her conversation with Doug and the other firefighters. They chatted about the parade, the baseball games and the next event, the spring dance. The firefighters were gearing up for the carnival and then the fireworks display that would close out the day's activities.

Several times, Sylvia noted that Doug was scanning the building crowd under the big tent and around the perimeter. She had an idea who he was looking for. Her suspicions were confirmed when Satarah Josephine walked up the lane under the pergolas covered with bougainvillea to the entrance of the tent. Doug excused himself and made a beeline for her.

"She looks just like Mariah at that same age, doesn't she?" Bernard Alexander asked, as he circled his wife's waist with one arm and kissed her temple.

"She's stronger than my sister, and maybe just a little more beautiful," Sylvia said, her eyes glossy with unshed tears.

Doug strode up to Satarah, whose back was turned toward him. He noticed the white confection she wore against her glossy brown skin. There was a network of strings intricately woven from her shoulders to her waistline. He saw no bra strap and mentally fought his hardening member for control. The front was bib-like, cinched at her small waist and a flirty little skirt draped to her knees. When he got closer, Doug noticed the skimpy little high-heeled sandals that tied what looked like a magnolia blossom across her toes and strapped above her ankles. The shoes with the flowers made her legs look sexy as hell.

When Mary Ella acknowledged his approach, Satarah turned and smiled brightly. Her hair was pressed sleek and smooth cascading over her shoulders and down her back. She had parted it on the right side, covering part of her face and a big, fragrant, white blossom pinned behind her right ear. Cowrie shell earrings dangled from her earlobes. She had done something to her face, too. Her eyes seemed larger, her mouth more rosy and her skin smooth and supple looking. It took him a moment to catch his breath and tune in to the fact that people were talking to him.

"Are you all right, Doug?" Satarah asked, concerned.

"Uh, sure. Why do you ask?"

"I don't know, but you seemed to have gone into some kind of trance. You were just standing there staring at me. What's that about?"

"Something on my mind. Uh, I thought you had a date. Where's St. Clair?"

"Jacque?" Satarah asked, confused. "I don't know. Probably in Columbia. My date wasn't with him."

"Oh." He shifted uncomfortably and noticed how Satarah, Mark and Mary Ella were staring at him. "What?" he asked.

"Satarah is my date," a familiar voice spoke.

Doug looked down into the upturned, grinning face and gold teeth of Bigger Thenham.

Bigger took Satarah's hand. "Come on, darlin'. Let's dance."

And dance they did; to every selection the band played. Doug sat at a round table on the sidelines with Donovan and others watching the women, some in beautiful floral tea-length dresses, being whirled around the temporary dance floor under the fans in the big-top tent. Even Jonathan and Jeffrey were dancing to the intricate country, line-dance steps. Doug had seen the Electric Slide, but it was a two-step compared to the jazzy country line or square dances. He could barely understand what the man on the bandstand was saying, but the dancers didn't miss a step in the alaman left or reel this way or that. The choreography was like watching a type of country ballet. Bernard and Sylvia Alexander were stepping with the best of them. So were Chuck and Vivian, Mayor Olivia Dixon, her husband, Romelo, and their twin sons, Donald and James with their wives, Cecil and Janice.

Bob Sweeny and Jennie Jones looked right at home while Mary Ella Baker was teaching Dr. Mark Brooks how to dance country style. He saw others, so many people he now knew by name and could call friends. People he met in his capacity as Fire Chief or at the hospital or at the barbershop. He loved the old fashioned dry goods store where he would go to pick up supplies and end up 'sitting a spell' with some of the old timers. He drank real cold root beer while sitting in a rocking chair on a wooden porch watching the slower paced world go by. He heard many stories about the good old days in Summer County. It was a strange phenomenon to be greeted warmly by hundreds, old and young, who were now his friends and neighbors.

When one band took a break after a solid two hours of lively raucous music, another younger band started up on the other side of the tent. The daylight was fading while the tent lights were slowly coming up. The young adults who were dancing continued in a renewed burst of energy while the older adults took a break.

Donovan was rocking his shoulders to the new music. His crutches were on the floor under the table where he sat in a wheel chair.

Doug grinned at him. "Can you do what they're doing?" he asked Donovan.

He gave Doug a "get real" look and continued rocking and bouncing in his chair. Clearly, his spine had healed, because he snaked his upper body and popped and locked it like he had never had a near-death experience. Doug was snapping his fingers and enjoying Donovan's happy chair dance. When twelve-year-old Whitney Ivy Alexander slipped between the tables dancing, Donovan goggled. Doug held on to his merriment, but he had to agree with Donovan. Whitney, the eldest daughter of Benjamin and Stacy Alexander, was an absolute beauty with her golden-brown, flowing hair and dark eyes. Again, Doug was impressed with how uninhibited and confident the Alexander's grandchildren were.

"Come on, Donny. Dance with me," Whitney Ivy crooned, snaking her body and locking just as Donovan was doing. She reached under the table and got his crutches.

For a moment, Donovan had that scared Jackrabbit look on his face, then as if to say, a man's got to do what a man's got to do, he levered himself up and followed Whitney Ivy to the dance floor. He could not do much on the crutches, but what he did do was impressive. Soon the crowd was chanting "Go Donny" in a quick cadence. Doug watched the boy who had become his son enjoying himself. Doug took a swallow of his watery tea to force down the lump in his throat.

When Donovan ambled back to the table, he smirked at Doug. "Your turn."

"Is that a challenge?"

"Whatever," Donovan said, grinning.

"You got it, my man."

Doug stood and scanned the floor looking for Satarah. She was already dancing with her Uncle Bernard, so Doug snagged Sylvia Alexander's hand. Without hesitation, they began to rock to an Old School beat. Sylvia Alexander was handling him. The woman could dance!

When the song ended, they laughed and hugged.

"Hey, get your own woman," Bernard Alexander joked, as he simultaneously twirled Sylvia out of Doug's arms and Satarah into them. Fortunately, the next tune was slow, so Doug brought Satarah up close. With her high heels, they were almost eye level.

Satarah was eye-level with Doug's mouth, so she looked up away from temptation. "You aren't a half bad dancer."

Doug chuckled. "Your Aunt Sylvia is a challenge. I was just trying to keep up. Plus, Donovan challenged me, so what's a man to do? I couldn't let him front on me, could I?"

"Of course, not."

There was a pregnant moment before Doug said, "You look very pretty, Satarah."

Satarah leaned back slightly. "How much did that hurt?"

"What?" he asked, confused.

"The compliment."

Doug chuckled. "I didn't want Bigger to get mad and hurt me for complimenting his girl." He whirled her around and had her laughing. Her hair flew around her shoulders and back like black mercury.

When Doug sat next to Donovan again, he patted Doug on his back, gave him a pitying looked, and shook his head. "Practice, Dad. Practice."

Dad. Something monumental shot straight through Doug when he looked into Donovan's eyes. To keep their manly demeanor, Doug grabbed Donovan in a playful headlock. He gave his son a knuckle nuggy and had Donovan giggling until he yelled uncle. He leaned down and kissed the top of Donovan's head. They sat together in animated conversation; mostly Donovan talked about all the phine young hunnies in Summer County, particularly Whitney Ivy Alexander, until a group of youngsters asked whether Donovan could go with them to the carnival that was now open on one of the baseball fields. Doug consented, gave Donovan some money, and the group wheeled Donovan away.

"Looks like Donovan is having a good time," Bernard said when he sat down beside Doug, taking the space Donovan vacated.

"He's not the only one," Doug said, still watching Donovan involved with the other preteens headed toward the carnival.

"That's good to hear."

"He called me Dad." Doug turned to face Bernard. "He used to call me sir, but he called me Dad and I don't know; can't explain how that made me feel. Something— happened inside me when he said it. I consider myself an educated man, Bernard, able to be articulate, but I can't put into words what I felt."

"Then just call it love, Douglas. You felt love for Donovan and when he called you 'dad' instead of 'sir', he was feeling it too.

"Both of you have come a long way. I was watching the two of you. You're both falling into a solid father/son friendship and relationship. He trusts you and he respects you. He has learned to depend on you. He tells everyone that you're his dad. He's very proud to be your son. That will open a lot of opportunities for you two to strengthen your relationship."

"I didn't know that. I want so much for him; good things to happen for him. I want to help him do and be everything that he wants. I don't want to make any mistakes."

"Then you will fail him, Douglas. No one sent any of us to parenting school. We all have to feel our way through. That means that we will make mistakes. It's only human. Work at making a solid relationship with Donovan based on love and mutual respect and trust. The mistakes will be few and far between. Just remember the love you felt when he called you 'Dad' and you'll do fine."

"Thank you. I've learned a great deal since I've been here, but I know I have a long way to go."

"As we all do."

"Certainly not you. You've raised five successful children."

"I had a lot of help. Sylvia is not only my wife, she's my best friend. We're each other's best friend, we're partners. We love, trust and respect each other and we help and support each other, but we had fine examples in our parents and grandparents. Just as our children had their grandparents, aunts, uncles, cousins—family—to help us all grow up and develop. No one person does this alone."

"I don't have a family to offer Donovan."

Bernard chuckled. "Sure you do. Just look around you, Douglas."

Doug did and suddenly understood the meaning of the phrase: it takes a village. The people of Summer County had taken him and Donovan in and treated them like family from the moment they arrived, particularly Sylvia Alexander. She was more mother to him than his own had been. Doug turned back to Bernard.

"I guess I should confess that I've fallen a little in love with your wife."

Bernard hooted out a laugh. "Good, because my wife has fallen a little in love with you, too."

It was Doug's turn to laugh and he did so with Bernard Alexander.

❧

Satarah sat at a table with Bob, Jennie, Mark, Mary Ella and Bigger enjoying the spring dance and the cooling fresh air laced with the scent of spring flowers. When Little Willie came to the table and beckoned Bigger away, Satarah's focus on her tablemates wandered, much as it had all day, to Douglas. He looked so handsome in the horse-drawn carriage with the other county officials, and tossing out the first baseball for the start of the All-Star game. He seemed to be enjoying himself with Donovan and he and Uncle Bernard were having, what appeared to be, a very deep and interesting conversation. When they hooted in laughter, Satarah wondered what they were talking about.

Satarah decided she would join her friends and Doug at his table when Uncle Bernard patted Doug on the shoulder and walked away. Before she could stand, Laurel Mason, a radiology technician, sat down beside Doug. They talked for a few moments before they got up to dance.

Satarah tuned out the vision of Doug and Laurel on the floor dancing and decided to visit other family and friends at their tables. Perhaps a half hour later, Satarah made her way to where Chuck sat holding his baby daughter while he talked with Dakota Logan, her cousin, James Dixon and his very pregnant wife, Janice; and Kenneth Alexander and his wife, JeNelle. They were planning to go to the horse races and to look at horses for their farms.

"Satarah, could I speak with you a moment?" Bigger asked.

Satarah excused herself, rose from the table and followed Bigger outside the tent. They sat on the football field bleachers.

"I have a situation, Satarah," he began earnestly. "You see, it's like this: I've been kinda seeing Ms. Lucile Lindsey, you know, the woman who takes in laundry over in Centerville? Well, she's been pushin' up on marriage talk for some time yet, and I told her that I wasn't ready to get all committed, you see? So she says that if I didn't ask her to marry me, she was going to go out with Odell Perkins, who owns the dry goods store over in North Ridge. So I tells Ms. Lucile that if that's what she wanna do, then I wasn't gonna stop her. So we was quits. Then I asked you to be my date. So Odell, he brings Ms. Lucille to the dance, but when she sees me escorting you, she throws a hissy fit. She gets Mama Lou all upset and then Little Willie gets all upset. Then everyone is upset and fussin'. You see what I mean?"

Satarah nodded, but had absolutely no idea where all of this was leading, so she asked, "What is it that you want me to do, Bigger?"

"Well, it's like this, Sara Jo. I can't be taking you out for a while. Not a long while, mind you, but Ms. Lucille, she all mad because I started dating you just after her and me went quits. So Mama Lou said there should be a cooling off period. Ms. Lucile and me, we not 'spose to date nobody else for a spell. So, I have to stop dating you right this minute or Mama Lou said she's gonna box my ears."

Satarah tried mightily not to laugh. She agreed that she wouldn't try to date him during his 'cooling off period.'

"Lessen you ready to marry up with me now," Bigger said, expectantly. "I'll be callin' you for another date soon as the cooling off period is over."

"You do that, Bigger." She got up and walked away.

When she re-entered the tent, Doug grabbed her hand. "There you are. How about another dance?"

He didn't give her a chance to agree or not, as he brought her onto the dance floor. When that tune ended, a slow tune began.

"Please, Satarah, don't leave my side, yet. I beg you."

Satarah went back into his arms. "Okay, Doug, what's going on? Why are you afraid to be left alone?"

"She has whips and chains," he whispered, fervently.

Satarah shook her head as if to clear it, and squinted in confusion at Doug. "Who has whips and chains?"

"Laurel Mason," he whispered for her ears only. "She said she wants to chain me up and whip me."

It took a moment for Satarah to get the picture of big, strong Douglas E. Johnson in chains with Dominatrix Laurel cracking a whip. When she did, she began to laugh so hard, her legs were about to give out. She smothered her face in Doug's chest to contain her laughter before she wet herself.

Doug couldn't help it. He tried not to laugh, too, but it bubbled up and he buried his face in Satarah's hair as they danced and shook with stifled laughter.

"It's not funny, Satarah. She was serious!"

Satarah couldn't hold it in any longer. "If you don't get me out of here, I'm going to wet myself."

They left the tent and went into the high school so Satarah could relieve herself. When she left the girls' restroom, she took one look at Doug and burst into laughter again. He joined her, holding himself up against the wall.

"A big, strong man, like you is afraid of Little Laurel. Jeez, Doug, she's not big as a minute."

"But she's got skills, Satarah. She told me what she likes to do to big, strong men like me—and it wasn't pretty!"

"At least you didn't get dumped at the spring dance," Satarah deadpanned.

"Dumped? Bigger dumped you? Why?" Doug asked, incredulously.

"Ms. Lucille Lindsey."

Doug stared at Satarah a beat. "The Amazon woman who runs the Centerville Laundromat? And Bigger?"

Satarah nodded sadly.

"Wait a minute; I can't quite get that image in my head. Four-foot-eleven-inch Bigger Thenham and six-foot-four-inch Lucille Lindsey." Doug shook his head. "Bigger must subscribe to the theory that more is better."

"Like I'm not enough woman for him!" Satarah said, pouting.

"Ah, come here, little girl," Doug teased and hugged Satarah to him. "Don't be sad. When you grow up, you'll be enough for any man."

"Miscreant," she said, laughing, and pushing out of Doug's embrace.

"Don't be mad. Come on, little girl, I'll take you to the carnival and buy you a cotton candy," he said, wiggling his eyebrows up and down.

"Pervert," she said, as Doug slung an arm around her shoulder and turned toward the corridor leading to the baseball field where the carnival was in full swing.

As they passed a door leading to a stairwell, they heard moaning and strange unintelligible sounds. Fearing that someone was hurt or injured, Doug pushed through the door with Satarah hot on his heels. Almost to the landing between floors, they were brought up short and goggled.

Dr. Reynard Steward and Doug's fire investigator, Louise McCrary, in various states of undress were uncoupling from one another.

When Doug picked his mouth up off the floor, he asked, "Dr. Steward, Louise, are you alright?"

Hastily stammering, "It's not what it looks like. You understand?" Rey said, trying unsuccessfully to stuff his member into his shorts with a full condom still attached.

"What does it look like?" Doug asked, straight-faced. He felt Satarah bury her face in his back. When he felt her shaking, he knew she was laughing though not a sound echoed in the stairwell.

"This could be misconstrued as a—something."

"I suggest you two continue your—communication in a more private location. We wouldn't want anyone else stumbling in on your—something." Doug winked and guided Satarah back down the steps and out of the stairwell. Once they were out of earshot, they looked at each other and burst out laughing. "Pit stop," Doug said, between gales of laughter and hustled into the boys' restroom.

When Doug and Satarah finally got to the carnival, they found the boys and wandered around, ate cotton candy, hot dogs, rode the Ferris wheel, drove the bumper cars on an oval track and played games at the booths for three hours. The spring dance was still going strong, as was the carnival. By the time the fireworks ended, the boys were knocked out. Doug carried Jonathan and Jeffrey in his arms while Satarah pushed a sleeping Donovan and a mound of stuffed animals in his wheelchair.

Once they got home, they worked together to get the sleepy boys out of their clothes and into bed. Then they plopped on opposite ends of the divan in the media room and kicked off their shoes. Doug took Satarah's feet in his lap and massaged them. She did the same for him while they recounted and laughed over the events of the day.

When they woke at dawn, they were still stretched out at opposite ends of the divan with a throw covering them.

❧

Doug walked into the training center at the end of Bob's session. He greeted the departing firefighters then approached Bob.

"Are you going to the house for lunch?" Doug asked.

Bob yawned hugely. "Nah, Mark and I are picking up Mary Ella and Jennie and going to the park for a picnic. You want to join us?"

"Thanks, but I'm heading home for the day. After all the preparation and activities at the Spring Fling, I'm beat."

"I heard that. I want to crash, too, but Jennie has other ideas. Would you tell Satarah that Mark and I won't be in for dinner? We're going to Columbia to sightsee and later to a dinner theater."

"Sure. What about, Louise?"

"She's heading to that conference in Myrtle Beach. She's on the program."

"I forgot about that. She'll be back on Sunday, right?"

"That's what she told me."

"I'll remind Satarah."

Bob looked at Doug expectantly and then said, at length. "I like her."

"Louise?" Doug asked, teasing.

Bob flushed. "No, I mean, yes, I mean not in *that* way. I'm talking about Jennie Jones. I like her. A lot," he said, a sappy smile on his face. "She's got those big, brown eyes and baby-fine, platinum hair. I know she has a lot of energy. She just wears me out and she's such a little woman, but she's got such a big heart." He gazed into the middle distance as if seeing Jennie in his mind.

Yeah, he's toast, Doug thought, not uncharitably.

"And she thinks the world of Satarah," Bob continued, bringing his attention back to Doug. "Jennie says it's not right that Satarah got suspended because she saved Donovan's life. Mary Ella doesn't talk about it much, because she's not supposed to. But she's agreeing with Jennie." He licked his lips, nervously. "I like her, too, Chief. I mean, she's something special. She knew what could happen to her for doing what she did, but she did it anyway. That took a lot of courage. I've never known anyone like her."

"It must be interesting falling for three women at the same time."

It took a second before Bob's eyes bucked and he quickly stood. "Oh. No, Chief. I mean, I like Louise. She's smart and knows her job. I mean she's a professional, but I don't want to date her or anything. But Satarah, I mean, I thought about asking her out a few times, but she's too much woman for me. Frankly, she scares me to death. Then I met Jennie, so—. Why are you laughing, Chief?"

"She scares me, too. And, you're right, she's something special."

Bob relaxed, somewhat. "I know it's none of my business, but you don't blame Satarah for what she did, do you?"

"No, I don't. I'm grateful to her."

"Then is there anything you can do to help her? I mean, Donovan being your son and all?"

"If Satarah wants my help, she's got it. Donovan's too."

"But, she would never ask anybody for help."

Doug patted Bob on the shoulder. "Don't worry about it. I've got that covered, too."

15

oug entered through the kitchen door from the recently rebuilt *Porto cohere*, ready for one of Satarah's great meals. When he did not find her there, he called out her name.

"I'm in the vestibule, but don't come in here."

"Why not?" he asked, and then stumbled to a halt at the sight of Satarah's rear end up in the air. She was scrubbing the tile floor on her hands and knees. And attacking the grout with what looked like a tooth brush.

"What are you doing?" he asked, for want of anything to say. The sight of her wiggling fanny was more than he should have to endure without satisfaction.

She looked up at him over her shoulder and narrowed her eyes. "I'm dressing for a ball. So scram."

Satarah heard the bitterness in her voice, but after Rey Steward had the gall to come to her home that morning to try to coerce her into his bed, she had a right to be a little salty. In exchange for her sexual favors, he offered her his support on her pending investigation. He would see to it that the hospital charges were dropped and her position restored with full back pay. Then he tried to put his clammy hands on her. She shuddered at the memory. And he thought she couldn't resist him? What a crock! She scrubbed harder. The man is delusional. Unzipping his fly and wagging his pencil-thin—.

"What!—What are you *doing?*" Satarah sputtered when she found herself being hauled to her feet.

Doug turned her around and held her at arm's length. It was either get her up off the damn floor or dissolve into a puddle from sexual heat.

"Okay. Now tell me what's got your mad on."

"I don't have to tell you anything. Let go of me, you big ox."

He hauled her up to her toes and was about to do something rash to that delectable mouth of hers; something he had been thinking about for far too long. However, when the front door slammed, they both looked over. A man, with long processed curls like a girl's, glared at them.

"Oh hell," Satarah mutter on a long, windy breath. "Just what I needed today." Doug released her and she turned to the intruder. "Hello, Reverend."

The man puffed up with indignation. "Jezebel! Harlot! You flaunt yourself around wearing nearly nothing and having assignations with anybody who lays a hand on you. Living openly in sin in front of those little bastards—," he continued.

Who *is* this man? Doug wondered, his temper rising as the man continued issuing disparaging remarks to Satarah. The man went on in a singsong voice as if he was on a pulpit delivering a sermon full of hell fire, brimstone, and damnation to a congregation. If this was the minister from Satarah's church, though he had not known her to frequent any church service, Doug decided he would hold his temper only for a moment or two more, as the man continued raging insults at Satarah.

"And the Lord will smite you down, whore that you are!"

That did it! Doug stalked slowly, but menacingly toward the minister, flicking off Satarah's grip on him. She dug in her heels, but Doug's forward motion had her sliding on the wet floor.

"Oh, hell no!" Doug said before he realized he had spoken. "I don't give a rat's ass that you're a man of the cloth. You will *not* disrespect this woman in her home and expect me to stand here and listen to this filth!"

Satarah could not get a grip on Doug's thick arm muscle, especially when they were bunched hard as rocks, so she hooked her hands in his belt at his back and pulled. She tried to dig in her heels, but she was pulled along as if she was on water skis over her wet floor.

"Hold on, Doug!" She tried desperately to hold him back, but gave up trying to get his attention over Doug's and the Reverend's rancorous voices. She scrambled around Doug until she could wiggle between the two combatants. Pressing her back against Doug's chest, she dug in her heels and stopped his forward motion. She flung her arms back to contain Doug while the two men continued the tirade of shouted insults at each other.

"Stop it!" Satarah repeatedly shouted until the vitriol subsided and heavy breathing was the only sounds echoing in the vestibule.

"You should leave, Reverend."

"You would tell me to leave this house!" he shouted, indignantly.

"Quickly. I cannot hold this man back."

"This *heathen*," he spat the word, "has no right to be here!"

"This *man* lives here. You don't."

"This house, this property belongs to *my* family. I have every right to say what goes on here! I have a mind to use it for my congregation. I will *not* have it used as a house of ill repute!"

"Oh, so that's the reason for your unwelcome visit? Now that this house is being restored you want to step in and take over."

"It's my right!"

"And pigs fly. This land and its buildings belonged to my great grandparents. My mother and her family inherited it from their parents and deeded it to me free and clear after my mother left you."

Understanding dawned for Doug. "This is your father?" he asked, incredulously. "This is the man who lied to you and your mother? The same man who forced you to give away your baby?"

"Lies! All of them lies! I am the head of my house, the leader of my flock! The harlot, Mariah, is my wife. I will not be denied what is rightly mine!"

"I suggest that you go tend to your flock and pray, Reverend. And while you're at it, I suggest that you *not* lay hands on Belinda Adele again or on Blanche Marie. They are not even sixteen years old yet. If you won't keep your hands off of them, I may have to speak with Mr. Bartholomew and Ms. Eldora about what you do to their daughters in the loft after Wednesday night choir practice!"

The Reverend swelled up like the Tasmanian Devil about to explode. "I will see you in hell before I let you and that bitch——."

Doug's hand snaked out and was around her father's throat, lifting him to his toes before Satarah's brain had time to register the swift move.

"Have a good damn day, Reverend," Doug said between clenched teeth. "I don't ever expect to see you again."

Doug released her father who made haste getting out of the door. Satarah leaned her head back against Doug's chest and looked up at him.

"Well. That was pleasant. Want to have sex now?"

Doug, caught in a phalanx of receding anger, breathed hard and slowly. He rarely lost his temper, but when he did, it wasn't a pretty sight. He was nearly calm again when he finally looked down at Satarah's upside down face. Her expression was so comical that he hooted a laugh, leaned forward and kissed her upside down mouth lightly. Satarah turned in his arms to face him, rose up on her toes, and hooked her arms around his neck before she devoured his mouth. He grabbed her thighs and boosted her up while she locked her legs around his middle.

"This is not going to be a one-night stand," he said, as they kissed each other senseless. "Or a quickie."

"I hadn't planned to do it standing up, but if it has to be this way, I want it hard and fast. At least the first time. We'll worry about the second time when we get to it."

"Okay, but I want to be on top. At least one of those times."

"Agreed," Satarah said, grinning against Doug's mouth before she ripped open his starched uniform shirt and attacked his pecks with teeth and tongue.

Doug had a moment to register that what he had in his arms was a wildcat, before he whimpered with blinding need. One handed, he pulled off her T-shirt and then feasted on the bountiful globes, which, thankfully, were unbound. Satarah reared back to give him space to tend to her hardened nipples as he stumbled into her bedroom, kicking the door closed with his foot. She rode his waist, rubbing her center against his hardened ridge. "Hurry," she gritted out. They made quick work of their clothes and then dived at each other, limbs tangling trying to touch and taste and pleasure every inch of each other all at once. Doug held her hips and, kissing the underside of her thighs to her center, shot her up and over the brink.

"More," she panted out. "More."

And he gave her plenty more. With nerves dancing, he sheathed himself and drove into her, swallowing her cries with his mouth. She pumped him hard and long bringing him to the edge of sanity just before he was ready to explode. He slowed the tempo to steady the blood racing wildly in his veins. Tangling his hands in her wild hair, he reset the rhythm and had her gasping out his name. Every muscle in Doug's body bunched taunt. Her short nails raked his moist back as she heaved up and down to take more of him in. The scent of her coalesced into blinding lust, making him greedy to devour and ravish.

Stunned by her own violent need, Satarah wrapped her strong thighs around Doug's waist and milked him, clenching, then releasing her inner muscles. Heat raked through him, pushing him to peak. When he drove her up and over again, sweat had pooled between her trembling breasts, but he could not seem to get enough of her. He was dangerously close to the edge of oblivion, but her open-mouthed gasps were like a siren's song. He wanted her with a blind desperation, a rush of need so huge that it swamped and swallowed him like a tidal wave. The taste of her mouth, the scent of her skin, the feel of her hair tangled in his fingers, heated to melt down his core until he peaked and let himself go.

Satarah was blind. She knew she was still horizontal, that there were damp sheets at her back, and there was a lovely hum in her blood. If she had to sacrifice one of her senses to float in this beautiful utopia, it was a good deal.

"Don't move," she said, when Doug started to uncouple.

"I'm heavy."

"I know," she purred it while lazily strumming her fingers over his back and butt.

"The kids—."

"Pizza night. Sleep over at James' and Janice's." She stretched lazily.

"Oh. Well, then," Doug said, and reversed their positions. "In that case, it's your turn to be on top."

Satarah grinned at him, reached between them and found his member. Doug jolted, still sensitive.

"Hey! Hey! I need a minute here."

"That's all the time you get," she said, straddling his thighs, dumping the used condom and covering him with a fresh one.

When Doug jack-knifed up, raising his knees and torso simultaneously, Satarah tumbled against his chest, laughing. He rested his arms on his knees, effectively keeping her enclosed. She rested her back against his long, powerful thighs.

For a long moment, they simple regarded each other. Tentatively, she reached out and touched his face much like a sightless person might, tracing his features with fingertips. Then she brought his face to her with both hands.

Light brushes of her mouth over his face were so achingly tender and warm. He watched her watching him. He wanted to speak, to say something, to tell her how much he cared. As if reading his mind, she put her fingers to his lips, shook her head slightly and continued to fill him up inside; filling his heart, his soul. He yielded to her soft mouth on his cheek, his eyes, his chin, the side of his mouth. His mind disconnected from his thoughts and he floated with Satarah while their mouths and tongues danced.

Her face was so arresting in the afterglow of lovemaking. The sunlight slanted across her face, her breasts; a gentle breeze ballooning the sheer, white curtains; the scent of her flower garden perfuming the air along with the aroma of mind-blowing sex. Doug mouthed her plump nipples then blew across them watching them peak and harden.

Satarah reached between them and on a tattered breath inserted his hardened member into her warmth. The raw need clawed at her as she slowly rocked and gyrated her hips like a belly dancer. She could hear the breeze through the trees, the birds chattering crazily in the outside world, the distant lonely sound of a train whistle, but her focus never wavered from Douglas. As her breath began to hitch, yet again, she rocked slowly watching him watching her.

He let her take her fill; take all of him that she wanted before he reached between them to play his fingers over her clitoris. She gasped, her head falling back over his up-raised knees as her breath trembled on each moan. He played her core with one hand, her nipples with the other while she rocked and gyrated. He watched her vision blur, go opaque; then he swallowed her jerky gasps before he took his fill.

Sometime later, Satarah jerked awake from the feel of her toes in Doug's warm soft mouth. Orienting herself was a challenge. Her head was hanging off the foot of her bed. With her eyes closed, she extended her arms from her sides to get her bearings. She found Doug's feet to her right, which were crossed at the ankles and walked her fingers up his legs, past his thighs until, at the apex of his body, she found his warm member and took him in hand. They lay quietly for a spell, touching each other lazily, until Doug took her ankles in his firm grip and pulled her up more securely onto the bed. "You're going to fall on your head, if you're not careful."

"How did I get down here in the first place?" She leaned up on her elbows and then grinned wickedly at Doug. "Oh, now I remember."

"I'll just bet you do." A smirk lifted the left corner of his mouth.

Her grin became more salacious as she leaned to plant lazy kisses between his thighs until she reached her goal.

Doug leaned forward, catching her under her arms and pulled until he brought her head to rest against his chest. "Go back to sleep before you kill me again," he said, laughter rumbling in his chest against her cheek.

His arms clamped around her when she snuggled in. She opened one eye and noted she was a breath away from his flat nipple. She waited until she heard him lightly snoring. Then her tongue whipped out and, bringing her mouth and teeth to bear, captured his nipple.

Doug jerked awake and swore liberally, but his curses died on a long, hard moan. His hands tangled in her thick hair, as she transferred her ministration from one hard, flat nipple to the other. He was as hard as an oak when he parted her thighs and slipped inside her. Palming her fleshy bottom, he closed his eyes while she feasted on him. He was so content; he never wanted to leave the peace and tranquility of Satarah's arms.

He loved touching her in the late afternoon, sliding slowly in and out of her while she played his body like a concert pianist. He wanted to go on for a lifetime of touching her in the afternoon heat, in the midnight clear, and in the morning quiet.

Doug and Satarah showered together then prepared a simple meal of steaks, baked white potatoes with sour cream, butter and chives and a field-greens salad. They lit citronella candles and ate on the back lanai. When they finished eating, they snuggled and watched Mother Nature's kaleidoscope of colors paint the sky and landscape until dusk fell.

"Are you going to tell me why you were so angry before your father arrived?"

"I don't want to, but I will if you promise not to get angry."

Doug looked at her askance. "Why would I get angry?"

"I want your promise."

He shrugged his massive shoulders, laconically. "All right."

Satarah recounted Rey Steward's visit and proposition. The more she said, the more his muscles constricted in rage. Outwardly, he remained calm, but Satarah felt and read his body language, even in the dim light. When she finished talking, there was dead silence between them before he spoke.

"Except for the time in Atlanta, have you given him any reason to think that you're interested in having an intimate relationship with him?"

"Not hardly. I mean, the man is a legend in his own mind."

"Performance problem?"

"And an equipment problem. All I wanted was a little innocent sex with someone. He was available, so—," she said, hunching her shoulders.

"And when you left him at the hotel, you did so to spare his feelings."

"Exactly! But did he buy a clue?"

"Apparently, not. Uh, you're not going to up and disappear on me in the morning, are you?"

"I live here, don't I? Why would I leave? If I'm going to do anything in the morning, it will include jumping your bones often and continuously."

Doug laughed at her sincerely confused tone of voice and hugged her to him. "And I'd let you do it too.

"What about your father's threat? Are you worried about it?"

"No, not really. Vivian handled the property transfer. She's scary when she's in her lawyer mode and she's death on details. My mother is one of seven children. They unanimously agreed to give the property to me before I knew anything about the gift. I'm not a lawyer, but I don't like his chances if he tries to take legal action. If the Reverend thinks there's a nickel to be made, he is likely to do anything. He may try to sue. It's true that my mother inherited her share in the property after she and my father married. I don't know whether they are legally divorced. I never asked and Mama never said."

"Maybe you should ask her or at least talk with Vivian. Chuck mentioned that they are going back to Maryland after Easter."

Satarah swung around to face Doug and sat with her legs under her. "Would you understand if I said that I really don't want to involve my mama's family? That they have done too much for me already?"

"Yes, I would understand, but would you understand if I said I don't agree with you?"

"Why? Because they are wealthy and can afford to help out a poor relation?"

"That's beneath you, Satarah," Doug said, taking umbrage. "Either you don't respect me or yourself. Your family is something I never had, something I didn't realize I needed. Their wealth has nothing to do with it. They weren't giving you a hand out. They gave you a hand. They do what most families neglect to do: they take care of their own. Are you going to slap away the hand they are reaching out to you or do you love them and yourself enough to reach out to touch them?" Doug stood, gathered their dishes and went inside, leaving his question for her to ponder.

⚬⚬⚬

The next day, Saturday, Doug was still angry with her, as well he should be, she thought, morosely. That was a cheap shot; taking her anxiety out on him for no good reason other than he was right. Her mama's people were wealthy and well respected. But that had never shown in their demeanor toward her or toward anyone else that she knew of. Anyone of them would give her the shirt off of his or her back without being asked. They never asked anything of her, except to be a part of them; a member of the circle that made up the family.

She was close to her Aunt Sylvia because she trained her to be a nurse practitioner and guided her through JoJeff's and Carlotta's betrayal, offering whatever help she seemed to need. Uncle Bernard and Aunt Sylvia became as near to surrogate parents as she would let them. She still felt that she was always the needy one and the one who let everyone down by becoming pregnant and then giving her baby away. In the Alexander and Benson families, people were held close, not given away.

She couldn't change the past, but she sure could show them that their love for her was not in vain.

She washed the gold family chain and dried it. It sparkled in the sunlight; a tangible symbol of family unity and loyalty: characteristics that she had waited far too long to express. It took a firefighter from Richmond, Virginia, to make her realize how precious her family was to her. They were not to be ignored or avoided. It was a lesson well learned.

She would go down stairs and see whether Doug and the twins would let her play with them in her workroom. After all, she had some fence mending to do.

Satarah slipped down the winding staircase to the basement. Against the cinderblock walls, pink insulation was tacked between the freshly-installed, two-by-six, Georgia-pine framing, a heavy plastic sheathing covering over all except the electrical boxes with white insulated wires protruding. Bob's work, she noted with a satisfied look on her face. The nine-foot ceiling mirrored the walls. Miniature canister lighting fixtures were evenly spaced and once the wallboard was installed, lights and ceiling fans would be installed. Satarah looked at the dusty paper covering the newly install Corinne floor. She, Bob and Doug had let the boys help with the floor installation working the sixteen-by-sixteen tiles into the adhesive over the heating floor coils. Starting from the center of the room outward to the edges, they had worked on their hands and knees for a full day until the floor came together like a giant checkerboard of royal blue and bone white squares. The large fireplace still needed to be refaced and the brick mortar pointed up, but that could wait until she had the chimney cleaned and checked. The house was so old, she didn't know whether the fireplace, that back in the day was used for cooking, was still functional. All in all, it was shaping up nicely.

Satarah was so intent on her scrutiny of the structural work that she didn't hear Doug's approach. He slipped his arms around her waist and guided her into a slow dance. That's when she heard the music. Something warm, yet wily. She couldn't place the singer or the music. Yet, she liked it—very much. She wound her arms around Doug's neck, looked up into his face and accepted the mind-numbing kiss he placed on her mouth. Angling closer, she felt his heat. When they parted mouths, she had a sappy look on her face.

"What was that?" she asked.

"Kemistry," he said, still swaying to the music that had changed to another soul-stirring melody.

"I'll say." She grinned at him. "But I meant the music."

"I know. It's a band led by a brother. His name is Kem and the group is called Kemistry."

"I haven't heard them before, but I like the sound."

"We'll go hear them perform the next time they're in the area."

She waited a bit before she asked, "Are you still mad at me?"

He kissed her temple. "I was never mad at you, Satarah, just disappointed."

She pressed her cheek to the solid wall of his chest and her right hand to his heart. His steady heartbeat comforted her, as he cocooned her in his powerful embrace and his cheek to the top of her head.

Their slow dance said "we're okay" and she sighed contentedly.

16

aster Sunday dawned bright and warm. Church services in the Village of Goodwill, Summer County, were packed to overflowing. Survivors of the February blizzard who were still in the area and their relatives attended the various services offering up their appreciation to the community for their many acts of kindness and support. Church socials at the Academy were to be held for parishioners and visitors after the Easter church services ended.

After leaving church, Satarah, Doug, Donovan, Jonathan and Jeffrey were in Doug's big SUV headed for the Easter fête at the Alexander/Benson family compound. The long procession of cars snaked around and through the narrow lanes and parked just off the road on freshly filled gravel beds. The family homes circled a park-like setting in a wagon-wheel design with lanes representing the spokes. Big oak, pine, elm, maple and dogwood trees in full bloom provided shade and dappled sunlight. Picnic tables dotted the pristine landscape that Doug thought had to represent at least five acres. He had seen the landscape snow covered in what looked like a winter wonderland, but in the warm sunlight, the green, freshly cut grass was so bright it hurt to look at it. The flower beds burst with color and scents too numerous to count. Engineered water features wound through the park, adding to the natural woodland setting. Birds sent up a cacophony of sound as if cheering the humans arrival. The forest edged the properties as if protecting what was inside the park.

Before he turned off his ignition, Doug checked his GPS system. As he expected, it was malfunctioning again. The problem did not occur in any other part of the county except here. He looked over his shoulders, to his right and left and forward. He saw no towers or electrical poles that could interfere with his reception; not even a roof-top antenna or satellite dish, but he was certain that something in this area caused the GPS malfunction.

"Are you coming?" Satarah asked, coming around to stand at Doug's open car door.

"Yes," he said, absently. Then turning the ignition switch to the off position, he swung out of his seat. Before he closed the door, he removed his tie and cufflinks, all while looking at Satarah. She wore a yellow sundress with spaghetti straps, a straight slash across her bosom, and a matching waist-length jacket. The bodice was snug, but the skirt floated around her hips, down her incredible legs to just below her knees. She also wore strappy, yellow, icepick heels. Her hair was a mass of curls pulled back behind her ears and held in place with cowry shell combs. She had tiny, gold studs and the beautiful, gold, family chain around her neck. The glimpse of the top rounded edge of her breasts drew Doug's eyes from hers as he rolled up his shirtsleeves. When he looked into her eyes again, they sparked with mischief and merriment.

"Later, baby," she purred and winked.

Much to her surprise, he took her hand and strolled toward the family gathering.

Hours later, after two plates of food, with a toothpick in the left corner of his mouth, Doug upped the ante in the poker game. Then held pat. He shifted his eyes to Donald Dixon, whose poker face revealed absolutely nothing when he tossed in his chips. Romelo Dixon grinned at his son and raised the stakes.

"You're bluffing, Uncle Romeo," Gregory Alexander chided, checking his cards again.

"You'll have to pay to play, kid," Romelo parried. "You know how we do it. You're a stockbroker. You know about taking risks, don't you, boy?"

"Calculated risks, yes. Okay, I'll see you and raise you," Gregory said, gamely.

Eyes shifted to Bernard Alexander who met his youngest son's challenge.

Doug laid down his two pair of queens over deuces.

"Not bad," Donald commented, laying down two kings over fours.

Romelo added four-of-a-kind.

When the play got to Gregory, he laid a flush on the table and reached to rake in the pot.

"Not so fast, younger," Bernard said, smugly, to his son and laid a royal flush on the table, one card at a time.

Jeers went up around the table and from those looking on.

"How does he do that!" Doug lamented, not as a question, but as a statement of frustration. He rose from the table with Donald. They were both out of chips. James Dixon, Donald's twin, took a seat and Benny Alexander took the other.

"Walk with me," Donald said to Douglas.

They dodged Frisbees, and watched as family members tossed horseshoes, kids played on the swings or climbed up into a multilevel tree house, toddlers built sandcastles, the teens played full-court shirts-and-skins basketball or baseball or tag football. Some rode ponies in a corral. Still others played volleyball, badminton or tennis.

After stopping briefly to watch various events, Donald and Douglas continued their stroll cutting across one of the lanes, through a leafy path with ponds and water features on either side of a decorative, yet functional drawbridge. Don stopped long enough to put a hand on what looked like a mirrored globe before continuing.

Doug looked around at the beautiful landscape and, through the trees ahead of them; a sleek, architectural wonder came into view: a subterranean structure. Don opened the front door of his home and Doug followed. He didn't want to goggle at the indoor waterfall that cascaded down a granite wall two stories deep into a stream of water, but he turned to Don in wonder.

Don shrugged. "My wife is an oceanographer. Cecil loves the water," he said in answer to Doug's silent query "She's associated with and she's on the board of the Scripps Institute of Oceanography, several universities and international organizations. She does much of her experiments here. It gives new meaning to the term telecommuting." As Don led the way down a flight of stairs, Doug stopped midway down and this time he did goggle. Surrounded by thick glass housing an under-the-sea world the likes of which he had only seen at theme parks, Doug couldn't believe his eyes. Schools of fish swam silently, their beautiful array of colors enhanced by the clear sunlight. Flora and fauna swayed in some invisible current, their colors no less enchanting than the fish.

"This is incredible." He looked up to the sunlight streaming in from the overhead glass-domed ceiling. "The floor is made of glass too, isn't it?"

"Yes, it is. Spooks the hell out of me sometimes," Donald said. "Makes me feel like I'm walking on water. I expect to fall in any time. Our children think it's cool. I think they're only half air-breathing mammals." He continued down the stairwell until he came to tunnels leading off in different directions. Now the water world was all around, above and below, like walking into the depth of a seashell.

When Don stopped walking, he put his hand on a plate in the wall, his eyes to a scanner and keyed in a series of numbers. The wall—that looked like water—slid silently apart.

Doug stood outside the portal, reluctant to go further. He sensed something edgy about Donald Dixon that he couldn't quite identify, but this setup had him unnerved and suspicious. He looked around him at the light shifting through the water. Then he looked at Don who gave him a come-ahead jerk of his head.

When Doug stepped through the opening, the door automatically closed at his back. Now he was in some type of glass-enclosed anteroom encased by solid walls with no hint of sunlight. Through the glass partitions, Doug would have believed he was in a fully-equipped space station. People moved about the space quickly and essentially ignored him and Donald. He couldn't hear what the people on the other side of the partition were saying, but whatever they were doing looked very important. He heard installations like this while he was in the Marine Corp and about government agencies that were so secret that they didn't have the benefit of an acronym, but he certainly never expected to be in contact with anyone who was involved in clandestine operations and definitely not in a small, rural village in South Carolina. The phrase, hide in plain sight, came immediately to Doug's mind. He looked up at one of the many monitors on the walls. Displayed on one group of monitors, in changing views, was the family gathering in progress. The views on other monitors covered different places and angles around the compound. Doug turned to look at Donald who was leaning on a see-through, stationary desk, arms folded across his chest, legs crossed at the ankles.

"I don't understand," Doug said.

"Satarah. She's sort of my first cousin on my Uncle Bernard and Aunt Sylvia's side of the family. She, nor many others, has ever been where you're standing now, but she knows enough to mention your concern about your GPS system to me."

"I couldn't get a signal whenever I was near here. This is the reason, isn't it?"

"It is, yes. It's also the reason that you don't see electrical lines or aircraft overhead. Why the forest is so dense."

"You work for some type of government agency?"

"World organization with authority to operate in every country."

"Why have you brought me here?"

"This is the first opportunity I've had to speak with you since the day I helped paint The Summer House. You have assumed the Fire Chief's position and needed to know certain things, even though your predecessor was not brought into the loop. If you had taken your truck in to have the GPS system replaced or repaired, the same problem would continue to occur—."

"Someone might have gotten suspicious."

"Yes, and it's just that type of serendipity that could make our operation vulnerable. A number of things can be controlled, but not everything. We've had far too many experiences with terrorists and renegade multinational corporations to overlook details, even minute ones."

"But you hardly know me."

"On Screen Four," Donald said nodding upward, without taking his eyes from Doug's. "Bring up Johnson, Chester Earl."

One of the screens digitized at Donald's back displaying an overhead view of the terrain of the United States from overhead, then narrowing to a truck stop somewhere in Nevada. A group of men stood against a split-railed fence drinking beer, smoking cigarettes and talking. The screen continued to digitize as the scene lowered to ground level and zoomed in on a man about to lift a beer to his mouth. Doug moved closer to the partition, pressed his palms against the glass and squinted at the monitor. When the man on monitor laughed at what one of the other men said, Douglas recognized his father.

Nearly seventeen years had passed since he had seen the man and, he admitted to himself, he would not have recognized him if he had passed him on a street. He looked so much older than Doug remembered. They were not pals as some fathers and sons would wont to be. Rather they were more like people occupying the same space for a period of time and, then, moving on.

When he was a child, his father was rarely at home. He drove for a trucking company and was at home at odd times. Rarely did they have meals together; not even on holidays. On birthdays, for him or his brother, his mother would take them on the bus to one of the fast food restaurants in a mall and buy them some toy, clothing, or shoes, but his father was never with them. They would take the bus home and that would be the extent of their birthday celebrations.

His father was absent for PTA nights as well. When his mother could get home in time to go, she would hustle them in and out with barely a word to their teachers. Neither he nor his brother were exceptional students, but she didn't seem to care about that. She only wanted them to behave in the classroom and not have her summoned to school and lose time from her job.

It was bracing, Doug thought now, that he had grown up in his parents' home when they were approximately the same age he was now, and know little or nothing about the people his parents were.

"Your father drives an eighteen wheeler, usually between New Orleans, Louisiana, and Seattle, Washington. He works for a company called Land Lines. The company is owned by BlackHawk International; a part of the conglomerate's transportation arm. Black Hawk International is a part of the BlackHawk Holding which is owned by Ambassador Jake Hawkins."

"And Jake Hawkins is the father of JaiHonnah Hawkins Baylor and LaiLoni Hawkins Logan. JRock Baylor's wife, JaiHonnah, and Vivian's close friend from college. I met her and her husband today. LaiLoni is the former Dakota Sinclair, the wife of Jefferson Logan, dean of Summer County Academy."

"Yes. Your father has worked for Land Lines for about five years. They change his route every couple of years. He's getting seniority soon, so he'll be able to select the more favorable routes, shorter distances, quicker turnarounds. He is fifty-seven years old, lives in an efficiency apartment on the south side of Seattle, Washington, and just purchased his first CD player.

"On Screen Five. Johnson, Chester Earl, Jr.," Donald continued.

When another screen digitized and adjusted for height, Doug saw his brother in a used-car lot making a pitch to an elderly couple. The scrawl across the bottom of the screen read: Peoria, Illinois.

"Your brother likes to be called by a street name, Buster. He has knocked around the country: Philadelphia, New York, Chicago, etc. He's seeing a waitress at the Golden Goose, a diner not far from the used-car lot where he's been working for the last sixteen months. Your brother and the waitress, Gail Simmons, dated on and off for almost two years and moved in together three weeks ago. She still steps out on him with a few of her regular customers, now and again. Mostly, because he's been stepping out on her with a bank teller, Emily Malone, at the bank where he buys money orders to pay his bills.

"You and Lily Stone met in high school. She and her parents kept the fact that she was bipolar a secret."

Doug's head snapped toward Donald, his face a mass of confusion. "Bipolar?"

"I see from your expression that you did not know."

Doug stared at Donald in stunned disbelief as he continued. Then a picture of his deceased wife flashed onto another screen. It was a photo of her in their high school yearbook. Other pictures followed; one of them at the military chapel where they married followed by pictures of Lily's parents.

"Lily's parents moved to Oklahoma City, Oklahoma, not long after you two adopted Donovan. They assumed that, since she had a child, something she always wanted, she would stay on her medication. Apparently, she did, for several years, at least. Then she stopped taking them. She told you the medicine was for menstrual cramps. There was no record of her filling a prescription from five years ago. Less than a year after she stopped taking her medication, she hung herself in your living room."

Still starring at Donald, Doug reached back to feel for the chair before his legs gave out on him. He plopped down, winded. "I thought—."

"You thought that you were responsible for Lily's death?"

"Yes, I mean, I was rarely at home. I was working four-and five-day shifts. When I was at home, I was writing articles for the *Firefighters' Monthly*, working on the fire training and safety manuals, working on my master's degree. When Lily's behavior became erratic, I took her to a doctor for a check-up. Then we went to a marriage counselor. I even took her to a therapist, but Lily refused to continue the treatment program." He thought about her blind jealousy and the way she came to the fire station and made a scene, leaving Donovan alone in the house except for Mr. and Mrs. Diggs next door. "I was at my wits end. I was going to take her to a private clinic so she could rest and calm down, but before I could get time off to take her, she committed suicide.

"All those years—." His words lingered, as he palmed his face and rubbed vigorously. "I never knew," he said, anger rising in his psyche. "I thought her death was my fault because I didn't spend enough time with her, making her feel safe and secure in our marriage. Now you tell me that it was because she and her parents kept her condition a damn secret; that she could have been helped with medication?"

Donald nodded. They talked a while longer until Doug felt steady again.

"You thought that I didn't know you. I know more about you than you probably know or remember about yourself, your family and acquaintances, but unless you ask, I'll consider it irrelevant. What I needed to know was whether you could be trusted with this much information; about this installation. When the investigation concluded, I was more than satisfied with what I know about you."

"I don't understand all of this," Doug said, looking through the glass partition at all the monitors and the people working a different stations with data streaming on reader boards. "How do you find people so easily and find out so much about them?"

"You probably would be surprised how many times you're photographed every day. In some places, major cities, like Richmond, Virginia, up to five hundred times in twenty-four hours. On highways, almost all routes are monitored by local law enforcement agencies. Your father is standing across the parking lot from an ATM. Your brother is near a camera-controlled intersection. Inside the restaurant, where your father had breakfast, is a security camera system. One is also located inside the car dealership where your brother works.

"If you have a numbered account anywhere: telephone bill, credit card, checking account, dentist bill, auto mechanic, shoe store, the Patriot Act makes all information accessible. Data is collected from telephone calls, text messages, e-mails, any type of communications verbal or electronic.

"Satellites circumnavigate the globe; their sole purpose is to collect information, data, find something or someone. If they can read the serial number off a dime on a sidewalk, they can find anything you're looking for."

Doug looked into Donald's eyes. "Even a missing child?"

Donald thought a moment until realization dawned. "Yes. Even a missing child."

⚬

When Doug and Donald strolled back toward the festivities, they came from a different direction through the woods. A battle was being waged between three factions shooting paint-pellet guns at moving targets two hundred feet away. They stood behind the contestants and watched. Three women—Stacy Greene Alexander, Dakota Sinclair Logan, and Aretha Grace Alexander, Bernard's and Sylvia's youngest daughter—stepped forward, took aim and hit their targets squarely in rapid succession. Red, black and green paint flew with a solid smack against the pinwheel targets.

The targets were repositioned twice more to three hundred and then five hundred feet. The results were the same.

"Dead even," Kenny Alexander announced, grinning. "That's it, folks. It's another tied game."

The contestants' high-fives were thunderous. Doug was impressed with their accuracy; sharpshooters and snipers in his Marine Corps squad were at this level of precision. "They're very good," Doug commented to Donald.

More than you can imagine, Donald thought, but only nodded his head in agreement. People who were sitting in the shaded stands, watching the contests, was making their way back through the woods toward the open-spaced farm park. As they drew closer, they could hear a rousing rendition of *We Are Family* played by a family band. Doug spotted Satarah standing behind the boys, singing and clapping with the music. She looked very happy. When he reached her, he circled her waist with one arm. She turned her head in his direction and smiled up at him. He leaned down and gave her a brief kiss. The boys giggled.

"Today is a special day for our family. We welcome a new family member," Bernard said, turning toward Chuck and Vivian. Chuck passed their daughter to Bernard who kissed the baby and then passed her to Chuck's father, Steven Montgomery, who kissed his granddaughter and snuggled her close while Bernard continued. He looked out into the assembled crowd and asked Doug and Satarah to join them on the stage.

Surprised, Doug escorted Satarah to the raised platform. Chuck stepped forward. "It would honor Vivian and me if you would accept the responsibility as godparents for our daughter, Eden Ann Montgomery."

Stunned, Satarah took an automatic step back and bumped into the solid wall of Doug's body. No less surprised, Doug looked from Vivian's pretty, smiling face to Chuck's mischievously grinning one. Silence fell over the crowd. Satarah wanted to turn and run, but Doug moved forward to accept the baby girl. That simple act brought tears to Satarah's eyes. She reached for Chuck and Vivian and hugged them both, as she cried. Turning, she looked up over her shoulder at Doug who nodded encouragingly for her to do the honors.

Whipping tears from her face, she stepped forward. Still full of tears and with a trembling voice, Satarah said, "As you know, Eden Ann was sent to us as a gift by The Creator and The Ancestors in the middle of the worst blizzards in South Carolina's history. We had record-making snow that not only brought a crisis to our community, but also new friends. Donovan," she said, motioning him forward. He moved to the platform and was lifted onto it, as Satarah placed him in front of her, draped her arms around his shoulder and continued, "—and Douglas Johnson came to us through that crisis. They have remained with us as friends, as a part of our community. Douglas and I accept the responsibility as godparents for Eden Ann. We ask that Donovan Johnson and Jonathan and Jeffrey Whitfield," she said while motioning her boys to join them on the platform, "accept the responsibility as god brothers to Eden Ann."

Douglas placed Eden in Donovan's arms, who looked down at the bright-eyed bundle. She grabbed his finger and brought it to her pink rosebud mouth. Donovan looked in absolute wonder at Douglas who nodded and then at Jonathan and Jeffrey who flanked Donovan on both sides. Then he looked back at the little girl's toothless smile. "Yeah, I mean, yes. We accept Eden Ann as our god sister, but, uh, could we call her Edie Ann?"

There wasn't a dry eye around, when the crowd broke up in uproarious laughter and applause.

Later, when Chuck offered to feed the baby, Donovan asked whether he could do it. Chuck said, "Hey, of course you can. She's your god sister."

Donovan beamed a smile as bright as a new copper penny.

Doug, Satarah, Sylvia and Bernard sat at an adjacent table eating when Bernard said, "That was a good thing that you did for Donovan and the twins. We're very proud of you, Sara Jo. I know you and Douglas were put on the spot, but—."

"I couldn't be happier, Uncle Bernie, about becoming Edie Ann's godmother. I promise I'll do everything in my power not to let her down. She's mine now and I know what that responsibility means." She reached across the table and took Bernard's and Sylvia's hands in hers. "I want to thank you for the opportunity."

Doug put his hand on top of theirs. "*We* want to thank you."

"It was really Chuck's and Vivian's decision."

Vivian walked up behind her father, kissed the top of his head and said, "Then, of course, Chuck and I have so many children, we were running out of godparents."

Everyone laughed and looked on as Chuck showed Donovan how to burp the baby.

"I'm not sure Donovan is going to let us get our hands on Edie Ann," Doug muttered, frustrated.

Everyone laughed.

"He hasn't had to change her diaper yet," Satarah commented.

Laughter again filled the air.

⁊⁊⁊

Later that night, Doug and Satarah went into the boys' bedroom to get them to go to bed. They were stacked like bookends watching pictures of the Easter gathering on the computer screen.

"We're almost finished," Jeffrey said, as he clicked from picture to picture. Doug and Satarah sat down to watch. They goggled when a picture of them kissing came on the screen.

Donovan turned to them, asked, "Are you, like, in love or something?"

Doug and Satarah looked at each other and said, in unison, "Or something."

The next day, Easter Monday morning, Doug snuck into Satarah's bedroom and eased into bed beside her.

Sleepily, Satarah rolled toward him and put an arm around his waist. He snuggled her close and kissed her temple.

"Did the boys get off okay?" she asked, without opening her eyes.

"Kenny picked them up. They were anxious to get to see Edie Ann and spend as much time with her before Chuck and Vivian leave for Maryland." Doug yawned.

"Good. Considering the number of Easter eggs the children dyed yesterday, it will take them half the day to find them all," Satarah said before she fell into a light sleep.

Doug thought about Donovan's question from the night before: whether he and Satarah were in love? He was glad he and Satarah seemed to be on the same page with their relationship. They had only known each other for a little over three months. When it came to the L word, he was not sure what it was all about. Nor did he feel confident that he could trust his own instincts where women were concerned. Sure, he was older now than he was when he met or even married Lily. Nearly thirty-five; but did age alone make him wiser?

His thoughts segued to Lily and his discussion with Donald Dixon the day before.

He had known Lily Stone for four years during high school or, at least, he thought he did until Donald Dixon enlightened him about the facts. He was in the Marine Corps when he and Lily married at twenty-two years old. He loved her for eight years as much as he could love anyone at that point in his life, yet he did not know about her mental and emotional challenges. Did he really want to know her that well? Or was what he felt for her more hormonal than emotional? What he wanted from his marriage was normality, but their life together was anything but normal. He wanted someone to be there when he came home, but never realized he was coming home to a stranger.

Lily wanted him, too, he admitted, but, in hindsight, which was twenty-twenty, it seemed for very different reasons. She wanted someone to take care of her, to support her financially. She finished a paralegal course while he was still in the Marines, but she never really wanted to be a career woman. Still living at home with her parents, she took in over-flow typing from several law firms in the area, but didn't want to work in an office.

What Lily also wanted was to have children immediately after they married, but at twenty-two years old, Doug was ambivalent about starting a family so soon. Nevertheless, she forced the issue. They bought a home, an investment really. An attached duplex with garages at the rear of the property. He rented the other part of the building to the Diggs and settled into what he hoped would be normality. After two miscarriages, Lily begged him to agree to adopt a child. He tried to convince her they were a family, just the two of them, that they had just bought a home, and should wait until they were a little older and more financially able to raise a child, but she went into icy sulks or despondency until he had no choice but to agree. After they got Donovan, Lily was happy again for several years until Donovan was old enough to start school. Then, as Doug's career began to take more of his time, Lily begged him to adopt more children. The trouble between them started when he refused.

Lily accused him of infidelity because he was away for days at a time. Nothing could have been further from the truth. Her suspicions compelled her to come to the fire station one night, wearing only her nightgown and slippers, in an attempt to catch him in a lie. When he was home, she followed him around the house like a stalker. She listened in on what few telephone calls he received, read his mail, searched his things. When he heard her yelling at a telemarketer, accusing her of being his lover, Doug realized Lily needed professional help. He took her to see a therapist, but she refused to return after a few sessions.

Their life together was spiraling down the drain. The therapist advised him to have her committed because he feared Lily was a danger to herself. Initially, Doug resisted the idea. After all, they had Donovan to consider, but when things between them deteriorated further, he felt he had no choice.

He was out on a fire emergency call when word reached him to get home immediately. Mrs. Diggs called because she and Donovan could not get into his home after Donovan got home from school. Lily piled all the furniture in front of the doors and windows. When the police and fire company arrived, they broke in and found Lily hanging naked from a ceiling fixture. Her suicide note was rambling, but said she wanted to die because he did not love her anymore and she could not give him children.

Now he knew the truth. He called her parents who confirmed what Donald Dixon had told him. Lily was bipolar. They were very apologetic, but Doug was hard pressed to forgive their duplicity.

Doug leaned his head against Satarah's padded headboard. The great load he carried around for many years since Lily's death was lifted from his shoulders with Don's revelations. Lily had been dead for more than four years, yet he was unable or unwilling to form another close, intimate, committed relationship with a woman. In his misery, he had closed up, shut down, and closed out everyone, including Donovan.

Until he met Satarah.

He would not make comparisons between Lily and Satarah. From the very beginning, Satarah was like no other woman he had ever met. She was nakedly honest and forthright with no pretense or posturing. Given all she suffered—a disreputable father, a disloyal sister, a philandering husband, and the responsibility of raising her nephews/stepsons on her own—she had every right to be bitter. Yet, she had risen above it all and succeeded in making a life for herself and her boys. She was strong and resilient, sexy and sensible. She gave a lot, but asked for nothing in return. She was a woman to be loved, appreciated and admired. He wondered whether he was up to the task of being in a committed relationship with her.

He looked down at her sleeping face in the crook of his arm. As usual, her hair was everywhere, just like he liked it. He gently brushed it away from her face so he could look at her.

"Are you finished thinking?" she asked without opening her eyes.

"I thought you were asleep. I didn't want to disturb you."

She ran her hand down his body until she could cup him. He drew in a breath between his teeth at her warm touch.

"I felt your thoughts in my sleep. When you're awake and feeling amorous, you like to touch me awake. When you're in deep thought, you hold me and play in my hair. I decided I would not disturb you until I could have your undivided attention. And just look at how lucky I got for being patient," she teased fondling him until his thickness swelled in her hand.

Doug slid down under the covers and kissed Satarah with the need to mate with her becoming all-consuming. After she rolled the condom into place, he slipped inside her. They moved slowly together in a leisurely, soul-stirring need to possess and to fill each other up with what had been missing in their lives.

Doug's body felt so good, so strong, inside her that Satarah palmed his head in her hands to ravish his mouth. Her body went on a pleasure overload, eliciting groans from Douglas that thrilled them both. He knew how to work his body and hers, too. He drove her up and over a crest, then intensifying his movements, shot her up again. She shuttered like a plucked bowstring with the intensity of her orgasms. When he reversed their positions, she rose above him, rode him like a rocking horse. Clamping his hands to the damp sheets by his wrists, she took him harder and faster. He was breathing like a long distance runner nearing the finish line with victory within his grasp.

Doug came so hard and long, he thought he was dying. His lungs burned, his muscles constricted, he could hear his heart's rapid tattoo in his ears. He wanted to touch Satarah, but she held his wrists immobile at the sides of his head.

"Damn! A nurse will kill a brother," he groaned. He felt Satarah's laughter on his ultra-sensitive penis while still buried deep insider her.

17

$\mathcal{D}$OUG EXITED THE HALLWAY FROM the family wing of The Summer House. He was brought up short at the sight of Mark Brooks and Mary Ella Baker wrapped up in the heat of a passionate kiss at the front entrance. Doug quickly and quietly walked past them. When he reached the kitchen, Bob had his head down on his folded arms on the table.

"Coffee?" Satarah asked Doug, as she put a mug full in front of Bob.

"Please," Bob groaned pitifully. He grabbed the mug in both hands and brought it unsteadily to his mouth.

"Yeah, you, too," Satarah said, chuckling at the shadows under Bob's bleary eyes. She poured a mug for Doug and gave him a salacious look under lowered lashes. If he didn't have to go to work, he would take her back to bed and have her sweating beneath him until she begged for mercy.

He sat in time to watch Mark limp into the kitchen and gingerly ease into a chair. Yeah, Doug thought, sympathetically, nurses would kill a brother.

Everyone perked up when Satarah placed a platter of fluffy eggs, tender grilled steaks and a basket of sugar-powdered baguettes on the table. The grapefruit sections were tart and cold, the marmalade was warm, and the coffee was hot and aromatic. Everyone tucked into his or her meal with gusto.

"Why didn't you ask Mary Ella to stay for breakfast, Mark?" Satarah asked, putting a healthy dollop of marmalade on her piping hot baguettes.

"Early shift at the hospital," he said sprinkling Tabasco sauce on his eggs. "She was running a little late. We, uh," he hesitated and looked around the table self-consciously. "We jogged a couple of miles this morning. She only had time to shower and change and, uh, stuff. She said that she'd call you later."

"Where do nurses get all that *energy*?" Bob lamented, shaking his head. He reached for another steak. "Jennie was up early for Sunrise service yesterday, worked on her dad's farm milking cows and gathering eggs and cooking three meals so she could meet up with us for Dr. Alexander's family fête. She was just as bright and perky when we left for the hospital party at eight o'clock last night. We danced until she had to start her shift at eleven o'clock. I swear I don't understand it."

Satarah grinned at Doug who pulled a face at her. Louise strolled in five minutes later and sat down. She looked at the men and said, "You guys look like hell. Did we have a five alarm or something? What did I miss?"

No one said a mumbling word, but tucked back into their meals with renewed gusto.

Doug was heading out the front door when Satarah asked for a moment of his time. He told Bob, Mark and Louise that he would be out shortly and then closed the front door behind them. He faced Satarah, curious about what she wanted to say. She seemed serious.

"It's about earlier, when you were thinking." She looked into his eyes.

"Yeah?" His voice held a hint of suspicion.

"I don't know what was on your mind, but if it had anything to do with me; with what we do together, I just want you to know that I don't expect this sexual heat to turn into something, you know, permanent or anything, but—." She was rambling she knew. This was virgin territory for her. She hadn't slept with a man she cared enough about, except Jacque St. Clair, to offer him a way to ease out before their relationship got complicated.

She didn't expect to be hauled up on her toes and kissed until her toes curled.

"I want to take you back to bed this very moment, but intimacy is only a small part of what I want for us. I haven't felt this way about any woman. I don't know what the future holds, Satarah," he said, a breath away from her mouth, "but I'm not going to be afraid anymore to find out. Being here with you, around your family makes me want to know what love is; what it feels like for a man who is about to be thirty-five years old to experience a mature, committed relationship with a phenomenal woman like you. So, if you're not opened to where this relationship might go, I suggest you pack up and move to another country, because I'm not going anywhere.

"Now kiss me so I can go to work."

Satarah grinned at him, laid a lip-lock on him that had his toes curling. And, if his enormous erection wasn't difficult enough for Doug to handle, what she whispered in his ear made him whimper with lust.

He looked into her dancing eyes and impish expression. "You're a wicked woman, Satarah Josephine Whitfield."

He could have pogoed out of the house on his third leg without the assistance from his feet.

A few weeks later, Doug sat with his team in his office. "Apparently, it was a good conference," Doug said, after Louise gave a report of her meetings in Chicago.

"One of the better ones I've attended. A lot of heavy hitters in the industry, good literature and valuable information. The five firefighters who accompanied me each had good things to say about what they learned."

"Put together an outline for a training course on sexual harassment and equal employment for me, would you? I don't think we have an existing problem, but I want to add it to the training course," Doug said, making a note of it. Sitting at the conference table in his office with Louise, Bob and Mark they were going over their reports of the previous week and planning for the weeks to come. He looked up at Mark. "I sat in on a few of your classes with the emergency medical technicians. I wasn't there for all of them, but from what I did see, they seemed to be coming along pretty well."

"Better than I expected. Especially Jeff Logan. He handled a few field accidents before I could get to the scene. A few others have been performing extremely well, too, on the medical rotation. No one is slacking off. It was a good idea of yours to have Mrs. Alexander include her senior nursing students for ride-a-longs. The Fire Department's Ambulance Service needs people on board with medical skills. I'm working with her to make this pilot project a permanent part of the curriculum for her graduating nurse practitioners and our emergency medical technicians. We should have an outline prepared by the end of next week. I'll be taking seven firefighters to one of the better medical conferences in Dallas, Texas, next month."

"Good work, Mark. I want to rotate all of the firefighters in and out of that program. Would you work that into the training scheduled, Bob?"

"Can do," he said, his head bowed while he made notes. "I noticed Jeff Logan's confidence and competency, too, Mark. He actively participates in training sessions and shows real leadership qualities."

"I like him, too," Louise interjected. "He handles the administrative stuff and I had him doing the paperwork on those house fires. You'd never know that this kid is a multi-billionaire and an heir to the Montrose fortune." She looked over at Mark. "You know his family, don't you?"

"Mmm," he hummed in his throat and gave a careless shrug. "A few of them. My parents know them very well."

"Logan will probably be voted the MVF Award by the other firefighters," Bob added into the thick silence. Mark didn't talk about his family's wealth nor did he depend on it for his livelihood. He shunned his family's demands that he enter one of their many enterprises. After he got his medical degree and credentials, he headed straight for the Ship of Hope to tend to people in need of his medical expertise. While he was tending to patients in economically-challenged countries, he trained the local medical staff on new or novel techniques. Doug was grateful Mark was volunteering his services to the Summer County Fire Department and the Summer County Hospital, but knew that eventually Mark would move on to other places before the Fall. He would be missed.

"Okay, Bob, where are you on the training schedule?" Doug asked.

"On schedule." Bob distributed a copy of the schedule and progress so far. "Since we're going to add two more sessions, I'll have to revise this schedule to reflect the new programs. I want to put these in before Burn Week."

"Burn Week is vehicular, structure fires and night forest fires?" Mark asked and, at Bob's nod of agreement, gave a low whistle. "That's a lot to cram into a week."

"Every firefighter needs this training. They could have any combination of these incidents in a single day. Louise will select a team to set the fires and then test the others on fire investigative techniques. We have—." Bob stopped abruptly when the signal for a two-alarm fire emergency came over the loud speaker. They were all moving before the alarm ended.

⚜

It was raining like a monsoon had struck, but Doug could see the thick, black smoke rising a mile away. Two of his fire companies were already engaged and he could hear sirens from a third coming from the opposite direction. When he reached the entrance to Bigger Thenham's farm, lightening lit the sky moments before a boom of thunder rocked the earth. The sooty storm clouds were low and nearly as black as the smoke from the fully engulfed barn that glowed bright orange.

The word coming over Doug's radio had him dawning his chemical fire mask and fire retardant gear. When he parked across the road to block any civilian traffic, he left the klieg lights on his vehicle rotating. He was racing up the rise toward the farmhouse when Firefighter Laureleen Gunter covered Mama Lou, Bigger and Little Willie Thenham with fire-retardant blankets and led them through the water-soaked field and thick smoke toward the road.

Suddenly, explosions erupted sending flaming balls like cannon fire in every direction. Doug looked up in his race to reach Laureleen. A blackened paint can landed two feet to his left. *Oh, God,* he thought as he finally reached Laureleen and her charges.

"Paint?" Doug yelled through the heavy rain and choking smoke.

Bigger coughed violently. "Yeah, about sixty cans and fifteen five-gallon buckets." He coughed again. "Varnish, solvents, gasoline, turpentine—all of my machines, farming equipment, hunting rifles and ammo. Manure, fertilizer, in the back silo."

Doug ordered his firefighters to pull back. The barn was a powder keg and their gear was not bulletproof. "Bob, get the ladders up from the road and douse the house." He gave instructions on how to attack the fire that the rain was having little effect on containing. He stood in the open field and watched as the ladder company worked the crane-like equipment into position. The heavy gauge hoses were unfolded, hooked to the Pumpers. Thick streams of foam shot out, inflating the hose to capacity. When the second ladder tilted up, they were attacking the flames from two directions. Doug's concern was for the rising wind channeling the foam away from its target. He kept an eye on the lightening and ground strikes, too. Although the ladder was insulated, if a strike hit it, then his firefighters could be jolted from their perches.

Doug's attention was on the ladders and listening to Bob's instructions, but he felt the ground beneath his feet begin to vibrate like a building earthquake. When the ground shook, Doug saw a herd of panicked cattle barrowing toward him through the smoke and rain. He and Bob would surely be trampled because there was nowhere for them to run.

Satarah stood on top of her jeep, hoisted the rifle to her shoulder, and fired rapidly hitting each of her targets. Stacy Alexander was advancing up the driveway, firing her riffle on the run. Dakota Logan was perched on a fence firing her weapons with both hands. The bill of her baseball cap leaked water like a faucet.

The lightening was touching down in jagged streaks while the paint cans flew, the fire ragged, the rain poured, and the thunder boomed for what seemed like an eternity.

Satarah scanned the field for what she could see through the smoke, looking for anything that might endanger the firefighters. She grabbed a heavy gauge shotgun, fired both barrels knocking a flaming projectile out of its trajectory toward Doug.

"Coming at you!" she yelled into her hand-held CB radio.

"We see them," James Dixon yelled back.

She heard Benny Alexander curse through the radio as his airplane flew over the barn, dousing the farmhouse with a heavy deluge of water before zooming off toward the lake again. A second aircraft flew in low over the confused cattle, turning them toward James and his father, Romelo, who were on horseback with whips and whistles. Others joined in to herd the skittish cattle to safety.

When the cattle were out of sight and away from Doug and his firefighters, Satarah plopped down on the rooftop of her jeep. She gave Stacy and Dakota a hand up. They reloaded their weapons, waiting and watching for any more projectiles while the firefighters waged war on the remaining flames.

One minute a herd of cattle was hell-bent on stampeding everyone in its path and the next moment pulling up short. For a moment, Doug didn't believe his eyes. Red, black, or green paint splatters on the faces of cows and then projectiles were shot out of the air. He could hear, through his headgear, his firefighters working hard to attack the conflagration. The thunder was so loud he could not hear much else.

When the cattle veered away wearing strange face paint, he breathed a sigh of relief. About ten feet away, Bob was standing stone still seemingly rooted to the ground. They looked at each other and moved forward simultaneously.

"Damn, Chief, what just happened? I nearly wet my pants!"

"Damn if I know."

"Behind you, Chief," Laureleen called out through the radio microphone.

Doug and Bob turned toward the road and squinted through the rain and smoke. Three women were standing on top of Satarah's jeep with rifles resting on their shoulders.

"That's Satarah, Chief. And the other two look like Stacy Alexander and Dakota Logan. What the hell—?" Bob said, confused.

"Let's get this fire knocked down and then we can find out."

Three and a half hours later, the fire was contained, but the rain still poured. They saved the farmhouse, but the barn and silo were just blackened heaps on the landscape.

Bob was conducting the mop up, so Doug started across the high-grass field to where Bigger and Little Willie sat on the split-rail fence. His boots, full of water, sloshed as he walked and his gear was coated with soot and splashes of paint. He pulled off his heavy gloves and headgear.

"How you doing, Bigger, Willie?" Doug asked when he reached them.

"Fair to middlin', I s'pose, Chief," Little Willie said.

"How about you, Bigger?"

"Well, Chief, I don't guess I'm gonna make it."

"Are you hurt?" Doug asked, concerned.

"Only in my heart. I guess I gotta marry her now," he said, sadly, looking at what was left of his barn. Sitting on the top rail of his fence, Bigger was nearly eye level with Doug.

Doug shook his head, confused. "What are you talking about, Bigger? Marry who?"

"Ms. Lucile. You see, I was working up on asking Satarah Josephine to marry up with me. My mama, she said that the barn burning was a bad omen that I was asking for the wrong woman's hand in matrimony. I didn't want to believe my mama, 'cuze I had my cap set on marrying up with Satarah Josephine, but my mama, she believe in all that old country stuff: gris-gris and juju cuz you know she a voodoo and all. Then I saw Satarah Jo, Ms. Stacy, and Ms. Dakota shootin' my cows so they wouldn't hurt you or Bobby Sweeny or nobody, and I just knew that Satarah wasn't for me. So I gotta marry up with Ms. Lucile."

"I'll marry up with Ms. Lucile, Bigger, if you don't want to," Little Willie said, sheepishly.

Bigger's countenance lit into a brilliant smile. "You'd do that for me, Little Willie?"

"Sure, I would, Bigger. That's what brothers are for, ain't they?"

"Sure nough! Let's go tell mama, she gotta boy of hern gettin' hitched!"

They scrambled down from the fence and started away. Bigger turned back and shook Doug's hand. "Good job, Chief. You and your people, they done a real fine job. And, by the by, would you tell Satarah Josephine I'm comin' a courtin' soon as I get Little Willie hitched up to Ms. Lucile?"

"Glad we could help out and I'll be sure to pass that message for you, Bigger," Doug said, *but hell would freeze over and the Devil would go ice skating before I'll let you take my woman away from me,* he thought silently. Speaking of whom—. Doug eyes scanned the crowd that gathered on the road. When he spotted Satarah, she was sitting on the hood of her old Jeep in the pouring rain laughing, drinking a beer and high-fiving Stacy, Dakota and Benny. Doug scaled the fence and headed in her direction.

Satarah saw Doug coming toward her, being stopped and congratulated by people from the community and patted on his back. She kept her eyes on him. He looked good, absolutely delectable all suited up in his firefighter's gear with his helmet under his arm, a radio clipped on his broad shoulder and his heavy gloves snapped in the epilates on the opposite one. His big fire retardant coat was open and he was soaking wet. Rivulets of warm water poured over his thick, curly hair and down his soot-covered face. When he turned his obsidian gaze on her, she felt her blood go warm and moisture dry up in her mouth. Gradually, he separated from the crush of humanity. Someone slapped a bottle of water in his hand. He drank it as he stalked toward her, never taking his eyes from hers.

"Hey, Doug. How you doin' this fine day?" Stacy asked, cheerfully, a grin edging her mouth, rainwater flowing off the bill of her cap.

"Oh, fair to middlin', I guess," he said, as he scooped Stacy and Dakota up in a bear hug and kissed both on their cheeks.

"Whoa, soldier. I usually want drinks and dinner first," Stacy joked.

"You got it, babe, but first I need a minute with the other sharpshooter." He dropped both women on their feet and took Satarah's hand. "Excuse us a moment."

He took her to the ambulance and pulled her inside locking the doors behind them. In moments, he had her pinned against a wall and her panties in shreds. She blinked and laughed lustily when he boosted her up and slid inside her. She wrapped herself around him. Doug clamped his mouth over hers when the orgasm hit her. By the time the next one was on her, she was boneless in his arms. He finally let himself fly to a place where only consummate lovers play.

"Jeez, if a fire stokes you up like this, I better get an electric stove," Satarah croaked out of a parched throat.

"Nah, baby, you lit my fire."

A laugh bubbled up in Satarah's throat. "That phrase is so played, it has whiskers. You can do better than that," she said giggling.

"Oh yeah? Then let's try this one on for size: I'm trying desperately not to fall too deeply in love with you, but I'm failing pitifully. So when Bigger comes a courtin', tell him you've got a man."

Satarah's eyes searched his warily for a moment. "Doug, you don't have to say that to get me into your bed, or in this case, up against a wall in an ambulance, but I have to admit I'm having one helluva a hard time trying not to fall in love with you too."

They stared into each other's eyes, then Satarah rested her forehead on Doug's. "We have to take this slow, Doug. We have damn good sex together. I just don't want either of us to make a mistake because fate has thrown us together or to get hurt. Also, we both have children who depend on us. They have to be considered not just what we want from each other."

"We have worlds to discover about each other, Satarah. And even then, we won't know everything. Right now, I don't understand what I feel for you. I need to be sure. Maybe we'll know enough to make the best decisions for our children and for us. I want to take our relationship very slowly, too."

She kissed his gritty forehead. "Thank you," she whispered before outlining his mouth with her fingertips.

"No, Satarah, thank you, for saving my life out there. I didn't realize that I was in the middle of a grazing field when I ordered the crews to pull back. Bob and I were right in the path of the stampede when it started."

"You're welcome, but actually it was Dakota's quick thinking. We didn't want to kill Bigger's stock, but Dakota had the foresight to give us the paint-pellet rifles. Being hit between the eyes with paint stunned the herd long enough for James and Uncle Romeo to get mounted on Bigger's horses. Aretha flew in low over the herd, turning them."

"I don't care how it happened or who did what. When I turned around, I saw you standing on the roof of your Jeep in the pouring rain and billowing smoke with a shotgun over your shoulder. Your hair was plastered to your head and your shirt and skirt were molded to your incredible body. You looked like some mythological goddess protecting what's yours. And I am yours, Satarah. No one has ever done what you've done for me. No one."

Tears stung the back of her eyes. He was right, exactly right. When she saw him in the path of the stampede, her heart pounded like African war drums. When she raised her rifle and started firing, her hands were steady and sure on the trigger. If she could have run as fast as Dakota or been as sure of her aim as Stacy is, she would have stood in front of Doug and shot anything that threatened his safety.

She was deathly afraid that sometime during the last four months, she had tumbled into love without feeling herself fall. She swallowed convulsively. She needed time alone to think about this revelation.

"Put me down, Doug. You're getting hard again. If you keep this up, we may never get out of this ambulance."

"Okay," he said, but ground himself into her again.

"Okay? What does that mean?"

"Okay, we may never get out of this ambulance."

"Oh no you don't, pal." She unhooked her ankles from his waist and stood, breaking their connection. "It's too close to time for my period to play Russian roulette with a full condom. Been there, done that."

"Do you want more children, Satarah? I don't mean this second, but maybe in the future?

"You expect me to think and talk when you're still this close to me?" she asked, confused disbelief bunching her brow.

He kissed her head and then her mouth. He would let the matter drop for now. He still had work to do on getting his own life into focus.

18

NO MORTAL FEMALE SHOULD HAVE to suffer high heat and humidity, a head cold and monstrous menstrual cramps simultaneously, Satarah thought, when she dragged herself into The Summer House behind not only Donovan, Jonathan and Jeffrey, but also her cousins', James' and Janice's, three boys and baby daughter; and Donald and Cecil's four boys and twin daughters. To top it off, she agreed to let the children go swimming in the recently refurbished pool before dinner—and they were bouncing off the walls like ping pong balls in a Lotto game. They would be with her for the weekend while their parents went to the horse races in Camden and bought horses for their farms from the thoroughbred country north of the Savannah River. It was only fair since Donald and James spent so much time helping her renovate her home.

Noticing her father's brand new Cadillac parked in her driveway, had her temples beating a rapid tattoo against her clogged sinuses. She didn't have time for him today. Not after spending most of the week at Bigger Thenham's farm helping with the cleanup after the fire and the barn raising. It struck her that all of her family's precious heirlooms would have perished in that fire while Bigger was working on restoring them. He lost nearly everything. It was only fair that she donate four of her prime, old-growth trees to set the four corners of his new barn. Although she didn't have to hoist the huge beams into place, she did make enough potato salad and chocolate cake to feed a small nation. She also withstood Mama Lou Thenham giving her the fish-eye every moment she spent on the Thenham farm.

What was worse, her father was not alone, Satarah noted as she entered the house. Sister Clarice Flowers, a deaconess, from her father's holiness church, Brother Phineas Roberts, the church treasurer, and a man with green eyes and flowing silvery-blond hair she did not recognize were being lead through her Rose Parlor by her father, as if he owned the joint.

She schooled her features, when the man stepped to her and extended his hand.

"Isaac Ocher, Esq., Mrs. Whitfield, attorney for the Holiness Retreat. Reverend James has been kind enough to show me around." He pumped her hand. Even in the draining heat and high humidity, his hand was cold and clammy to the touch. On closer inspection, his eyes were a cold grey-green and kept sliding from hers to her breast.

For form, Satarah nodded a greeting to the pinched-faced Sister Flowers and the puffed up countenance of Brother Roberts. For her father, she did not spare a glance in his peacock-strutting direction. "The bed and breakfast isn't open for business yet, Mr. Ocher. The grand opening will be held on July 4 and I am booked solid. If you're interested in booking accommodations, I'll have to put your name on a waiting list."

His laugh was hardy when he placed an inappropriate arm around her shoulder and guided her toward the others standing in the parlor. "Oh, no, Mrs. Whitfield, I'm not here to avail myself of your—services," he said in a way that clearly indicated he meant the reference to "services" with a sexual connotation.

He had the nerve to sit on her great grandmother's settee, stretch his arms across the back and cross one knee over the other. The others followed suit and sat down, as if it were high tea and she was the servant. She stood her ground, though, her body was in no shape to cope with what she expected was about to happen.

"You see," the attorney continued, "I thought it would be advantageous to have a little talk. You know, to iron out a few problems and avoid a pesky legal morass."

"Legal morass?" Satarah asked, with a cocked eyebrow. Out of her peripheral vision, she noted Sister Flowers possessively running her pudgy fingers over her great grandmother's side table.

"Well, yes," he said, clearing his throat. "You see, going through the courts could become rather costly for you and could go on for many years. However, if we could reach an amicable out-of-court agreement for the transfer of this property and its contents, of course, then the expense would be kept to a minimum. You understand that my client could not permit this property to be used as a so-called bed and breakfast in the interim."

"A bordello!" Sister Flowers impatiently interjected, her face pinched to the point of puckering.

"Amen!" Brother Roberts chimed in.

Into the ensuing silence, Satarah heard Jeffrey, Jonathan, and Donovan enter the parlor. From their expressions, she knew they had heard every word spoken.

"Boys, I need a few moments," Satarah said as calmly as she could.

"Mama Satarah, he can't do that. He can't take our home away, can he?" Jonathan asked, fearfully.

Jeffrey wrapped himself around her waist, sobbing. Satarah rubbed his back and placed a comforting hand on Jonathan's shoulder. She looked into Donovan's angry expression. He was staring daggers at the people seated in the Rose Parlor.

"Donovan?"

"Yes, ma'am?" he answered, never taking his eyes from the other adults.

"You're the oldest. Would you take care of the children for me for a little bit? Maybe play outside?"

Slowly, he looked at her, his expression one of surprise that she would entrust him with such a task. "Yes, ma'am," he said, and wrapped his arms around Jeffrey and Jonathan, encouraging them to leave the room. "Come on, guys. We have company. Ms. Satarah and my dad will take care of everything."

Donovan had so much faith in her and Doug's ability to handle whatever came his way. They had taught him—together—to lean on them in times of trouble. He felt safe and loved in this home, in his relationship with her boys and in her and Doug's care. She would not let him down.

Satarah took a deep breath before she turned around and her eyes bore into her father. "Reverend, get out of my home and take your pack of dogs with you. And if you *ever* put your foot on my property again without my express permission, I'll have you arrested for trespassing." She then focused on the attorney. "Mr. Ocher, the Holiness Retreat will be in bankruptcy before I will." She reached into her wallet and pulled out a business card. "You will be hearing from *my* attorneys." She placed the card in Ocher's hand and was a bit gleeful when the attorney read the card and then paled considerably. "Now, get out!" she said sternly, an arrow straight finger pointing the way to exit.

"Listen here, girl!" the Reverend said, belligerently, and continued hurling insults and threats.

Satarah's tenuous hold on her patience snapped rending the air blue.

When the uninvited guest hightailed it out of there, slamming the door behind them, Satarah fled to her bedroom. She needed a minute to calm down before she went to see after the children. She swallowed two Ibuprofen and then sat on the foot of her bed, her face palmed in her hands.

That's how Doug found her fifteen minutes later.

Donovan's excited call to his office saying that Satarah needed him right away had him leaving a briefing session with Bob, Mark and Louise. There was no leaving his team behind though. Four fire department vehicles peeled out of the county office-building parking lot, sirens blaring. They cut the sirens when they reached the driveway and Donovan met them at the front door.

He told them what he had overheard. While Bob, Mark and Louise went to entertain the children by taking them swimming, Doug sought out Satarah.

Her bedroom door stood open so Doug went in, sat beside her at the foot of the bed and put an arm around her shoulders. She laid her head against his cheek. When he kissed her temple, she was burning up.

"Satarah?" he said, concerned. He lifted her chin, but her eyes were closed. "Open your eyes for me, baby."

"I can't," she whined. "I have a headache.

"And you're burning up with fever." Doug scooped her up, placed her on the bed, and undressed her. After he tucked her listless body under the covers, he brought Mark in to examine her. Doug stood by until Mark finished.

"Exhaustion, a cold, a fever, and menstrual cramps," Mark said to Doug as they stood outside of her bedroom door. "She needs twenty-four to thirty-six hours of rest. Plenty of fluids. She'll be fine though."

"I'll see to it," Doug said.

"I know. Let her sleep. Bob, Louise, and I will take care of the kids."

"Thanks, Mark."

Satarah slept as if she was in hibernation, barely moving. Doug checked in on her frequently while he grilled hot dogs and hamburgers for the children and his team. Thank goodness Satarah had a tub of homemade potato salad in the refrigerator. Louise made the lemonade with fresh-squeezed lemons and iced tea. Mark raided Satarah's garden for tomatoes, cucumbers, lettuce and green peppers for the tossed salad. Bob stayed at poolside while the children played.

After supper, when the sun went down, they made a campfire and read stories. Louise bathed the baby girls and put them to bed in her bedroom suite, while the boys camped out on air mattresses in Jeffrey's, Jonathan's and Donovan's room.

After the children were down and out for the night, Bob and Mark left for dates with Jennie and Mary Ella. Louise went upstairs to her suite to read and watch over the little girls. Doug sat up in Satarah's bedroom sitting area with his feet up on an ottoman reading a novel.

It was nearing midnight when Donovan came into the bedroom. "Dad?"

It still made Doug's heart swell with pride and love to hear Donovan call him Dad. "Yes, son, is everything alright?"

"Yes, I mean, I just wanted to see if Ms. Satarah was all right."

"She's going to be fine. She just needs a little rest." He patted the space next to him. Donovan sat down and leaned his head against Doug's shoulder. Doug placed an arm around him and held him close.

"Did I do right, Dad, when I called you to come home?"

"You did exactly right, son. I'm very proud of how you handled yourself and the situation."

"Ms. Satarah asked me to look out for the children. It was too hot outside for the little ones, so we stayed inside and played games in our room and watched cartoons until you came home."

"That was a good thing to do, Donovan."

Donovan yawned hugely. "She trust me to do it."

"Yes, she did and you were a big help to her."

They sat quietly for a while before Donovan said, "I love Ms. Satarah, Dad. I know you stayed here because I was in the hospital and all. I'm all better now, but I want to stay here. I don't want to go back to Richmond."

That surprised Doug. "Why, Donovan?"

"I like it here. I like the Academy and everybody. Mrs. Sylvia and Dr. Bernie and Ms. Jennie and Ms. Mary Ella and Jeffrey and Jonathan. Everybody. Ms. Vivian and Uncle Chucky P said that if it was all right with you, I could come to their home in Maryland when Jeffrey and Jonathan go during the next school rotation break. Then Gregory and Aretha Alexander said that they want to take us to New York and to Boston again. Then on the next rotation, we're invited to go to California with Mr. Kenneth and Ms. JeNelle. Ms. Satarah said that if everything goes all right, she would like to take us to Paris, France, to visit her mother. And—. Why are you laughing, Dad?"

"I guess Richmond, Virginia, doesn't stand a chance against Maryland, New York, Massachusetts, California *and* France." He chuckled softly.

"But if we went back to Richmond, we couldn't go to all those places, could we?"

Doug brushed a hand over Donovan's head. "Eventually, perhaps, but certainly not in the next twelve months. I may want to take you to Ohio and the State of Washington for a visit, though."

"Can Ms. Satarah, Jeffrey and Jonathan come with us?"

"Absolutely. We will see whether they want to go when the time comes."

"And maybe Mr. and Mrs. Diggs could come to visit us here at The Summer House?"

Doug chuckled. "Why don't we ask Ms. Satarah before we ask them to make sure it's all right?"

"Okay, dad, but you're not going to let anybody take The Summer House away from Ms. Satarah, are you?"

"No, son, no one is going to take anything away from Ms. Satarah. That's a promise."

"Okay. I'm sleepy now. I'm going to check on the children before I go back to bed." Donovan rose, hugged Doug, and tiptoed to Satarah. He kissed his finger, placed it gently on her cheek before he said goodnight and left the bedroom.

Doug sat contemplating how much better his relationship with Donovan had become since moving to Summer County. Donovan was much more confident, secure, and looking forward to going to school every day. He was actually a happy kid, on the verge of becoming a teenager with hopes and dreams of traveling to different places. Doug wanted that kind of positive exposure for Donovan.

Actually, Kenneth Alexander invited him and Donovan on a male-bonding ski weekend to Vale, Colorado. Apparently, the men in the Alexander and Dixon families took their children on a three-day ski vacation just before Thanksgiving every year. It gave their wives free time to do whatever they wanted to do and, of course, to buy and hide the Christmas gifts. Doug had never gone skiing, but he was looking forward to the experience. He would bring Donovan, Jeffrey, Jonathan and hopefully one other on the trip. Hell, there was a lot of living that he had never considered, but he would enjoy doing it with *his* and Satarah's boys.

Doug was so lost in his thoughts that he didn't notice that Satarah was up, until he heard her leave her bathroom. She had showered and was wearing a long, blue nightgown. She walked toward him, took the book from his lap, and doused the light.

"Come to bed, Doug," she said, reaching out to him.

He did as she asked, stripped down to his jockeys and crawled into bed behind her.

"How do you feel?" he asked.

"Like a limp dishrag, but my fever broke and my period started."

He rubbed her flat stomach. "Cramps?"

"Not so bad now, especially when you're holding me."

"Do you need anything?"

"Just you," she said, snuggling against him and yawning.

He kissed her cheek. "Go back to sleep."

Satarah turned in his arms to face him. "Doug?"

"Humm?"

"I love your son, too."

He kissed her lightly on the mouth and held her gently. "I know. In a very special way you gave him life."

⟨⟩

The library was one of Doug's favorite places in The Summer House—a close runner up to the workroom in the basement. Of course, his all-time favorite was anywhere he could catch Satarah for a little afternoon delight. She was still resting on this second day of her "confinement." At least that was what she called it, in a very annoyed way. She was not accustomed to being idle and did not suffer it well. He was firm with her when he crawled out of her bed this morning before anyone else was up. She actually thought she was going to get up, cook and clean house, and tend to ten active boys ages eight to twelve and three girls, ages four and five—and she was serious! He put his foot down and threatened to tie her to the bedpost if she moved one muscle. Of course, what she said about bondage had his blood draining into his groin like a faucet. She is truly a wicked woman. His morning shower was on the tepid side, on purpose. She couldn't possibly feel up to doing what she had suggested, but he sure didn't want to test that theory.

After he was dressed, he checked on her again. She was sleeping, so he quietly left her bedroom. While he started the coffee going, he put out cold cereal, juice, yogurt and fruit for the children and watched the heat rise over the meadow with the sunrise while he drank his coffee. Today everyone would have a continental breakfast. He would figure out something for lunch and dinner. The meals weren't his primary concerns though. He needed to figure out what to do with thirteen active children for two days.

Of course, they may want to spend time in the pool, but, if the temperature was going be in the mid-nineties, he did not want them outside for long periods. The game room was geared toward more adult games like pool, darts, etc. and was still under construction, so that was out. They had videos to watch, books to read, and a rack of board games, but those things would not hold their attention for the entire two days. He would have to ask Satarah, when he took her breakfast tray in, exactly what she had in mind for the children's entertainment. That settled, he sat back to wait for the house to come alive.

Two hours later, Doug and Bob were cross-eyed trying to deal with the banshees who had invaded and turned Satarah's clean and orderly kitchen and family room into a toxic disaster area. He carried two of the grinning alien creatures under each arm like footballs. And, they were enjoying themselves immensely. Bob was crawling around on his hands and knees under the tables and in the cabinets, hunting for one of the twin girls. Doug wasn't sure exactly which was which, especially with finger paint everywhere on them. Bubbles were floating in the air, building blocks were crashing, Legos were under foot and remote-controlled cars were zooming here and there around Cheerios lost during the food fight. There were unidentifiable splotches on what was his favorite Million Man March white T-shirt, Play-Doh hanging out of the pockets of his shorts. He started out wearing a pair of leather sandals, but one was now MIA.

He and Bob were on the floor with them under a makeshift tent they constructed out of four high stools and sheets from Satarah's linen closet. Pots and pans became mountain quests for the math game using an army of three-inch-high wooden people. Satarah's little kitchen window herb garden became the forests in the obstacle course, when it wasn't being used for the racing track barriers.

And Doug was having the time of his life!

Kids, God love them, were a bunch of fun! Who knew?

Doug was making airplane sounds for the two boys currently under his arms when he noticed the mayhem had subsided. When he looked up, everyone's focus was on something behind him. He turned around to face two women who did not have a smile anywhere in the vicinity of their faces. He swallowed hard.

"Uh, good morning, Sylvia. Olivia."

"Gotcha!" Bob shouted, triumphantly. A little girl squealed and giggled. "I told you I'd find you. You can't get—oops!" Bob said when he stood with the other twin over his shoulder. "Uh, hi, uh—." he trailed off.

With hands on hips, Sylvia Alexander imperiously raised one eyebrow while Olivia Dixon crossed her arms over her impressive breasts and patted one foot to some soundless beat that could have been a death march.

"Douglas, Bobby," Sylvia said, without cracking a smile, "Children." The kitchen was so quiet you could hear a pin drop in the Alaskan Tundra. "Olivia and I are going to look in on Satarah Josephine for approximately thirty minutes, then *we will be back*," she enunciated the later part of that statement as if she had taught Arnold Schwarzenegger the language. They turned on their heels and were gone.

Sylvia cackled. "You should have seen them! I tell you, Satarah, it was the funniest thing I've seen in a month of Sundays!"

Olivia was laughing so hard she could hardly catch her breath. "I tell you, if I could have taped that scene, I would win a mint on The World's Funniest Videos." She hooted out another laugh.

"I thought I would pee my pants when Doug and Bobby finally saw us standing there. They stood in the middle of that pandemonium like deer caught in headlights. They had finger paint on their faces—." She couldn't stop laughing.

"There—there—," Olivia couldn't get the words out for laughing. "There they were, these two, big, strong firemen with babies hanging off of every appendage like they were filming a battle scene from Star Wars!"

"Stop! Please!" Satarah begged, laughing hysterically. "I'm on my period and about to have an accident!"

Lying at angles on their backs on Satarah's bed, for a while only heavy breathing could be heard as they desperately tried to calm down. Then they started giggling again.

"How much rope did you give them?"

"Thirty minutes," Sylvia said, checking her watch.

"What the heck, Aunt Sylvia, give them thirty-five for good measure."

"Oh, why not? This was such fun. Douglas and Bobby will never live this down." She sat up and wiped the tears from her face. She looked at her niece. "You look better."

"I do feel better, physically."

"What is it, Sara Jo?" Olivia asked, noting the concerned expression on her face. "What's happened?"

"My father. He was here when I came home yesterday." She told them about his claim to the property.

Sylvia and Olivia glanced at one another. Satarah saw the look.

"You already know about it," Satarah surmised.

"Clarice Flowers couldn't get to Minnie Mae's beauty parlor fast enough this morning to spread the word about your behavior. Your Uncle Bernie and Romelo got an earful at the barber shop from Phineas."

"Bad, huh?" Satarah asked.

"Did you really call Clarice a dog?" Olivia asked.

"Not directly," Satarah said, chagrin. "But have you noticed how her face always looks like she sucked on a lemon? Like a Pekinese or something," she asked rhetorically. "I was trying to say 'witch' and got it wrong." She looked up at her aunts' disbelieving expressions. "That's my story and I'm sticking to it." She defiantly raised her chin.

"Sassy Jo," Olivia said, calling Satarah by her childhood nickname and remorsefully shaking her head. "You will never change—thank goodness!"

"You are so much my sister's child," Sylvia said, stroking Satarah's cheeks, a beatific smile on her face. "It's been so long since I've seen that vim and vinegar surface in you. It does my heart good. I love your independence and your vigor, but you were taught to respect your elders."

"When they deserve it. My grandparents taught me to respect those who respect me—but, you're right. I should not have called her out her name," Satarah said and huffed out a breath. "I'll apologize to her, but my heart won't be in it."

"And then there is the matter of calling Phineas 'numb nuts'..." Olivia added.

"Oh, hell," Satarah moaned and dropped her face forward into her bed sheets. "I lost my temper." When she felt the bed vibrate and heard her aunts' stifled coughs, she raised her head and looked at them crossly. They were laughing silently, covering their faces.

"*Numb nuts!*" Olivia bleated before everyone collapsed into another fit of giggles.

Satarah sobered first and shook her head, recalling to her mind her behavior toward her father and his cohorts.

"What do you want to do about this situation, baby?" Sylvia asked.

"I already did it. I gave lawyer Ocher Bill Chandler's business card. He went all pale when he read Bill's name and law firm. I thought he was going to faint."

"Good," Sylvia said, as she rose from the bed and kissed Satarah's temple. "Well, my work is done here."

"Not so fast," Olivia said to her sister-in-law while looking at Satarah. "You'll not block us out anymore, Satarah Josephine Whitfield. When you have trouble, we all have trouble. Is that understood?"

Olivia's stare was commanding. Satarah nodded and embraced her aunt and was hugged fiercely in return.

"Yes, ma'am. I love you," she took Sylvia's hand and squeezed, "both of you so very much."

For a few quiet, monumental moments, the three women held hands in an unbroken chain; a show of unity, a family link, much like the ones they each wore around their necks.

❧

"They've been in there a long time," Bob whispered to Doug who was frantically wiping up the last of the finger paint.

The children silently trouped back in, their attire spic and span. The kitchen and family room were spotless; order restored.

Everyone turned when Sylvia and Olivia entered. The women inspected each child, the family room and the kitchen. Then Sylvia rose on her toes to kiss the cheeks of Doug and Bob.

"Boys," she said, an eyebrow lifted, "We're running late. Bernie and Romello are building pizzas for lunch. The children are supposed to help. We will be back later tonight."

"Uh, Mrs. A? Could I come with?" Bob asked.

Sylvia nodded once. "Go wash the paint off your ear and meet us at the vans. Come along, children, let's get loaded up."

Doug followed them to the eight-seat SUVs and helped to strap in the children. As Sylvia started her ignition, she winked at Doug and was gone. He released a breath.

"Whew! That was a close one," he said, but then grinned. They had big fun! He dug his hands in the pockets of his clean jean shorts and whistled his way back into the house. After he checked on Satarah, who was asleep, he settled into the library again and pulled out his video cam. He laughed periodically through the replay. The existence of this particular video would remain his and Bob's little secret.

When he shut off the video, he picked up the latest Eleanor Taylor Bland novel and got caught up in the Marti McAlister mystery where he left off before breakfast.

19

Let the record show that this is a preliminary fact-finding hearing to determine whether criminal or civil charges should be brought against Satarah Josephine James Whitfield for her actions on February 18 of this year.

"Let the record also show that present are the attorneys for Summer County Hospital; Dr. Reynard Steward, Chief of Medical Services for Summer County; Gill Dunston, Chief of the South Carolina Medical Board, the appellants. For the defense are William Anthony Chandler and Vivian Alexander Jackson Montgomery, Attorneys-at-Law, though Mrs. Montgomery is a sitting federal judge, acting as a friend of this court; and Mrs. Satarah Josephine James Whitfield, the defendant.

"I am County Court Judge Malcolm Galloway. The record should note that I have personal relations with both Dr. Steward and Mrs. Whitfield. Nevertheless, I have been asked by all parties to mediate this matter and render an opinion.

"It is alleged that on February 18, Satarah Whitfield, in her capacity as Head Emergency Room Registered Nurse did, with forethought, conduct a medical procedure on a minor, Donovan Johnson, not permitted under the terms and conditions of her license as a Nurse Practioner. Moreover, she did so without the knowledge, guidance or consent of a duly licensed physician in attendance."

While Judge Galloway continued to cite the facts and charges against her, Satarah tuned them out. Not because she was disinterested, but rather because she was reconciled with whatever the outcome would be. The salient point, to her way of thinking, was that, given the same set of circumstances and even knowing the probable consequences, she would do exactly the same thing. She wasn't exactly sure that was a good position to take, but her conscience was clear.

"In addition to the briefs filed by the parties present, investigative reports were filed by Richardson Medical Investigations and statements independently filed by The Nurses Association, The Summer County Fire Department, The Doctors' Association, individual patients and their relatives, and the sole parent of the minor, Douglas E. Johnson.

"I have reviewed all pleadings entered into the record. Emmaline?"

"Yes, Judge Holloway?"

"We will go off the record," he said and waited for the court stenographer to take her equipment out of the judge's chamber. When the door closed, the judge leaned back in his seat, removed his glasses and pinched the bridge of his nose.

"Sara Jo, you have caused the killing of more trees for your hour of work on Donovan Johnson than you have on that tree farm of yours." He looked at her, perturbed. "You've got everyone's panties in a pinch over this. I know you have one of the best mouthpieces in this country to speak for you in Mr. Chandler here, but I want to know what you have to say for yourself. Do you regret what you did?"

"No, Judge Galloway, I don't regret it, and if your next question is going to be, would I do it again, the answer is yes I would. I'm guilty as charged."

"Hump!" The Judge shook his head. "Just as I thought. Sara Jo, I've known you since you were a gleam in your mama's eyes. You've always been up front and told the truth, even when I caught you stealing peaches off my trees, but you've never been a hot head or held a grudge, and the Good Lord knows you had every right to do exactly that.

He looked at Vivian. "Vivian Lynn, you got something you want to say about your cousin's behavior?"

Vivian took off her stylish glasses, folded them neatly, and placed them beside her laptop. She looked directly at the judge who had bounced her on his knee when she was a baby. Then she gave him a quick grin. "I am as guilty as Sara Jo, Your Honor. If you had looked up in your peach tree you would have caught me too."

It took a moment while the judge stared at Vivian's sterling smile and devilishly dancing eyes. Then he threw back his head and laughed heartily. He shook head and smiled at her. "I should have known better than to ask you an open-ended question like that, Madam Justice. You are truly your mama's child."

"Thank you, Your Honor. She likes you too."

"Rey," the judge said turning to face him, "you and I play golf once a week and though you have a nice stroke, you are hell to deal with when you lose." He held up a hand to stave off Rey Steward's protest. "You placed Sara Jo and the rest of your hospital staff in an untenable position. You pulled all of the doctors out of every department and pressed them into surgical duty, even Garrison St. Clair who's a podiatrist, for pity's sake. Though he is the Head Resident in the Emergency Room, he is an administrator and hasn't performed an operation since he was a resident at the hospital twelve years ago."

"I had no choice, Mal. There were so many people injured and in need of surgery. We were working around the clock for more than five days!"

"And you did an admiral job, Rey, but you disregarded your Disaster Plan and left everyone else unsupported. You're an excellent surgeon, but a lousy manager. Your job is to set policy, manage the hospital, and its staff. Fortunately, you have excellent, well-trained department heads to carry the extraordinary load you placed on their shoulders. That includes Sara Jo as the head of the Emergency Room nursing staff. I've read account after account of how she saved lives and managed to keep the hospital functioning according to the Disaster Plan until more staff could get through the blizzard to the hospital to help. She pulled people out of Maintenance to move patients into rooms. Had the administrative staff working with the patients and their families to evaluate their needs and the kitchen staff making room deliveries, as if they were pizza delivery people. She was doing not only her job, but also the jobs of three or four others, including yours. Not once in those five days did you check on how she or anyone else was handling the emergency. Thank goodness Sylvia Alexander and the volunteers were doing a lot of the grunt work.

"Now I know that these were extraordinary circumstances, the likes of which I never hope to see again, but, damn it, Rey, Sara Jo did you and the hospital proud. I've read Chuck Montgomery's report and the report of the Doctors' Association. The surgical procedure she performed was exactly what was required and the post-operative report indicates that she should have been in the surgical wing instead of Garrison.

"Jeez-o-flip, Rey, just look at all this paper," he said, picking up the briefs and letting the stack of paper slam down onto the polished table. "And then you had to go and put your hands on her in a public corridor of the hospital in front of witnesses? Everyone, including your own hospital board of directors, wants this matter dropped, except you. And don't think for one minute that everyone on your hospital staff doesn't know the reason why."

Rey looked absolutely popeyed. "I don't—uh; I have no idea what you're talking about."

"Sure you do, Rey. According to Garrison St. Clair, who happens to be the older brother of Jacque St. Clair; a man Satarah dated a few summers ago, you've been hot to trot after her for more than a year or two. And you've been jealous of any relationship that she developed. You told him and others in the doctors' lounge that you finally had her exactly where you wanted her. Sound familiar?"

Rey said nothing, but his face flushed.

With a nod, Judge Holloway said, "That should be it. Okay, I've read and heard enough. Emmaline!" he shouted. The court reporter entered too quickly for her not to have been listening at the door. "Did you get all of that, Emmaline?"

Guilt was written all over her suddenly pink cheeks and all too innocent expression. Without a word, she sat poised and ready to resume the official transcript.

"I am now ready to issue an opinion. Satarah Josephine James Whitfield did, on February 18, perform an unauthorized surgical procedure on Donovan Johnson that exceeded the terms and conditions of her license as a Nurse Practitioner. She was reprimanded for that action by suspension from her position as head of Emergency Room Nurses for one hundred twenty days without pay.

"Based on the record before me, I find nothing criminal in her action. The State Attorney General has declined to bring criminal charges against her. I find that civil charges could be brought against her. The only party with standing, however, is Douglas Edward Johnson, father of the minor, Donovan Johnson. He has submitted an affidavit evidencing his refusal to take any action against Satarah Josephine James Whitfield. However, he holds in abeyance his right to take action against Dr. Reynard Steward and/or Summer County Hospital.

"Therefore, it is my opinion that no further action be taken in this matter."

All heads turned to the court reporter when a little 'yip' of agreement came from her.

"Something you want to add, Emmaline?" the Judge asked, amused.

"No, sir, Your Honor," she said it with a straight face, but the energy was shooting off her in waves.

"Very good. Then," he said, looking around at the pleased expressions, except, of course, Rey Steward's. He leveled his eyes on his golf buddy's and said over the top ridge of his glasses, "this matter is closed."

⌥

Doug waited outside Judge Holloway's chambers with other concerned friends, family, and people, many of whom were patients from the hospital, while they shook Satarah's hand, hugged her, and congratulated her. Doug noted that Rey Steward skirted the well-wishers and when he spotted Doug, Rey made an about face, and headed in the opposite direction. Bill Chandler stood beside Satarah while she was interviewed by the news media.

Doug stood apart from the others, glad for the opportunity simply to observe Satarah in her trim, navy-blue, pinstriped suit with a skirt that stopped just above her knees. The nude, silk stockings did wonderful thing to her glamorous, strong, long legs. He got a little thrill looking at her pretty feet in icepick, navy-blue pumps and the white, lace, high-neck Victorian blouse that lay against her throat. He wanted to nibble just below the gold studs in her earlobes.

With a jolt to his system, Doug knew in that instant that he was undeniably and irrevocably in love with Satarah Josephine James Whitfield.

It wasn't a high school kid crush the way it was with Lily Stone; a relationship that was built on youthful heat and loneliness that should have run its course after they were on their own. At twenty years old what did he really know about, for lack of a better words, "true" love, or commitment? They grew older, but not together. Lily was still stuck in her silly games only presenting a false front. Yet, because he hadn't looked deeper, the fact that she had a mental illness flew over his head while she heated his sheets with her young, nubile body.

However, Satarah was a full-grown woman dealing with the tragedies of life and succeeding in spite of the pitfalls. She could construct cabinets from scratch, manage a staff of Emergency Room nurses, and raise two energetic, well-rounded boys. She could also cook up a storm, run a tree farm, shoot a gun with precision, and nerve, and deliver a baby. She soothed the fears of a man, charmed a twelve-year-old boy, danced like there was no tomorrow, and made love like a hurricane, all-encompassing, and, yet, kept herself on a level plane. How could he not fall in love with a woman like Satarah?

What he needed at twenty was far cry from what he wanted at thirty and likely what he would need at forty. However, Satarah would be a woman for all seasons and for the rest of his life.

Vivian smiled at Doug as she approached him. "How are you doing, Chief?"

Doug returned her smile. "That depends on what happened in Judge Holloway's chamber."

"Oh, I think things went as well as can be expected. No further action will be taken against Satarah. The hospital board voted yesterday to have her reinstated with full back pay and with no break in service. In fact, she will likely receive a commendation for action above and beyond."

Doug released a breath. "That's good. She deserves it."

"And a break, too."

"I've got that covered. Thanks for taking the boys to Maryland again with you. Donovan is so excited he could hardly eat this morning."

"My pleasure. I'm taking the entire crew of cousins with me. I'll only have them for a week before Gregory and Aretha come to get them. Then they and six of mine are off to New York and then Boston. By the time they get back, they will be ready to go back to school for some peace and quiet."

"You're a brave woman, Vivian. I had some of the Cousin Crew last month. They are a handful."

Vivian laughed. "Yeah. Mama and Aunt Olivia told me about that lost weekend."

"They didn't have any evidence to back up their allegation, Judge Montgomery."

"Only because you swore all the witnesses to secrecy."

"That's my story and I'm sticking to it."

"And it's going down in the annals of family folklore to be told over and over again."

Doug did not miss the reference to his being in the family. He was proud of the connection, and, if he could convince Satarah to make it legal sometime in the future, he would be a very happy man.

"I've got to go round up the Cousin Crew. We're flying out shortly and my brood has called twice, wondering why we're not in the air already." Vivian hugged him and kissed his cheek. "Take good care of my cousin," she said before she left to join Bill who took Vivian's hand and waved goodbye to Doug.

Satarah stood in the now empty hallway and faced Doug. She glimpsed him while she thanked everyone for their support and answered questions for the news media. She declined offers to go on a speaking tour or make the media rounds. She wanted only to get back to her life—and to Douglas.

They started toward one another, eyes locked.

"Hi," they said in unison before they kissed each other softly.

"Ready?" Doug asked.

"Yes, I'm ready."

They locked hands and strolled out of the courthouse.

"Doug, you missed the turn."

"No I didn't. We're not going home for a few days."

"Oh? Where are we going?"

"Charleston. I've never been there before."

"Charleston? I can't go to Charleston without packing something to wear."

"That's already taken care of. Your luggage is in the back. Not that you'll need clothes much while we're there."

"Promises, promises," Satarah quipped while easing her seat into a reclining position, a grin edged her mouth.

❦

"God! You drive me crazy, woman!" Doug said, expressively, as he tried to catch his breath.

Satarah's laugh bordered on malicious. She rolled off of Doug, stood up, and then twirled her blissfully naked body around and around in the suite, arms extended up over her head. "I feel wonderful!" she exclaimed.

"I'll say," Doug parried, and grinned at her as he watched her twirl. She looked like an exotic nymph with her bushy skein of hair flying about her face and down her back.

It was the morning of their third day in Charleston. The city was a surprise to Doug with its historic charm, beauty and genteel nature. Horse-drawn carriages, cobblestone streets, and an abundance of antique shops and boutiques had been on Satarah's list of places to take him.

On the first day in the city, they visited her Aunt Adeline's Sweet Grass Basket Boutique and watched artisans making the coiled baskets by hand, just as they did centuries before in the Manu River Region, Senegambia and Angola-Congolese regions of West Africa. Doug learned, from the little historic stories the artisans told as their busy hands worked, that originally men made workbaskets out of bulrush. Later women began making smaller baskets out of sweet grass for storing and serving food. The process evolved into an art form and then a cottage industry.

Satarah's aunt had a thriving mail order and catalog business in addition to her basket boutique that served customers worldwide. Each year, she selected a small group of interested high school students to learn the art of basket weaving and, as they went off to colleges and universities elsewhere, they continued to work for her for their pocket money or school necessities.

He and Satarah left her aunt's shop and hauled a bountiful bunch of baskets back to their suite at a bed and breakfast on Chalmers Street near the Old Slave Mart Museum. She would use the baskets as decorations in The Summer House and take orders for sales that she would send to her aunt to fill and mail. This new little venture would add nicely to her profit statement. Later, they dined alfresco in the warm night air overlooking the harbor in Beaufort County with Satarah's aunt, her husband, Phillip, a former sea captain with the Merchant Marines, and two of their five adult children, Martin and Septima. Beaufort, one of the Gullah/Geechee Sea Islands, offered Doug a glimpse into the Gullah people through Phillip whose pathos was thick with the dialect as he regaled them with stories of his ancestors and childhood.

Martin and Septima, both teachers, invited him, Satarah, and the boys back for the Penn Center Heritage Days Festival and Gullah Festival, both nationally acclaimed events.

On their second day in Charleston, they had a light breakfast and then toured the Avery Research Center for African American History and Culture. It was a pleasant journey through the preserved history and cultural heritage of African Americans in the region. Doug and Satarah spent hours there in the reading room while she showed Doug her family's history with great pride printed in the book in the Research Center. Later, they had She-Crab soup in the old City Market while they watched the Andante Drum and Dance Company perform traditional West African dance styles.

Last night they strolled into jazz and blues clubs and had dinner on the Charleston waterfront.

Today they were going to the beach to lay in the sun and sand—if they ever got out of bed. As Doug watched Satarah's lush body twirl, his member hardened: a reaction that did not bode well for the planned beach adventure.

"So, are you going to tell me where we're going?" Satarah asked Doug for the umpteenth time.

"Yes," Doug grinned as he listened to the GPS directions while he drove.

A beat later, Satarah said, "Well?" Exasperation was evident in her tone. "When are you going to tell me?"

"In a few minutes."

"Doug," she said on a lengthy sigh.

He chuckled at her long-suffering agitation, but did not answer her question.

After a few more turns and a successful search for a parking space, Doug turned off the engine and, turning toward Satarah, planted a brief kiss on her mutinous face, before he got out of his truck.

Satarah looked out the front window at the College of Charleston Auditorium as Doug came around the front of his truck to open her door. People were getting out of cars all around them and heading toward the building in droves. She took Doug's offered hand and then looked up at him. "What's going on here?" she asked perplexed.

"You'll see," he said, cryptically, and guided her toward the building.

When they entered the vestibule, the press of humanity jammed them together, but Doug's bit, muscular body edged toward the auditorium door and produced two tickets for entry. An usher guided them to excellent seats in the front center section. Satarah looked up at the tall, closed curtains and at the rapidly filling auditorium before turning her questioning gaze on Doug again. He put his arm around the back of her seat and whispered, "Relax," before delivering a quick kiss to her pouty mouth.

Nearly three hours later, Satarah was dreamy eyed and languid. The first performer was Paul Taylor whose virtuoso horn playing set a beguiling mood and lulled the packed audience into an appreciative silence. Keiko Matsue, the world acclaimed pianist, followed taking the charged audience to another level of appreciation, but when the curtain again rose on Kem and his band Kemistry, the audience was in a heightened state of anticipation and excitement—and they were not disappointed.

Satarah's face was rapturous throughout the young musical artist's performance. After the end of the evening's performances fans stood patiently in line to receive autographed copies of promotional material and CDs from each artist. Then Doug and Satarah spent the remainder of the evening dancing slowly on the terrace of their suite to the romantic sounds of the artists' CDs.

"Satarah?" Doug said, as they swayed to the music.

"Yes?" she answered languidly, her head against his heart.

"Remember when I said that I was trying not to fall in love with you?"

She raised her head, snaked her arms around his neck, and smiled into his eyes. "Yes, I remember."

"Well, it didn't work. I failed and I've fallen in love with you."

She grinned at him. "You want me to help you get up out of love?"

"No, I like it where I am."

"Good because I'm right with you. I'm in love with you, too. Now, how did that happen I wonder?"

"I think it happened when you opened your front door to a complete stranger and took me in. You took care of me when I didn't know that I needed being taken care of."

She kissed him softly and smiled. "And I thought that it was my coffee that hooked you."

"That, too," he said and kissed her with purpose.

❦

The week after Doug and Satarah returned from their extended weekend trip to Charleston, Doug sat in Jinx's Juke Joint with Donald Dixon, drinking a surprisingly good, cold beer. Donald called Doug to meet him for lunch. They ate two, thick burgers with all the fixings and fries that were perfectly golden brown. They had a corner booth in the back of the lunchroom. The music on the jukebox was just loud enough so that no one could over hear anyone else's conversation.

Donald wiped his hands and mouth with the paper napkins and then tossed it on the empty platter that had once held his burgers, fries and coleslaw all while intently regarding Doug.

Doug noticed Donald's pointed stare and similarly cleaned his hands and mouth. He then leaned forward, crossed his arms on the table and waited.

"You're going to a conference in Chicago next Thursday, so clear your schedule. You'll leave on Wednesday night and you'll be spending the night on Thursday and possibly Friday, so pack a bag with a suit and tie."

"Okay," Doug said slowly. He wasn't completely sure about what was going on but he trusted Donald Dixon without question. He knew enough, however, to understand that the trip to Chicago was the cover story that he was to tell his staff, Satarah, and Donovan.

He awakened early that morning, violently aroused to find Satarah under his covers with her mouth between his opened thighs working quickly to bring him to a catastrophic orgasm. She rocked his world and left with the stealth with which she had entered his room. When he woke again, his bed was absent one Satarah Josephine Whitfield. It was time to step up his pace.

The sun was hot and the air steamy in late June and noon was hours away yet. Satarah put the last of the breakfast dishes away and stood at the kitchen window over the sink to watch Douglas with her boys and Donovan in the swimming pool. The water was waist high on Doug as he instructed Donovan on how to hold his breath under water.

Her boys were introduced to the water before they were a year old. Now they could qualify as lifeguards and they weren't even teenagers. During the season, she and her boys like to swim daily. She, too, was an excellent swimmer and would often join them when time permitted. Shortly, her time would be limited. She was cleared to return to work as head of the Emergency Room nursing staff. Since she received her back pay and a hefty bonus for her work during the February emergency, she decided to delay her return to work until after the 4th of July family reunion.

As she continued to stand and watch Douglas, she mentally went over what she needed to do in preparation for the event. Her teenaged cousins asked to camp out in tents on her back lawn around the pool and, in exchange, they would act as the cleaning crew for The Summer House for the duration of the festivities. She desperately needed the help since every bedroom in the massive old mansion was booked. She planned to hire some of the locals to handle work at The Summer House when she returned to work, particularly Miles Logan, Jefferson Logan's middle son who was studying hotel management. His deceased mother's family owned hotels worldwide and he wanted to make that his career objective. He was an heir to the huge Montrose fortune, but he asked her to let him work with her and she had agreed. Besides, a number of her cousins on the Benson side of the family, her mother's and her Aunt Sylvia's siblings and their offspring would be attending the reunion and staying at The Summer House. She wished her mother would be one of them. It would be very special indeed to have her mother come home for a visit. However, she couldn't dwell on that. She had too much else to concern herself with.

She had to find additional temporary refrigeration units so she could prepare some meals in advance and freeze the food until needed. They would be running two tours a day at 10:00 A.M. and 2:00 P.M. for the seven-day reunion. Lunch would follow the early tour and dinner after the later tour. Other family remembers would be attending the informative classes that family members agreed to conduct at the Academy. Vivian was doing a class in consumer law and another in careers in law. Her cousin, Gregory Alexander, Vivian's younger brother, would be teaching classes on the stock market and investments. He was a partner in a prestigious investment firm on Wall Street. There would be other classes for every age group and interest. There were fun things, too, like crafts, and, in the evening, a carnival, family performing arts entertainment and dancing. The Olympic-sized swimming pools at the Academy would be opened for swimming. That reminded Satarah that she needed to order more towels for The Summer House to use at poolside.

She smiled as she watched Douglas climb out of the pool and her boys take over Donovan's swimming lessons. Donovan seemed to be getting his rhythm going, as he stroked the length of the pool with Jonathan and Jeffrey at his sides and beamed a big smile at his father when he reached the deep end before starting back. Satarah predicted that before too long they would have another preteen who could qualify for lifeguard duty. Every child who progressed through the Summer County Academy had water safety training as a apart of the school's standard curriculum. Along with all of the other classes that Donovan would take, he seemed to be doing very well and immensely enjoying himself.

"He's going to be good," she commented, as Doug came through the kitchen door.

He grinned at her. "He's so excited about learning everything under the sun. This is so different from his experience in Richmond. When he got back from visiting Vivian in Washington, Gregory in New York and Aretha in Boston, he couldn't get enough of finding out about all the places they visited. When he learned that Jonathan and Jeffrey have family all over the world who they communicate with virtually every day, he was enraptured. Geography has suddenly become his favorite subject. We're definitely going to have to find time to take the boys to France to visit your mother."

Satarah looked up into Doug's shining eyes and easy smile and her world narrowed to his face. Tears threatened the backs of her eyes. "I was just thinking about my mother and wishing that she could be here for the family reunion celebration."

"Great minds and all that," he teased and kissed her. "Go get changed and join us at the pool."

"I can't. I have so much to do to get ready for the holiday."

"Give it a rest, Satarah, and come have some fun with us. I promise that I'll help you with the planning later."

How could she resist this wonderful man who wanted to take her and her boys to visit her mother and to come have fun for a few hours? She kissed him quickly and then sprinted off to do as told.

As soon as Satarah was out of earshot, Doug pulled his special cell phone from the pocket of his terrycloth robe and pressed one button.

"What have you got?" he asked.

"A location and a plan. Are you still in?"

"Yes."

"Good. More soon."

Doug clicked off and pocketed the small device, as he considered the implications. If all went well, Satarah would be enjoying the upcoming family reunion in a major way. Her Uncle Bernard Alexander's nephew, Donald Dixon, had located Satarah's son and had a plan to unite mother and son soon. Doug didn't know the details, yet, but whatever it took, Satarah would reunite with her son.

Doug was also informed that Satarah's sister, Carlotta, and former husband, JoJeff, were still together living in Las Vegas, Nevada. Carlotta sang and danced at a club and JoJeff dealt Blackjack at one of the casinos. They started an escort service on the side and were doing quite well for themselves until a bigger, mobbed-up service moved in, and stole all of their male and female escorts. JoJeff and Carlotta still worked their side business themselves from time to time, but, if times got hard, in addition to his job as a Blackjack dealer, JoJeff would work as a mechanic in any of the garages around the area. According to Donald, Carlotta and JoJeff did not seem inclined to return to the slower lifestyle of Summer County, South Carolina.

To that bit of news, Doug could smile at the beautiful vision Satarah was as she approached him wearing a one-piece swimsuit that made his blood warm.

Satarah cocked her head as she drew near Douglas. "What's that grin all about?"

"You, Satarah Josephine, are absolutely any man's hot dream fantasy.

"You keep looking at me like that, pal, and I'll have to take you back to my bed and have my way with you," she teased.

"Promise that you won't be gentle?"

She hooted a laugh, took his hand and pulled him out of the kitchen to the patio to join their boys.

By ten in the morning, Bob and Mark had come out to join Doug, Satarah and the boys in the pool and a water volleyball match ensued.

"So what have you decided to do, Sara Jo?" asked Sylvia Alexander, as she reviewed and signed reports on her desk at the hospital.

Satarah stood with her hands in her jeans pockets, looking out of the top floor window. "I'm coming back to work fulltime after the 4th of July holiday and family reunion. I can't afford not to. Thanks to you, my young cousins are going to have summer jobs running The Summer House. They got some experience during their Spring break," she said chuckling. "I'll be there to supervise the morning meal and be at the hospital by nine in the morning."

"Sounds good. Heaven knows Bernie and I are thrilled to have our grands with us this summer until Labor Day. Vivian and Chuck are staying after the reunion and so is Aretha."

20

This is sudden, isn't it?" Satarah asked, as she sat on Doug's bed and watched him pack an overnight bag.

"Somewhat. I've had this trip on my schedule for some time, but wasn't sure when I would get the opportunity to go." He closed his bag and shifted to look at Satarah. "It's okay to leave Donovan with you for a day or two, isn't it?"

"Yes, of course, it is. It's just that... I don't know... you rarely have to leave on such short notice." She looked up into his unreadable expression. "Somehow this trip seems different."

"Just tell me that you're going to miss having me underfoot," Doug teased and hugged her to him. He hated lying to her and he wasn't any good at it. He needed to get out of there before he told her the truth and then where would they be? She would get her hopes up and want to come along.

"Well," she said, elongating the word with a sly smile. "I will definitely miss the great sex. I guess I'll have to see what Bigger's up to."

"I won't be gone long enough for you to have to tap another source for sex."

She walked her fingers up his chest and over his right shoulder. Then she plastered her front to his back and wrapped her arms around him laying her face between his shoulder blades.

"I'm going to have to have something to hold me until you get back." She unzipped his slacks and eased her right hand into the opening to find him hot and hard. Simultaneously, she unfastened his shirt buttons to allow her access to his hard flat nipples, which she aggressively massaged.

"Uh, what did you have in mind?" he asked around his labored breathing. He tilted his head back as she latched onto his right ear lobe for a little pain and pleasure with her teeth and tongue.

"I'll think of something... eventually. How much time do we have before you have to leave?"

"An hour, maybe two."

"Well then," she breathed the words in his ear, as she unbuckled his slacks, inserted her hands palming his hips, and letting his slacks fall to his ankles. In no time, his Jockeys followed. His dress shirt met the same fate.

He should have felt like a fool standing in his dress shoes and socks with his slacks around his ankles while Satarah had her way with him, but truth be told, sex with her could never be denied. She was so creative and enthusiastic that he could get a boner several times a day just thinking about her and her antics. Sex had never been like this for him with any other woman, including Lily. He reached back to grab her butt, as she ground her front to his rear. She continued exercising his penis and his nipples, putting him into a state of near asphyxiation from heavy breathing.

"God! You drive me crazy, woman!" he exclaimed on a strangled cry. He pushed his duffle bag to the floor and pulled Satarah from behind his back and onto the bed. He watched her as he toed off his shoes and slacks then dived for her, as she giggled impishly.

"Oh," she said around a moan when Doug was balls deep inside her. He set a grueling pace that had her climbing the bed and clinging with tenacity to the sheets. When he latched onto her breast to suckle, she found herself climbing toward an explosive orgasm only to be denied an ultimate release when he changed his rhythm to tease her.

21

There had been an air of danger when Donald Dixon drove a black SUV into an area of Chicago that Douglas admitted, even as a former Marine, he wouldn't have wanted any part of. Donald didn't seem at all concerned about their surroundings, as they drove into a dark alley and cut the engine. He was speaking to someone he called Explorer One through a tiny device looped around his ear. Then he said, "That's affirmative, Wind Breeze. Copy that, Luca Brodsky; you have the Con. Delta Dawn disengaging."

Shortly, three figures rapidly approached from the rear of the vehicle. Don unlocked the doors and the figures quickly got in and ducked down. No one spoke. Don started the engine and then waited. An identical black SUV backed into the alley ahead of them, engine idling. Two of the three figures exited Don's SUV and quickly got into the first one. Doug thought the figures were either particularly small men or agile women. He didn't ask and Don did not offer an explanation.

When both SUVs began to roll out, they veered off in different directions.

They were aboard a private jet and airborne before Doug was able to get a good look at Satarah's son, whose name was Michael.

"That other person said that you were gonna take me to my real mother."

"Yes. That's where we're going now. Your mother has been looking for you for a very long time, but she doesn't know that we've found you. She is going to be very surprised and happy to see you. And she's probably going to cry a lot, so you'll have to put up with a lot of hugs and kisses."

"But I don't ever have to go back there where you took me from?"

"No, you don't. We know that you never wanted to be in that gang. That they took you from the orphanage where you've been living."

"Bone, he ain't gonna like that I'm gone. He always make me count the money 'cause I'm good with numbers. I can add things in my head and once I see something, read something, I can't forget it."

"Don't worry about him. This time tomorrow, he and everyone in his crew will be in police custody facing a laundry list of criminal charges. They will all be convicted and spend the rest of their lives in prison. With the evidence that you were able to provide to the FBI and local police, you are out of all of it. You are in what's called the Witness Protection Program now. You remember what was explained to you?"

"Yes, my name is gonna be Benson James Whitfield. My mama is Satarah Josephine James Whitfield and my father is Jonathan Jeffrey Whitfield. I got two brothers, Jonathan and Jeffrey Whitfield, but we don't got the same mother. Jonathan's and Jeffrey's mother is Carlotta James, my mama's sister. She's really my aunt."

"That's right. This man is Douglas Edward Johnson. He's the fire chief in Summer County where you're going to be living. He and his son, Donovan, live at The Summer House where your mother and brothers live."

"Is that place some kind of orphanage like I been livin' before? She's shacking up..."

"No, Ben, your mother isn't that type of woman. She owns the place," Doug interrupted. "The Summer House is a bed and breakfast." At the child's blank state, Doug said, "It's like a hotel. I live there and so do my team of fire safety experts.

"What's really important is that this weekend starts your family's 4th of July family reunion. The Summer House will be filled with people who will be so happy to finally meet you."

"You said that my real father didn't live with my real mother anymore." Ben directed his statement to Don.

"That's right. He lives in Nevada. If or when you want to meet him that can be arranged."

"Was he trying to find me too? Is that why he's in Nevada?"

"I don't know the answer to that question. It's something that you may want to ask him if you decide that you want to meet him." Don looked up overhead at a flashing light. "Fasten your seat-belt. We're about to land."

Doug wasn't sure of his reception. He left Satarah and the boys days ago on a bogus business trip. He never wanted to ever have to lie to her again, but when he opened the front door to The Summer House, there stood Satarah and the three boys smiling, holding up a handmade welcome home banner. When Ben stepped through the door, everyone went quiet and the smiles slipped slightly. There was no question as to whom the new addition was. The resemblance to Jonathan and Jeffrey was extremely pronounced. Satarah stared, never blinking and then seemed to falter, as she took several shaky, stumbling steps forward. She reached out her hands and clutched Ben's shirt pulling him to her until she had him firmly, tightly in her arms. Her body shook violently as she cried. Slowly, Ben raised his arms and then held her just as tightly, his racking cries mingled with hers.

"Dad?" Donovan asked, obviously concerned by Satarah's heart-wrenching cries and tears.

"It's all right, son. This is Satarah's older son, Benson James Whitfield. Jonathan, Jeffrey, this is your brother."

"For real?" Jonathan asked, evidently pleased with the prospect of another brother.

"Can he stay and live with us, too?" Jeffrey asked, apparently as pleased as his twin.

"Yes, yes, he can," Satarah said holding Ben at arm's length touching his face, as if categorizing his features and form. Then wiping furiously at her still falling tears with one hand, she seemed to have difficulty letting him go. "Benson, I'm your mother, Satarah Josephine. I'm so glad..." her voice wavered. She took a deep, fortifying breath and tried again. "I'm so glad to have you home where you belong."

The boy was as overcome as she was and swallowed convulsively, obviously trying hard not to cry anymore. "I didn't know that I had a mother. I'm glad that you sent those people to help me."

"People?"

"We'll discuss that later," Doug interrupted. "For now, Benson, these two boys are your twin brothers and this young man is my son, Donovan Johnson."

"Hi," they all said in unison, somewhat shyly.

"You wanna go see the new games we got?" Jeffrey eagerly piped up.

"Uh, sure." He turned to look at Satarah. "Is that alright?"

She nodded too choked up to speak. She watched him go off to the boys' room and then turned to look up at Douglas. She went into his arms, crying hard into his chest.

"That's the way. Let it all out, babe. You've got your son back in your arms now. Everything's going to be fine."

Eventually, her tears subsided enough for her to lean back in his arms, looking up at him. "How did you find him?"

"Are the details important right now?"

She looked askance at him. "I suppose that it can wait, but something tells me that he was in trouble. He said that people came 'to help' him?"

"Yes, but now you have him safe and sound and secure under your roof. This is going to be new and unfamiliar territory for him. He was living in an orphanage until about a year ago. He's going to need time to get used to his new home and his multitude of family members. You know how to make him feel welcome just like you've done for me and for Donovan. And we will be here for Ben."

"I don't know what you've done to find him, but I love you so much, so very much more than I can say."

"Well, then, that's worth coming home to."

When Satarah came back to bed after checking on Ben for the fifth time that night, she snuggled up close into Doug's arms.

"Is he still okay?" Doug asked, teasingly.

"You're supposed to be asleep," she fussed, without heat.

"Not with you up every few hours all night." He picked up his watch from the nightstand and checked the time. He yawned hugely, stretched, and then brought Satarah's warm, pliant body closer to him. "I'm going to have to go to my own room shortly."

Satarah leaned up on one elbow over him and turned Doug's face to hers. "I think it's time for you to marry me, Chief Johnson. Have babies with me and make a family with our four boys. Watch our children marry, give us grandchildren and great grandchildren to spoil. Grow old with me, Douglas."

"Is that what you think?"

"It is, yes."

"Okay, but only if we can do it this week during the 4th of July family reunion. I hate having to get up so early in the morning to go back to my bedroom before the boys get up. And with so many of your relatives in the house, I won't have many opportunities to bury myself between your thighs." He got out of bed and reached into his pants pocket to retrieve a small, royal-blue box; something he made time to purchase while in Chicago. He knelt beside the bed and opened the box, turning it in her direction. "Since you asked me so nicely, I'll marry you, Satarah Josephine, have babies with you and make a new family with our four boys. We will watch our children marry, give us grand babies and great grandchildren to spoil. I will grow old with you and go on loving you until my last breath and beyond." He took the ring from the box and slipped it on her finger. It fitted perfectly.

"You planned this all along, didn't you?"

"Well, I did ask your Uncle Bernie and Aunt Sylvia last week whether I had their permission to ask you to marry me. I did that because we haven't known each other that long. They wanted to know what took me so long."

She kissed him, pulled him back into bed with her and snuggled into his arms again. "I'd probably want to know the same thing later after you put me to sleep."

"What I plan to do to you, Sara Jo, has no relationship to sleep."

He put his words into action. Neither one slept for a few hours more.

"I sure hope that we don't have any emergencies today," Bob Sweeny commented standing next to Doug.

Doug checked his watch for the umpteenth time and nervously scanned the building crowd. Vivian promised that she would get everyone there on time, and he trusted her to keep her word.

"Stop worrying," Bernard Alexander advised, patting Doug on his shoulder. "She'll be here. She won't disappoint."

If she's coming at all, Doug ruminated, pensively. This was such short notice, but it was so important. He searched the crowd again. His friend and mentor, Duke Patterson, sat in the front row with Mr. and Mrs. Diggs, his tenants and former childcare providers. His firefighters were still ushering people into available seating in the back rows on the shady side of The Summer House lawn. The tent was huge, but Doug didn't think that he'd ever seen so many rows of chairs even in the Marine Corp. A beautiful pergola had been constructed by Kenneth, Benny and Gregory Alexander it seemed like overnight. It had been covered in delicate looking fuchsia flowers and pink bougainvillea. A raised platform stood before the pergola. Streamers and assorted draping greenery fluttered in the breeze fostered by the tent's huge ceiling fans. Beautiful music led by Aretha Alexander and played by the family band was the backdrop for an almost mystical environment.

Then the music quieted and changed.

There, at the far end of the rows of chairs, a vision in cream appeared flanked by four nattily dressed boys who smiled broadly, as they escorted Satarah up the aisle. As they progressed up the grassy lawn, oohs and ahs sounded throughout the assembled family, friends and guests.

Doug lost his breath when Satarah looked up and smiled at him. She was stunning with flowers from her garden crowning her head, long flowing hair like a floral hairnet and in a drape in her hand. He forgot about everything else and his entire universe narrowed and became her. Then she was standing before him, looking up at him with such love and adoration. He couldn't resist. He leaned down and kissed her lightly on her pretty mouth.

"There will be none of that until after the 'I do's', you two," the minister teased.

The audience chuckled and applauded.

"Dear family and friends, we are gathered together on this beautiful day in this wonderful garden to join together Douglas Edward Johnson and Satarah Josephine Whitfield in the holy bonds of matrimony. Who give these people into this marriage?"

"We do, their sons,"

"Benson,"

"Donovan,"

"Jonathan,"

"And Jeffrey."

"His friend, Duke Paterson."

"And her mother, Mariah Benson," a beautiful replica of Sylvia spoke up, stepped forward, suddenly appearing to their left.

There were loud, audible gasps throughout the crowd. People half stood, craning their necks and bobbing their heads to get a peek at the incomparable songstress, actress, and toast of Europe, Asia and African known to the world as simply The French Mariah. When things quieted to a dull roar, the ceremony proceeded. Satarah was hard pressed to contain her joy. Happy tears flowed down her cheeks when she looked from her mother's gamine smiling face to Douglas. Somehow, she knew that he had a hand in arranging for her mother's unexpected arrival.

At a certain point in the ceremony, her mother's clear, warm, and soothing voice brought tears to everyone's eyes when she sang *One In A Million* while Aretha accompanied her on her electric piano and sang backup. It was clear why during the height of her career she had won so many Grammy and other music and acting awards. She had many gold records as testament to her unique and timeless sound that stood her apart from her contemporaries.

Doug didn't hesitate when the minister asked whether he took Satarah Josephine as his lawfully wedded wife. Nor did Satarah when she agreed to take Douglas Johnson as her husband.

"With the power vested in me, I now pronounce you husband and wife. You two already know what to do next."

Satarah immediately tossed her flowers over her shoulder. They landed in a very surprised Jenny Jones' hands, her gamine face going bright pink with pleasure.

Jenny smiled up at Bob Sweeny from under her lashes. Bob swallowed audibly.

Satarah laid a lip lock on Doug that had everyone hooting and clapping. Then she leaned up to whisper in his ear, "I missed my period."

He whispered back, "That's okay. I plan for you to miss many more in our future."

Epilogue

oug sat in the screened gazebo holding his daughter, Arianna Mariah telling her about the amazing woman who is her mother. He held the baby in his arms so that she could see her mother and four older brothers as they weeded the vegetable garden. Of course, Arianna Mariah couldn't actually see that far at two months old, but it didn't matter. He continued to talk with his daughter on this lazy Saturday morning.

He loved his life now, his wonderfully sexy wife, their four boys and her family. Satarah got a real kick out of tripping his trigger at the least provocation and in some of the most inappropriate places, like she had in his office at seven months pregnant. Some women craved unusual or exotic foods, but when his wife got a yen, she sought him out and jumped his bones.

Douglas did not regret leaving the Richmond Fire Department. He stuck it out returning only when his case came up in court. With Vivian Montgomery and Bill Chandler aiding his attorney, the Fire Department pleaded no contest and asked for an out-of-court settlement. He had not brought the law suit because of what financial benefit might be gained, but to insure that fire protection services were made available to all Richmond residents equally regardless of the neighborhoods they resided in. On advice of counsel, he agreed to the terms and conditions of the settlement, pocketed a hefty payment to settle the suit, and then retired from the Richmond Fire Department with full benefits. He actually never had to work another day in his life if he did not want to. However, he never could have given up being a firefighter and he loved being the Fire Chief in Summer County.

Bob Sweeney also resigned from the Richmond FD and talked so much about how great it was living and working in Summer County, South Carolina, that seven other seasoned Richmond firefighters moved, some with families, into Summer County to work with Chief Johnson. To date, none regretted their moves, particularly not Bob who was engaged to marry to Jenny Jones.

His friend, Duke Patterson, loved Summer County, too, and bought a small place, only fifty acres, in the county where he could become what he called "a gentleman farmer." Doug's tenants, Tom and Bertha Diggs, visited often and were due to arrive at The Summer House in a few days for an extended period. They came primarily to escape the cold winters in Richmond and to spend time with their adopted grandsons: Benson, Donovan, Jonathan, Jeffrey, and their newly adopted granddaughter: Arianna Mariah.

After a year assisting with the medical training needed by the ambulance medics, Doug's Marine bubby, Mark Brooks, rejoined Doctors Without Borders taking Mary Ella Baker with him. Mark established a solid program of medical rotations using young doctors on the ambulance team and Sylvia Alexander's senior nursing students. Mark also anonymously donated four fully equipped ambulances. Doug and Satarah received a post card from Mark and Mary Ella last week. They were somewhere in Africa that didn't show up on any map that Donovan could find.

Louise McCrary was Doug's lead Fire Investigator and trained and managed several other men and women on her staff of investigators. She still consulted for other fire departments across the country from time to time, but her burgeoning pregnancy limited her trips to few. So far, Rey Steward's pleas to get her to the altar were unsuccessful.

The Summer County Fire Department was rated the best in South Carolina. Douglas was asked by the state Fire Marshall to travel to other counties and advise on how to improve their fire safety programs. Instead of taking on the job himself, he hired Duke Patterson as a consultant and dispatched him to work with other in-state fire departments. Duke was enjoying his new role and Doug was enjoying being able to spend more time with his Satarah and his growing family.

Just before Thanksgiving, the Alexander cousins and friends, including Chuck Montgomery and Vivian's male law partners, took a trip to ski in Vail, Colorado, with their children. Doug, of course, took their four boys. It was another first for Donovan, Ben, and for Douglas too, never having gone skiing before. Nevertheless, they learned quickly and were, before the end of the trip, taking on the more challenging ski trails with everyone else. They even skied several of the night runs a few times. The kids had big fun sleeping in sleeping bags on the floor of the great room while the adult males claimed the beds. They shared housekeeping duties and looked forward to next year's trip, but were all very glad to get back to Satarah's home cooked meals.

Ben was acclimating very well to his new life, his huge family and new school curriculum. He was a very bright boy and quickly took to new things. Satarah held long talks and walks with him sometimes, just the two of them or with the other boys. She told him about the circumstances of her early teen pregnancy. Jonathan and Jeffrey already knew that their biological mother, Carlotta, and father, JoJeff, ran off together, leaving them behind with Satarah without a backward glance. The twins told Ben that they didn't harbor any ill feelings toward JoJeff and Carlotta because Satarah, to their way of thinking, was the best mother anyone would want. Now with Douglas as their stepfather, their new brothers, Benson and Donovan, and new baby sister, Arianna Mariah, they were happy with their family unit and extended family members.

Donovan and Ben had never ridden a horse before, but Jonathan and Jeffrey, being raised on a farm around animals, were avid teachers. They taught both Ben and Donovan how to care for the animals on Bigger Thenham's farm and Bigger let them ride his horses on a daily basis. Though Bigger was still miffed with Sara Jo for marrying Douglas before his "cooling off period" was over, he had a smile on his face now that he was married to the laundress, Lucile Lindsey. They were expecting their first child soon. Doug still couldn't quite visualize four-foot-nine Bigger and six-foot-four Lucile together, but he really was not trying very hard. What did surprise him more was that Little Willie, Bigger's six-foot-seven younger brother, married the Radiology Technician cum dominatrix Laurel Mason. Truly to Doug's way of thinking, that was a scary thought.

Surprisingly, The Summer House stayed fully booked since its opening last 4th of July. They were attracting a number of conferences, small conventions, and other group businesses to the point that work had started on renovating the old slave quarter cottages on the back lawn in a rustic style reminiscent of the days before slavery ended. There were only a few motels in the county and nothing as grand as The Summer House. The house was added to the National Registry of Historic Places and various history groups, schools, and universities regularly conducted tours through the house and around the grounds. The fine furniture and other rare pieces of Americana alone drew art aficionados from around the world. On weekends, Satarah booked entertainment in the large lounge, not to compete with whatever event was going on in the grand ballroom or other venues under their roof. The Summer House became a favorite wedding venue. They were also planning to have summer concerts on the south lawn in early evening performed by the talented students from Summer County Academy. The Summer House had events scheduled nearly every day of the week.

Satarah and Miles Logan were so busy and booked so many months in advance that Satarah had to give up her position as Chief Emergency Room Nurse at the hospital. They hired a large enough staff to ensure that everything ran smoothly.

She and Doug still found time to spend with their growing family. Even with all the activity, the boys, including Ben, loved living in The Summer House. Each morning, when Satarah and her helpers cooked for everyone in the house, she set aside food and a full two hours to sit, eat and talk with her family. Doug fed Arianna Mariah her morning bottle of breast milk. The boys claimed that was gross, but Doug told them that they didn't know what they were missing just to see them pretend to gag and hear them boo. The boys had to have a schedule to keep from fighting over who would feed Arianna Mariah her dinnertime bottle. Their family-only times together were precious to them all. Douglas proudly wore the gold chain that read **FAMILY** as did each of their boys.

In fact, after the upcoming family reunion, Doug and his family were looking forward to a trip to Paris, France, on one of Vivian's long distance luxury, private, executive jets. He and Satarah lost their minds and asked to take 'the Cousin Kids' with them. All of the Alexander-Benson grandchildren were eager to go, so they enlisted the aid of Bernard and Sylvia and Romelo and Olivia to accompany them. Satarah's mother, Mariah, was thrilled and busy planning a fun filled two weeks touring as much of France as they could fit in before everyone collapsed from sheer exhaustion.

"Excuse me, my brother," a man said standing just outside of Doug's peripheral vision.

"Yes, how may I help you?" Doug asked, turning his head toward the man.

"I asked inside where I could find my wife?" he said, hooking a thumb over his shoulder toward the house. "The girl at the desk said that she was out here."

"Your wife? Uh, no one's out here, except me and my family." He rose from his comfortable position on the chaise lounge and exited the gazebo with Arianna Mariah in his arms to go back into The Summer House. "Come with me. I'll try to help you find her."

"Thanks, brother. Awful nice place you got here and just look at that pretty little girl. She sure has a lot of hair for someone so small."

"Thank you. This little golden nugget is Arianna Mariah Johnson."

"You must be new in the area. I grew up here, but I don't think I know you."

"Sorry," he said extending his hand. "I'm Doug Johnson, Summer County's new fire chief. I moved here from Richmond, Virginia. I haven't lived here that long, less than two years. I don't think that we've met. What's your wife's name?"

"Sara Jo, Satarah Josephine Whitfield. Perhaps you've met her? I'm her husband, JoJeff; Jonathan Jeffrey Whitfield. Pleased to meet you, Chief Johnson."

AUTHOR BIO

Ann Jeffries is a native of Washington, D. C. She is an only child who enjoyed the benefits of a private school education at Allen in Asheville, NC, and a public education at the University of Maryland. She began writing fiction for her own amusement.

Ann is the recipient of many awards for leadership and public service. A speaker at colleges and universities and conferences and conventions, she has extensively traveled the North American continent, Asia and Europe. Among other things, she is an entrepreneur, an avid viewer of public television and a voracious reader of fiction.

Ms. Jeffries' pride and joy are her family, particularly her Fabulous Four grands. She lives in Maryland and South Carolina.

www.ingramcontent.com/pod-product-compliance
Lightning Source LLC
Chambersburg PA
CBHW031241120726
47905CB00002B/681